*F*OR a moment it was startling. Crouched in the chair, which was still on an even keel, was indeed a wart-horn. Its warty skin, its frog-like head and face with the forward pointing horns, made it anything but a pleasant looking object. But the way it crouched in the chair, its webbed forepaws even resting on the arms as it seemed to lever itself up to meet our gaze, always supposing that our actions here had activated the appearance of a twin screen for reception there and two-way viewing, gave it a disturbing air of intelligence, as if it had been about some secret business of its own in our alien structure and had been surprised.

Also by Andre Norton:

THE JARGOON PARD	23615	$1.75
JUDGMENT ON JANUS	24214	$1.95
SHADOW HAWK	24186	$1.95
SNOW SHADOW	23963	$1.95
STAR RANGERS	24076	$1.75
VELVET SHADOWS	23155	$1.50
THE WHITE JADE FOX	24005	$1.75

DARK PIPER

Andre Norton

FAWCETT CREST • NEW YORK

DARK PIPER

THIS BOOK CONTAINS THE COMPLETE TEXT OF THE
ORIGINAL HARDCOVER EDITION.

Published by Fawcett Crest Books, a unit of CBS Publica-
tions, the Consumer Publishing Division of CBS Inc., by ar-
rangement with Harcourt Brace Jovanovich

ISBN: 0-449-24328-1

Printed in the United States of America

First Fawcett Crest printing: September 1980

10   9   8   7   6   5   4   3   2   1

One

I HAVE HEARD it stated that a Zexro tape will last forever. But even a second generation now may find nothing worth treasuring in our story. Of our own company, Dinan, and perhaps Gytha, who now work on the storage of all the old off-world records may continue to keep such a history of our times. But we do not run our reader now except for a pressing need for technical information, since no one knows how long its power pack will last. Therefore, this tape may keep its message locked for a long time unless, ages from now, those off-world do remember our colony and come seeking to learn its fate, or unless there shall arise here people able to rebuild machines that have died for want of proper repairs.

My recording may thus be of no benefit, for in three years our small company has taken a great backward leap from civilized living to barbarism. Yet I spend an hour each evening on it, having taken notes with the aid of all, for even young minds have impressions to add. This is the tale of the Dark Piper, Griss Lugard, who saved a handful of his kind, so that those who walk as true men should not totally vanish from a world he loved. Yet we who owe him our lives know so little about him that what we must in truth set upon this tape are our own deeds and actions and the manner of his passing.

Beltane was unique among the Scorpio Sector planets in that it was never intended for general settlement, but instead was set up as a biological experimental station. By some freak of nature, it had a climate acceptable to our species, but there was no intelligent native life, nor, indeed, any life very high in scale. Its richly vegetated continents numbered two, with wide seas spaced between. The eastern one was left to what native life there was. The Reserves and the hamlets and farms of the experimental staffs were all placed upon the western one, radiating out from a single spaceport.

As a functioning unit in the Confederation scheme, Beltane had been in existence about a century at the outbreak of the Four Sectors War. That war lasted ten planet years.

Lugard said it was the beginning of the end for our kind and their rulership of the space lanes. There can rise empires of stars, and confederations, and other governments. But there comes a time when such grow too large or too old, or are rent from within. Then they collapse as will a balloon leaf when you prick it with a thorn, and all that remains is a withered wisp of stuff. Yet those on Beltane welcomed the news of the end of the war with a hope of new beginning, of return to that golden age of "before the war" on which the newest generation had been raised with legendary tales. Perhaps the older settlers felt the chill of truth, but they turned from it as a man will seek shelter from the full blast of a winter gale. Not to look beyond the next corner will sometimes keep heart in a man.

Since the population of Beltane was small, most of them specialists and members of such families, it had been drained of manpower by the services, and of the hundreds who were so drafted, only a handful returned. My father did not.

We Collises were First Ship family, but unlike most, my grandfather had been no techneer, nor bio-master, but had commanded the Security force. Thus, from the beginning, our family was, in a small measure, set apart from the rest of the community, though there was nothing but a disparity of interests to make that so. My father lacked ambition perhaps. He went off-world and passed in due course through Patrol training. But he did not elect to try for promotion. Instead, he opted to return to Beltane, assuming, in time, command of the Security force here that his father had commanded.

Only the outbreak of the war, which caused a quick call-up of all available trained men, pulled him away from the roots he desired.

I would have undoubtedly followed his example, save that those ten years of conflict wherein we were more or less divorced from space kept me at home. My mother, who had been of a techneer family, died even before my father lifted with his command, and I spent the years with the Ahrens.

Imbert Ahren was head of the Kynvet station and my mother's cousin, my only kin on Beltane. He was an earnest man, one who achieved results by patient, dogged work rather than through any flashes of brilliance. In fact, he was apt to be suspicious of unorthodox methods and the yielding to "hunches" on the part of subordinates—though, give him his due, he only disapproved mildly and did nothing to limit any gropings on their part.

His wife, Ranalda, was truly brilliant in her field and more intolerant of others. We did not see much of her, since she was buried in some obtuse research. The running of the household fell early on Annet, who was but a year younger than I. In addition, there was Gytha, who usually was to be found with a reading tape and who had as little domestic interest as her mother.

It must be that the specialization that grew more and more necessary as my species entered space had, in a fashion, mutated us, though that might be argued against by the very people most affected. Though I was tutored and urged to choose work that would complement the labors of the station, I had no aptitude for any of it. In the end, I was studying, in a discontinuous manner, toward a Rangership in one of the Reserves—an occupation Ahren believed I might just qualify for—when the war, which had not affected us very directly, at last came to a dreary end.

There was no definite victory, only a weary drawing apart of the opponents from exhaustion. Then began the interminable "peace talks," which led to a few clean-cut solutions.

Our main concern was that Beltane now seemed forgotten by the powers that had established it. Had we not long before turned to living off the land, and the land been able to furnish us with food and clothing, we might have been in desperate straits. Even the biannual government ships, to which our commerce and communication had sunk in the last years of the war, had now twice failed to arrive, so that when a ship finally planeted, it was a cause for rejoicing—until the authorities discovered it was in no way an answer to our needs but rather was a fifth-rate tramp hastily commandeered to bring back a handful of those men who had been drafted off-world during the conflict. Those veterans were indeed the halt and the blind—casualties of the military machine.

Among these was Griss Lugard. Although he had been a very close part of my childhood, the second-in-command of the force my father had led starward, I did not know him as he limped away from the landing ramp, his small flight bag seeming too great a burden for his stick-thin arms as its weight pulled him a little to one side and added to the unsteadiness of his gait.

He glanced up as he passed, then dropped that bag. His hand half went out, and the mouth of a part-restored face (easy to mark by the too smooth skin) grimaced.

"Sim—"

Then his hand went to his head, moving across his eyes as one who would brush aside a mist, and I knew him by the band on his wrist, now far too loose.

"I'm Vere," I said quickly. "And you are"—I saw the rank badges on the collar of his faded and patched tunic—"Sector-Captain Lugard!"

"Vere." He repeated the name as if his mind fumbled back through time for identification. "Vere—why, you're Sim's son! But—but—you might be Sim." He stood there blinking at me, and then, raising his head, he turned to give his surroundings a slow, searching stare. Now he gazed as if he saw more than his boots raising planet dust.

"It's been a long time," he said in a low, tired voice. "A long, long time."

His shoulders hunched, and he stooped for the bag he had dropped, but I had it before him.

"Where away, sir?"

There were the old barracks. But no one had lived there

for at least five years, and they were used for storage. Lugard's family were all dead or gone. I decided that, whether Annet had room or not, he could guest with us.

But he was looking beyond me to the southwest hills and to the mountains beyond those.

"Do you have a flitter, Sim—Vere?" He corrected himself.

I shook my head. "They're first priority now, sir. We don't have parts to repair them all. Best I can do is a hard-duty hopper."

And I knew I was breaking the rules to use that. But Griss Lugard was one of my own, and it had been a long time since I had had contact with someone from *my* past.

"Sir—if you wish to guest—" I continued.

He shook his head. "When you've held to a memory for some time"—it was as if he talked to himself, almost reassuring himself—"you want to prove it, right or wrong. If you can get the hopper, point her west and south—to Butte Hold."

"But that may be a ruin. No one has been there since Six Squad pulled out eight years ago."

Lugard shrugged. "I've seen plenty of ruins lately, and I have a fancy for that one." With one hand he fumbled inside his tunic and brought out a palm-sized metal plate that flashed in the afternoon sun. "Gratitude of a government, Vere. I have Butte Hold for as long as I want—as mine."

"But supplies—" I offered a second discouragement.

"Stored there, too. Everything is mine. I paid half a face, strong legs, and quite an additional price for the Butte, boy. Now I'd like to go—home." He was still looking to the hills.

I got the hopper and signed it out as an official trip. Griss Lugard was entitled to that, and I would face down any objection on that point if I had to.

The hoppers had been made originally to explore rough country. They combined surface travel, where that was possible, with short hops into the air to cross insurmountably rough terrain. They were not intended for comfort, just to get you there. We strapped into the foreseats, and I set the course dial for Butte Hold. Nowadays it was necessary to keep both hands on the controls. There was too apt to be some sudden breakdown, and the automatics were not to be trusted.

Since the war the settlements on Beltane had contracted instead of expanded. With a short supply of manpower, there had been little or no time wasted in visiting the outlying sites, abandoned one after another. I remembered Butte Hold as it had been before the war—dimly, as seen by a small boy—but I had not been there for years.

It was set on the borders of the lava country, a treacherous strip of territory that, in remote times, must have lighted most of this continent with titanic eruptions. Even the eroded evidence of these volcanoes was still spectacular. Of late years it was an unknown wilderness of breaks and flows, a maze of knife-sharp ridges with here and there pockets of vegetation. Rumor had it that, beside the forbidding aspect of the land itself, there were other dangers—from beasts that had escaped the experimental stations and found this forsaken range an ideal lair. No one actually had evidence of such. It was rumor only. But it had grown into tradition, and a man wore a stunner when he ventured in.

We left the road at a turn trace so dim by now that I could not have found it without Lugard's direction. But he gave that with the surety of one seeing markers plain in the sun. And very shortly we were out of the settled land. I wanted to talk, but I did not quite dare to ask my questions. Lugard was so plainly occupied with his thoughts.

He would find other changes on Beltane, less tangible than those of the abandonment of old landmarks but nonetheless sharp. The settlements had been drained of certain types of men: first the guard, and then scientists and techneers. Those left had unconsciously, perhaps consciously in some ways, changed the atmosphere. The war had not come close enough to make any great impression on our planet. It remained a subject of reports, of attrition of supplies and manpower, of growing irritation as men, buried in their own chosen fields of research, had been commanded to explore other paths for refinements in killing. I had heard enough to know that there had been a deliberate dragging of feet in sections that had been set to war problems. And there had been angry outbursts five years back, threats passed between the last commander and such men as Dr. Corson. Then the commander had been ordered off-world, and Beltane settled down to a peaceful existence.

The sentiment now on Beltane was pacifist—so much so that I wondered whether Lugard would find an accepted place among these men bent so strongly on keeping matters as they were and had been. He had been born on Beltane—that was true. But, like my father, he was of a Service family, and he had never married into one of the settlement clans. He spoke of Butte Hold as his. Was that literally true? Or did it mean that he was sent here to make ready for another garrison? That would not be welcome.

Our trail was so badly overgrown that I reluctantly took to the air, skimming not far above the top of the brush. If Lugard was the forerunner of a garrison, I hoped they would number among them some techneer-mechanics with training in the repair of vehicles. Already our machines had become so unpredictable that some of the settlements talked of turning to beasts of burden.

"Take her farther up!" ordered Lugard.

I shook my head. "No. If she parts at this height, we have a chance of getting out in one piece. I won't chance more."

He glanced first at me and then at the hopper, as if he really saw it for the first time. His eyes narrowed.

"This is a wreck—"

"It is about the best you can find nowadays," I replied promptly. "Machines don't repair themselves. The techneer-robos are all on duty at the labs. We have had no off-world supplies since Commander Tasmond lifted with the last of the garrison. Most of these hoppers are just pasted together, with hope the main ingredient of that paste."

Again I met his searching stare. "That bad, is it?" he asked quietly.

"Well, it depends upon what you term bad. The Committee has about decided it is a good thing on the whole. They like it that off-world authority has stopped giving orders. The Free Trade party is looking forward to independence and is trying to beam in a trader. Meanwhile, repairs go first for lab needs; the rest of it slides. But no one, at least no one with a voice in Committee affairs, wants off-world control back."

"Who *is* in charge?"

"The Committee—section heads—Corson, Ahren, Alsay, Vlasts—"

"Corson, Ahren, yes. Who is Alsay?"

"He's at Yetholme."

"And Watsill?"

"Drafted off-world. So was Praz—and Borntol. Most of the younger men went. And some of the big brains—"

"Corfu?"

"He—well, he killed himself."

"What?" He was clearly startled. "I had a message—" Then he shook his head. "It was a long time reaching me—out there. Why?"

"The official verdict was minor fatigue."

"And behind that verdict?"

"Rumor has it that he discovered something deadly. They wanted him to develop it. He wouldn't. They pressured him, and he was afraid he might give in. So he made sure he would not. The Committee like that rumor. They have made it their talking point against off-world control. They say that they will never put weapons into anyone's hands again."

"They won't have the chance—into former hands, that is," Lugard replied dryly. "And they had better give up their dreams of trade, too. The breakup is here and now, boy. Each world will have to make the most of its own resources and be glad if someone else doesn't try to take them over—"

"But the war is over!"

Lugard shook his head. "The formal war, yes. But it tore the Confederation to bits. Law and order—we won't see those come again in our time, not out there—" He motioned with one thin hand to the sky over us. "No, not in our time, nor probably for generations to come. The lucky worlds with rich natural resources will struggle along for a generation or two, trying hard to keep a grip on civilization. Others will coast downhill fast. And there will be wolves tearing all around—"

"Wolves?"

12

"An old term for aggressors. I believe it was an animal running in packs to pull down prey. The ferocity of such hunts lingered on in our race memories. Yes, there will be wolf packs out now."

"From the Four Stars?"

"No," he answered. "They are as badly mauled as we. But there are the remnants of broken fleets, ships whose home worlds were blasted, with no ports in which they will be welcomed. These can easily turn rogue, carrying on a way of life they have known for years, merely changing their name from commando to pirate. The known rich worlds will be struck first—and places where they can set up bases—"

I thought I knew then why he had returned. "You're bringing in a garrison so Beltane won't be open—"

"I wish I were, Vere, I wish I were!" And the sincerity in his husky voice impressed me. "No, I've taken government property for my back pay, to the relief of the paymaster. I have title to Butte Hold and whatever it may contain, that is all. As to why I came back—well, I was born here, and I have a desire that my bones rest in Beltane earth. Now, south here—"

The traces of the old road were nearly hidden. There had been a washout or two, over which the quickly growing guerl vines had already laid a mat. Now we were coming to the lava country, where there were signs of the old flows. The vegetation rooting here was that fitted to wastelands. This was midsummer, and the flowering period was nearly over. But here and there a late blossom still hung, a small flag of color. There were ripening yellow globes on the vines, and twice spoohens fluttered away, at the approach of the hopper, from where they had been feeding.

We circled about an escarpment and saw before us Butte Hold. It was a major feat of adaptation, the rock of the mountain carved away and hollowed to make a sentry post. It had been fashioned right after First Ship landing, when there was still doubt about the native fauna, meant to be a protection against what lay in the saw-toothed wilds of the lava country. Though the need for such a fort was soon known to

13

be unnecessary, it had served as a headquarters for all the outland patrols as long as they kept watch here.

I set down on the landing strip by the main entrance. But the doors were banked with drifting sand and looked as if they had been welded so. Lugard got out, moving stiffly. He reached for his bag, but I already had it, sliding out in his wake. By the looks of it, he was traveling light, and if there were no supplies within—well, he might change his mind and want to return, if only temporarily, to guest in the section.

He did not deny my company but went on ahead, once more in his hand that metal plate he had shown me at the port. As he came to the sand-billowed doorway, he stood a long moment, looking at the face of the stronghold, almost as if he expected one of those now shuttered windows to open and himself to be hailed from within. Then he stooped a little, peering closely at the door. With one hand he brushed its surface and with the other fitted the plate he carried over the locking mechanism.

I half expected to see him disappointed, my belief in the durability and dependability of machinery having been systematically undermined by the breakdowns of years just past. But in this case I was wrong. There was a moment or two of waiting, to be sure, but then the seemingly solid surface parted into two leaves, rolling silently back on either side. At the same time, interior lights glowed, and we looked down a straight hall with closed doors to right and left.

"You ought to be sure of supplies," I ventured. He had turned to reach for the bag I still held. Now he smiled.

"Very well. Assure yourself, come in—"

I accepted that invitation, though I guessed he would rather be alone. Only I knew Beltane now as he did not. I would have to leave in the hopper, and he would be, could be, disastrously on his own—marooned here.

He led the way straight down the hall to a door at the rear, raising his hand to pass it in a swift, decisive gesture over the plate set into its surface. That triggered the opening, and we stood on the edge of a grav shaft. Lugard did take precautions there, tossing his kit bag out. It floated gently,

14

descending very slowly. Seeing that, he calmly followed it. I had to force myself after him, my suspicions of old installations being very near the surface.

We descended two levels, and I sweated out that trip, only too sure that at any minute the cushioning would fail, to dash us on the floor below. But our boots met the surface with hardly a hint of a jar, and we were in the underground storeroom of the hold. I saw in the subdued glow shrouded machines. Perhaps I had been wrong to think Lugard would miss transportation when I left. But he was turning to the right and some alcoved spaces, where there were containers and cases.

"You see—I am well provided for." He nodded at that respectable array.

I looked around. There were weapon racks to the left, but they had been stripped bare. Lugard had gone past me to pull the covering off one of the machines. The plastic folds fell away from a digger, its pointed pick nose depressed to rest tip against the surface under us. My first hopes of a command flitter, or something like it, faded. Perhaps, just as the weapon racks had been stripped, so had such transports been taken.

Lugard turned away from the digger, and there was a new briskness about him.

"Have no doubts, Vere. I am well situated here." His tone was enough to send me to the grav, and this time he signaled reverse, so we rose to the entrance hall. I was on my way to the door when he stopped me.

"Vere—?"

"Yes?" I turned. He was looking at me as if he were hesitant to say what was in his mind, and I had the impression that he fought to break through some inner reserve.

"If you find your way up here again, look in." It could not be termed a warm invitation; yet, coming from him, I knew that it was as cordial a one as I would ever have, and it was honestly and deeply meant.

"I will that," I promised.

He stood in the doorway, a light sundown wind stirring up the drifted sand, driving some of it over the threshold to grit in the bare hallway, to watch me go. I deliberately circled once as I left and waved, to see his hand raised shoulder high in return.

Then I headed to Kynvet, leaving the last of Beltane's soldiers in his chosen retreat. Somehow I disliked thinking of him alone in that place, which must be for him haunted by all the men who had once trod its corridors and would never now return. But that it was a choice no one could argue against, I knew, Griss Lugard being who and what he was.

When I put the hopper down at Kynvet, I saw the wink of lights through the summer dusk.

"Vere?" Gytha's voice called from the house. "Annet says hurry. There is company—"

Company? Yes, there was the other hopper with the Yetholme code on its tail, and beyond it the flitter Haychax kept in flying order—almost as if we were entertaining half the Committee. But—why? I quickened pace and for a space forgot about Butte Hold and its new commander.

Two

IT MIGHT NOT be a full meeting of the Committee gathered under Ahren's roof that night, but the men whose voices murmured behind closed doors were those who would dominate any such meeting. I had expected to have to answer for the presence of the hopper and was prepared to stand up for Lugard's rights, only to discover that had I presumed to take a flitter, it would not have been noted then.

Annet, busy at dishing up before summoning the men now entrenched in her father's study, informed me of the reason for such an unusual convocation. The ship that had brought in Lugard and the other veterans had, in addition, a second mission. The captain had been contacted, as he came out of hyper into orbit, by a ship now above Beltane, of whose presence we had not been aware. And a plea had been delivered to the Committee.

It was as Lugard had predicted, though his view of the matter had been gloomy. There were ships now without home ports, their native worlds burned-out cinders or radioactive to the point that life could not exist on their deadly surfaces. One such load of refugees now wove a pattern in our sky and asked for landing rights and settlement space.

Beltane had, by the very reason for its settlement, been a "closed" world, its single port open only to certified ships. But that enclosure vanished with the end of the war. The truth was that the sector settlements occupied so little of the

17

continental masses that we were not even a true pioneer world, in spite of the permanence of the hamlets that radiated from the port. The whole eastern land mass was empty of any colonization at all.

Did the old restrictions still prevail? And if they did not—was the welcome signal out for any flotsam of the war? I thought of Lugard's dire prophecy that wolves ranged or would range the star lanes—that those without defenses could be looted, or even taken over. And would these men now conferring with Ahren think of that possibility? I believed not.

I picked up a platter of dunk bread and took it to the long table. Servo-robos were long gone now, save for a few in the labs. We had returned to the early state of our species and used our two hands, our feet, and the strength of our backs to work. Annet was a good cook—I relished what came out of her pots and pans more than the food at the port, which was still running by robo. The appetizing odor of the dunk bread made me realize it had been a long time since noon and that my port meal had been even less satisfactory than usual.

When I returned for a tray of dunk bowls, she was looking out of the window.

"Where did you get the hopper?"

"Portside. I had a passenger into the outback."

She looked at me in surprise. "Outback! But who—?"

"Griss Lugard. He wanted to go to Butte Hold. Came in on the tramp."

"Griss Lugard—who is he?"

"He served with my father. Used to command at Butte Hold before the war."

"Before the war" was even more remote to her than to me. She had hardly been out of a sector crèche when the first news of the conflict had come to us. And I doubted if she could remember the time before.

"What did he come for? He is—was—a soldier, wasn't he?"

Soldiers, men who made fighting their profession, were as legendary on Beltane now as any of the fantastical creatures on the story tapes of the young.

"He was born here. He was given the hold—"

"You mean there are going to be soldiers here again? But the war is over. Father—the Committee—they will protest that! You know the First Law—"

I knew the First Law—how could I escape it? It had been dinned into my ears, and supposedly my head, long enough. "War is waste; there is no conflict that cannot be resolved by men of patience, intelligence, and good will meeting openly in communication."

"No, he's alone. He is no longer with the forces. He's been badly wounded."

"He must be wit-addled too"—she began ladling the stew into the waiting tureen—"if he plans to live out in that wasteland."

"Who's going to live in the wasteland?" Gytha bobbed up, a collection of bowl spoons in her suntanned hands.

"A man named Griss Lugard."

"Griss Lugard—oh, Second-Commandant Lugard." She surprised me as she was so often able to do to all of us. Her mouth curved in a smile at our astonishment, and her two side braids of hair swung as she nodded vigorously. "I can read, can't I? Don't I? Well, I read more than story tapes. I read history—Beltane history. It's all in the old news tapes. And there's more, too. All about how Second-Commandant Griss Lugard brought artifacts from the lava caves—that he found Forerunner things there. They were going to send someone here from Prime Center to see—then the war came. And nobody ever came. I read a lot of tapes to find out if they did. I bet he's come back to look for treasure—Forerunner treasure! Vere, couldn't we go out and help him look?"

"Forerunner artifacts?" If Gytha said she had read it in the news tapes, it had been there. In such matters she made no mistakes. But I had never heard of any Forerunner remains on Beltane.

When our kind had first broken out of the solar system that had nourished our species, we soon learned that we were not unique in our discovery of the worlds of far space. We met others already free of the lanes between system and system. And, as the galaxy counted time, they, too, were newcomers, though they were centuries in advance of our own first timid star steps. Yet there were those who had gone before *them*, and others before and before—until one could not count the empires that had risen and fallen or know how many generations of creatures, many much longer lived than we, had passed since some of those Forerunner ships had planeted on long-forgotten worlds.

There had once been a brisk market in Forerunner finds, especially in the core planets of the inner systems where VIP's had wealth and wanted curiosities to spend it on. Museums bought, too, though the story was that a better deal could be made with a private collector. If the tape Gytha quoted had the truth, then I could understand Lugard's return to the Butte. Having been granted it, he would have legal title to any find thereabouts. But that such a luxury trade would be of use to him now—No, if conditions were as bad as his pessimistic account made them, one could tumble into a whole Forerunner warehouse and get no good of it.

However, there is always a pull to the thought of treasure, and I cannot deny that Gytha's reaction was mine—to go look for such. The thought made one's blood run a little faster.

The lava caves were no place for the prudent to venture unless a man knew something of the territory and went well equipped for all emergencies. They are not formed like usual caves by the action of water, but rather are born of fire. A tongue of lava flows down a slope and congeals on the outer surface, but the interior remains molten and continues to move, forming a passage. After ages, the roof of such a tube may collapse, opening it to the outer world. These long corridor caves can run for miles. The landscape around them is ridged with trenches where some cave ceilings have entirely collapsed, and in places natural bridges of rock span them. There are craters, broken volcanic cones, hazards that close the country to the casual traveler.

"Could we, Vere? Perhaps the Rovers could go?" Gytha clattered her spoons against each other in rising excitement.

"Certainly not!" Annet whirled around from the cook unit, a ladle dripping in her hand. "That is dangerous country; you know that, Gytha!"

"Not alone," Gytha returned, none of her excitement in the least dampened. "Vere would go and you maybe. We'd abide by the rules, no straying. And I never saw a lava cave—"

"Annet," Ahren called from the other room, "we're in a hurry, daughter."

"Yes, coming—" She went back to filling the tureen. "Take the spoons in, Gytha. And, if you please, Vere, the preserve crocks."

Her mother had not come in. This was not unusual, since experiments in the lab did not wait on meal hours, and Annet was long resigned to sending over a tray or keeping back a portion of a dish. Consequently, she most always gave us food that could be reheated or set out successfully for a second or even a third time.

The visitors and their host were already seated at the head of the table, and we took the hint to sit at the foot, not to interrupt. Not being truly one of their number, I usually found the conversation at such gatherings of little interest. But tonight might be different.

However, if I had hoped to hear more of the refugee ship, I was disappointed. Corson ate mechanically, as one whose mind was entirely elsewhere. Ahren was as taciturn. Only Alik Alsay paid Annet compliments concerning the food and finally turned to me.

"Good report you turned in, Collis, about the north slope."

Had he been Corson, I would have been pleased, even flattered a little. But I knew very well that my report was of small interest to Alsay, that he was merely making conversation. I murmured thanks, and that would have been that had not Gytha taken a hand for motives of her own. When she chose to fasten onto some project, as I might well have remembered, she generally, sooner or later, got her way.

"Vere was out to the lava beds today. Have you been there, First-Tech Alsay?"

"Lava beds." He paused in raising his cup of caff in open surprise. "But why? There is no authorized mapping in that direction—simply wasteland. What took you there, Collis?"

"I took someone—Sector-Captain Lugard. He is at Butte Hold."

"Lugard?" Ahren came out of his preoccupation. "Griss Lugard? What is he doing on Beltane?"

"I don't know. He says he was given Butte Hold—"

"Another garrison!" Ahren set down his cup with a clatter that slopped a little of the caff over on his fingers. "We will *not* have that nonsense here again! The war is over. There is no need for any Security force!" The way he said "security" made it sound like an oath. "There is certainly no danger here, and we will not have any of those controls foisted on us again. The sooner they learn that, the better." He glanced from Alsay to Corson. "This puts another light on the whole matter."

But what matter he did not explain. Instead, he demanded of me a full accounting of what I had learned from Lugard, and when I had given that, Alsay cut in.

"It would seem Lugard has the hold as a pension."

"Which could be only a cover-up he used with the boy." Ahren was still aroused. "But his port papers—they ought to tell us something. And"—once more he turned his attention to me—"you might well keep an eye on him, Vere. Since he accepted your help in getting there, he could well understand your dropping in again—"

What he was suggesting I did not like, but I would not say that yet, not before these others and across the table where I ate by his leave, under the roof he had made mine. Something in Lugard's return seemed to have flicked Ahren on the raw; otherwise, he would not have gone to the length of hinting I should spy on a man who had been my father's good friend.

"Father"—once more Gytha cut in, still intent on her own wishes—"can't Vere take us with him? The Rovers have never been to the lava lands."

I expected Ahren to quell her with one of those single glances he used with effect. But he did not, and when he made no quick answer, Alsay spoke.

"Ah, the Rovers. And what has been their latest adventure, my dear?" He was one of those adults who were never at ease with children, and his voice took on a stilted note, used earlier to a lesser extent with me.

Gytha could be polite when the occasion, by her measurement, warranted it. She smiled at the Yetholme leader, and she could smile winningly when she chose.

"We went to the gullat lizard hatchery and made a recording of peep cries," she replied. "It was for Dr. Drax's communication experiment."

I applauded her cunning. To remind her father at this point of some volunteered aid in the past was a bolster for her present demand to widen horizons.

"Yes," Ahren agreed. "It really was an outstanding piece of work, Alsay, showing great patience and perseverance. So now you would like to see the lava beds—"

I was startled. Could he actually agree? Across the table I saw Annet stiffen; her lips moved as if they were already shaping a protest. But Alsay spoke again and this time to me.

"Quite a useful organization, Collis. You are supplementing the teaching tapes very well. It is a pity we have not been able to advance to off-world study. But now that the war is over, there will be opportunities for that."

Did he really believe so, I wondered. The Rovers were more Gytha's idea than mine, though she had drawn me into it and locked me to her purposes so well that I could not now have dropped the project even if I wanted to.

When the settlers had come to Beltane, they had intended to train their children into a science-minded caste. In fact, experiments in such education had been part of the original plan. However, the war had interfered with this as with so much else. Off-world science during those years might have made some great strides. We suspected as much. But our knowledge had become so specialized and narrowed that, lacking fresh imports of taped information, we generally still went over ground ten years old by planet dating, perhaps a hundred by advances elsewhere.

To counteract this stultifying effect had been one of the tasks of the educators. However, the cream of them had been drafted for service. Those remaining—like the sector people—tended to be conservative, the older ones. Then there was a drastic epidemic in the third year of the war (caused said rumor—we always had rumor—by over-zealous experimentation for the Services that resulted in a battle between the sector chiefs and the commandant and the closing down of two projects). After that there were even fewer left to be concerned with the training of the next generation. By spasms parents came out of their labs and studies long enough to be excited for a moment over the lack of concentrated cramming for their children. Then some sudden twist in their own work, some need for complete concentration, took their minds off the matter.

There were never many children—at Kynvet now only eight, ranging from the seven-year-old twins Dagny and Dinan Norkot to Thad Maky, who was fourteen and considered himself—irritatingly at times—nearly adult.

Gytha early dominated. She had a vivid imagination and a total recall memory. Her use of every tape she could lay hand on, though she was barred from digging into lab recordings, had given her a wide range of the most miscellaneous and amazing information. But she differentiated clearly between fact and fiction, and she could spin a fantasy or answer a factual question in the space of a couple of breaths. To the younger children, she was a fountain of wisdom. They appealed to her general knowledge before they approached any adult, for the abstraction of their parents had become so much of a habit by now that this community was really split into two, marked by the difference in ages.

Having organized her followers, Gytha had worked upon me. And I found, whether I willed it or no, I was leading expeditions of the Rovers sometimes more than I was trying to further my own Ranger studies. At first I had rebelled at assuming such responsibilities, but Gytha's discipline held so well, her threat to any one of them of being left out was direful, that they did obey orders. And it came to be a source of pride to me that I was in part a teacher for those eager to learn.

Annet was not quite one of us. She always distrusted Gytha's enthusiasms and thought her sister very prone to reckless disregard for danger. But she did not give vocal vent to any worries when I was in command, for she knew I would not willingly lead them into trouble. Now and then she did join one of our expeditions, her role usually being that of managing the commissary. And, I will say this in her favor— she never made any complaint when on the march.

But to take the Rovers into the lava lands—no, that was where I joined with Annet and was ready to hold firmly to the negative. But Ahren leaned forward a little to question his younger daughter.

"You have a project in mind?" He at least knew how to talk to the younger generation, using the same tone of interest with which he would have greeted a remark from one of his colleagues.

"Not yet." Gytha was always honest. She never tried to conceal facts. "Only, we've been to the swamps, and up in the hills several times, and never there. It is to broaden horizons—" She fell back on her own general term for exploration. "We would like to see Butte Hold."

I noted that she said nothing of a hunt for Forerunner treasure.

"Broaden horizons, eh? What about it, Vere? You were in there today with a hopper. How was the terrain?"

I could not hedge, though I wanted to. He need only check the reading on the machine dial to know the truth, though I did not know why Imbert Ahren would do such a thing. Only, I did know him well enough to recognize a state of mind-made-up. He wanted us to go to the lava lands—or at least to Butte Hold. And the reason for that took little guessing—he wanted a report on Lugard. Perhaps he thought if he could not get it readily from me, he could from Gytha. Children's eyes are sharp, and they see much.

"Well enough around the Butte. I would not venture farther without a good survey."

"Gytha"—Ahren turned to her—"would a trip to Butte Hold enlarge horizons enough for the present?"

"Yes! When—tomorrow?" She demanded almost in one breath.

"Tomorrow? Well—yes, tomorrow might be very good. And, Annet"—he spoke to the older girl—"we shall be at the port. Your mother will accompany us. I think that the Norkots and the Wymarks will be going, too, for a general meeting. Why don't you make this a full-day outing? Take food for a—do you not say—cookout?"

Again I was sure she would protest. But in face of the firmness underlying that suggestion, she did not. Gytha gave an exclamation of delight. I thought she was already mentally listing supplies needed to uncover Forerunner treasure.

"Give my greetings to the Sector-Captain," Ahren said to me. "Say that we shall be very glad to see him at the port. We may be able to profit by his experience."

That I doubted. Ahren's opinion of the military had been stated so many times, forcibly for the most part, that I could not conceive of his listening to Griss Lugard on any subject without impatience and a closed mind.

Ahren was so eager to speed us on our way that he gave me permission to use the supply hopper, which I knew to be in repair and which would hold our whole company. Once supper was done, Gytha was off at light speed to warn her crew of the next day's promise.

I helped Annet clear the table and saw her frown as she fed the dishes into the one kitchen mecho that still ran—the infra cleaner.

"Father wants to know about Griss Lugard," she said abruptly. "He doesn't trust him."

"He need only go out and meet the man, and he'd know the truth." I was unhappy about the way we were being used. "Lugard is certainly not planning to take over Beltane! He probably only wants to be left alone—and I don't think he will welcome us too much."

"Because he does have something to hide?" she flashed.

"Because he must want peace and quiet."

"A soldier?"

"Even they can grow tired of war." I had skirted her prejudices before. They were rooted in what she had been taught all her life. My situation as more guest than family had made me talk and walk with circumspection ever since I had been sorrowfully and firmly put through a discussion session for defending my absent father's beliefs with my fists when I was all of ten.

"Perhaps." But she was not convinced. "Do you really think there is something in the Forerunner artifact story? That seems unlikely. There were never any traces of anything found on the surface."

"Not that we have searched very thoroughly," I countered, not because I did believe in any treasure, but to keep the record correct. It was true that we had aerial surveys of much of the western continent, plus the reports of all the early exploring parties, but although those made a network of the known across much of the land, it was a loose one, with perhaps something to be learned about what lay in the gaps between.

The land was wide and empty. Perhaps those of the refugee ship, were they permitted to settle, could even find a good place to the north, south, or father west, without changing much the course of our pattern.

We prepared for an early takeoff in the morning, but we were still behind those who left for the port. I gathered that they were assembling not only the full Committee, but also as many of the others as they could to hear the petition of the orbiting ship. But for the children, this subject took second place. The lava country had been so talked up by Gytha that I feared there might be some disappointment later.

So I sat in the pilot's seat, half facing around as we readied to go, and made it most plain to my passengers that our destination was Butte Hold and *not* the rough country behind it, which we had no intention of entering. Also, they were not to fasten on Lugard or enter the hold unless at his invitation, which secretly I thought would not be uttered. Were he wise and caught sight of us on any view screen when we landed, he would leave us to wander outside his wall.

Privately, I had also made it clear to Gytha that if Lugard did appear and be hospitable, she was not to mention Forerunners, treasure, or anything of the sort.

I was answered by her scorn. As if she did not know how to act! I was, she commented, getting to be as narrow-minded as Annet. And if that was what came of growing up, she would try to get some sort of retarding pills from one of the

27

labs and be herself for years yet. She *liked* to be the way she was, and she didn't try to make people over either!

The flight-hop from Kynvet was shorter than that from the port. In the old days, Kynvet had been the first link in the chain tying the Butte to the other settlements. In less than an hour, we touched down on the blowing sand of the old landing. I fully expected to see the Butte firmly closed, but its door stood open to the morning sun and there was Lugard, entirely as if he had invited and expected us.

Obeying orders, the Rovers hung back as I went to explain our presence, but I heard some muffled exclamations. The veteran was not alone. On one of his thin shoulders perched a herwin, as if it had known him since its hatching. And by his boots crouched a rock hanay, while between his fingers he held a slender dark red rod. He did not speak or hail us, but rather he raised the rod to his lips. Then he began to pipe—and at that trickle of clear notes falling in a trill as might spring rain, the herwin whistled its morning call and the hanay rocked back and forth on its clawed digging paws, as if the music sent it into a clumsy dance.

I do not know how long we stood there, listening to music that was like none I had ever heard before, but which drew us. Then Lugard set aside the pipe, and he was smiling.

"Magic," he said softly, "Drufin magic." He gave one last note, and the herwin took wing, sailing straightway up into the sky, while the hanay seemed to see us for the first time, gave a startled grunt, and waddled into hiding among the rocks.

"Welcome." Lugard still smiled. "I am Griss and you are—?"

The children, as if released from a spell, ran to him, and each called his name as if he wished to claim instant recognition from this worker of magic. He gave them greeting and then suggested that they explore the Butte, making them welcome to any room with an open door. When they had gone into the corridor behind him, he looked at me, at Annet, and back to me, and his face was darkly sober.

"The refugee ship"—his question was a command for an answer—"what have they decided to do concerning that?"

"We don't know. They have a meeting at the port today."

He limped on into the sun. "Lend me your hopper." Again it was more order than asking. "They can't be so stupid as to let them land—"

I stood aside without a question, so compelling was the force of his preoccupation. It was clear he harbored some thought to the extinction of all else.

He was in the cabin, raised from the ground, when Annet cried out, "Vere! He's going off with all our food—leaving us here! When will he be back? Stop him!"

Since this was now a complete impossibility, I caught her arm and pulled her out of the miniature dust storm raised in his takeoff, urging her to the Butte. She turned on me then with demands to know why I had let him go. And to tell the truth, I had no real answer for her. But I did manage to make her understand that Lugard's supplies could certainly be used by us under the circumstances, and it might be well to see what the Rovers were doing inside.

Three

"IT ISN'T REAL MAGIC!" We heard Gytha's voice raised from one of the rooms. "Don't you *ever* read tapes, Pritha? The vibrations, the sounds—they attract the animals and birds. I don't know what Drufin means—it's probably off-world. But it's the sound—and maybe a special kind of pipe to make it." As usual she was quick to distinguish the real from the unreal.

One of the thoughts I sometimes have crossed my mind then—what *is* real and unreal? Unreal to one people or species can be real to another. Beltane libraries are sadly lacking in information about other worlds—unless it deals with scientific matters. But I had heard stories from spacemen, and perhaps not all of those were tall tales told to astonish the planet bound. Drufin magic meant nothing to me either, but doubtless Gytha's explanation was right. But there were other things beside piping to start the thought of magic growing—

"With a pipe such as that," Thad broke in, "you could go hunting and never come home with an empty bag. Just pipe 'em up and stun 'em."

"No!" Gytha was as quick to counter such speculation as she had been to deny the supernatural. "That is a trap and—"

I moved on into the room. Gytha, her cheeks flushed, faced Thad, indignation expressed in every line of her thin body. Behind her the younger children had drawn together as if to form a support. And Thad had only Ifors Juhlan on his side. It was a clash that had occurred before, and I expected it at intervals. Perhaps someday such a difference of opinions would break Thad loose from the Rovers. He wanted action and more excitement than we could promise him.

"Second Law, Thad," I said now, though that sealed me away into the adult world. But the admonition was strong enough to keep his rebellion bottled.

Second Law—"As we value life and well-being, so does lesser life. We shall not take life without thought or only to satisfy the ancient curse of our species, which is unheeding violence."

There was no need to hunt on Beltane—save for specimens for the labs. And then sure care must be taken of them so that they eventually might be returned unharmed to the Reserves. These were scattered widely, each with its population to be studied. The prizes were the mutants of the over-mountain Reserves. Their intelligence had been raised, and a certain number of such animals had even gone to war, in "beast terms," aligned with human controllers. I hoped to qualify for work on such a Reserve. Since the breakdown of the educational chain, I thought I could persuade the powers in control that practical knowledge of the field type was as useful now as the stated requirements of off-world learning, which might never be in existence again.

I had gone a-hunting with a stunner, and I had shown visa-tapes of this to the Rovers. Perhaps that had been a mistake. Thad—well, we were a nonviolent world, with action mainly confined to cerebration and experimentation within four walls. There had been a case or two during the past few years of killing and pillage without cause. The perpetrators had been sent to the psyche lab at the port and the stories hushed up. But—perhaps not only machines broke under the circumstances that had gripped Beltane for the last decade. I had been thinking of the stalemate in education. If one did not go forward, one did not just remain still; one slipped back. Were we slipping back? We were still conditioned by the laws, intended to keep us at peace with each other and the life about us. But—

"Vere—" Thad changed the subject now, either because he wanted to escape Gytha's accusation or because he was really interested. "What is all this?"

He gestured to indicate the four walls of the room. Time had set lightly here. I believed the Butte must have been sealed airtight. The walls were as bright under the diffused light as if they were newly painted. Three were unbroken; the fourth, with the door, was separated by that into two tall panels. And what they all displayed were maps, each covering a quarter of our continent, north, east, south, and west. All the settlements were marked with small bulbs, unlit. In addition, I picked out some of the long abandoned Security holds, most of them mere sentry posts.

Below each wall was a board with a range of levers and buttons, and in front of each board a chair that slid with ease along the full length of the controls. The center of the room was occupied by a square platform a step above the surface of the floor, and on it was a fifth chair, made to face any wall, as Dinan Norkot had discovered, sitting in it to whirl dizzily about.

Memories of the past when I was about Dinan's age stirred. I had been here once and had seen my father in that center seat—not whirling but turning slowly to watch lights winking on the board. Blue—yes, blue for the sectors, red for the Security posts, and yellow—no, green—for the Reserves.

"This is a com post," I told Thad. Not a com post either, but *the* com post—more important even than the one at the port. Butte Hold had been the most secure of all the posts, and so the most necessary installations were here.

Did it still work, I wondered? The lights were out, but that might only mean that the boards were closed down, not really dead. I went to the one facing north. The port light—I leaned over the board, discovered that that was too uncomfortable, so seated myself in the chair, and compared numbers on board and wall until I found the button to press.

Voices boomed into the room so that I heard Annet cry out, and we all stared at the wall map from which they seemed to break with a clarity that would have been more natural had the men speaking stood before us.

Dagny Norkot ran over to stand beside my chair. "That's my father," she declared. "But he went to the port—"

"—satisfied with their statements. Then—"

It faded as if Norkot had walked away from an open com mike or else that the power installation weakened. Annet was beside me now.

"We're not supposed to be listening in on a Committee meeting," she said.

That was the truth. But somehow I wanted to know just how effective the whole system still was. I snapped up the port lever and depressed that of Yetholme.

Again we had a pickup. Not clear voices as Norkot's had been, but enough to know that the old setup was partially effective.

"You know"—Thad pushed between Annet and my chair—"this Griss Lugard, he can about hear all that is going on—everywhere—and stay right here! Voice pickup anyway. Isn't there any visa-screen relay?"

Again I remembered. Getting out of the seat before the north board, I went to that center control chair where Dinan had been spinning moments earlier. It took me two false starts before I either remembered, and was not aware of it, or lit by chance on the proper combination of two buttons in the chair arms, plus a foot lever. A section of the wall slid up to disclose a screen.

"Yah!" Thad expressed his excited interest. "Now what do you do?"

I glanced quickly over the rest of the map, having no mind to look at any occupied sector house. The easiest choice would be one of the abandoned Security ports in the far north.

"Thad, press the first lever, first row," I ordered, holding the screen ready with my own fingers.

He did so. There was a flicker on the screen and then a picture, so dim at first that I thought the power was nearly exhausted. But as I continued to hold, it built up into a brighter display, and we were looking at another room. This, too, had banks of controls, a couple of chairs. But there was a great crack in the wall behind the control board and—

"Look—a wart-horn!"

For a moment it was startling. Crouched in the chair, which was still on an even keel, was indeed a wart-horn. Its warty skin, its froglike head and face with the forward pointing horns, made it anything but a pleasant-looking object. But the way it crouched in the chair, its webbed forepaws even resting on the arms as it seemed to lever itself up to meet our gaze, always supposing that our actions here had activated the appearance of a twin screen for reception there and two-way viewing, gave it a disturbing air of intelligence, as if it had been about some secret business of its own in our alien structure and had been surprised.

We watched its throat swell and heard, muted but still recognizable, its harsh croaking grunt. It leaned up and out even farther, its face filling the screen, and I heard Pritha cry out, "No! No!"

I released the com buttons, and the screen not only went dark but also the wall moved to cover it again.

"I don't like it! It looked at us!" Pritha's voice became a wail.

I swung around in the chair, but Annet had already taken her in her arms.

"You know wart-horns," she said soothingly. "They are nothing to be afraid of. And if that one saw us, he probably was just as startled as you were. That"—she turned to me— "was an old sentry post, wasn't it, Vere?" At my nod, she continued. "And it's been left empty for years. I bet the wart-horn may have a den there."

"It looked at us," Pritha repeated.

"And we looked at it," Annet answered. "So we're even. And that place where it is is a long way from here!"

"Two days by hopper, Pritha," I cut in. "Nobody goes there any more."

"Vere"—Gytha was beside Thad, her hand poised above the levers and buttons—"let's try another one—maybe this?"

"No!" Annet snapped before I had a chance to answer. "There's been enough of this listening and peeping. And since Sector-Captain Lugard made off with our lunch, suppose we try to find out what is in the cupboards here. As you said, Vere, he owes us that."

"Indeed he does." I backed her up. But I lingered to make sure I was the last to leave the room, Gytha and Thad going reluctantly, gazing back at the tempting display of possible peeps hither and thither across our world.

"Vere?" A small hand slipped into mine. I looked down into Pritha's almost triangular face. The families that had been brought in to settle Beltane had not been homogeneous in the beginning but came from widely separated worlds, since it had been their special talents and training that selected them. So we did indeed represent types of many kinds, some of which had mutated physically from the ancient norm of our species.

Pritha Wymark, within one month of Gytha's age, was hardly taller than Dagny, five years younger. Her delicate bones and slender body, though, were not those of a small child. She had a quick mind, but she was timid, highly sensitive to things that perhaps the others were never aware of or felt only lightly. Now there was a shadow on her ethereal face.

"Vere," she repeated, and her voice was hardly above a whisper. "That wart-horn—it—it was watching us!"

"Yes?" I encouraged, for behind that statement of fact something troubled her. Dimly I felt it also—that the way the thing had squatted in the chair before the screen, its stance aping that of a man minding the control board, had been disturbing.

"It—it was not—" She hesitated as if she could not put her troubled thoughts into words.

"Perhaps it was just the way it was hunched in the chair, Pritha. Wart-horns have never been submitted to the upraying, you know. They are two low on the learn-scale. And that was a sentry post we picked up, way out in the wastelands. It was not on one of the Reserves."

"Perhaps—" But I knew she was not satisfied.

"When we get back, Pritha"—I tried to reassure her—"I'll report it. If by chance some wart-horn *has* been up-scaled and escaped, they will have a record of it. But one does not have to fear even an up-scaled animal—you know that."

"Yes, Vere. I guess it was just the way it sat there, looking at us."

But still she kept her hand in mine until we reached the last of the open doors and looked in upon a scene of activity as Annet examined labels on ration cans taken from a case recently opened and made choices to set out on the table that must once have served the whole garrison for mess.

Lugard's cooking arrangements were simple. He had attached two portable cooking units. And there was another case of mess kits clipped together, which Thad now unpacked with no small clatter.

Against the far wall were the huge units that were dial food, but Lugard's plates were enough for our purposes. Gytha handed the containers Annet selected to Ifors, who fitted them into the heating clips. It was all very brisk and efficient.

"It would seem we are not going hungry," I commented.

Annet wore an excited expression as she turned to me.

"Vere, real caff! Not just parx-seed substitute! And a lot of off-world things. Why, here are camman fowl slices and creamed fass leaves—things we haven't seen for years!"

"Lugard must have been using officers' mess supplies." I crossed to read the labels on some of the cans. We ate well enough on Beltane—perhaps our common fare would have seemed luxury on some worlds, since the bio labs produced new strains adapted to growing here in great variety—but for a long time there had been no imports, and we had heard, if we had never had a chance to taste for ourselves, nostalgic mention now and then of some particular viand our elders remembered.

Prudence finally controlled Annet's selection, and she picked for our eating not the more exotic things she had found, but those that promised few if any upsetting reactions from stomachs unaccustomed to the unknown. We ate cautiously at first and then with our usual good appetites to be satisfied.

When we had done, Annet lined up a small company of containers and looked at me wistfully.

"Do you suppose he would trade?" she asked. "If I could have some of these for Twelfth Day feasting—"

"No harm in asking. He ought to like some fresh dunk bread, or your partin-berry preserves, or even a freeze dinner out of the deep store. Canned rations, even if they are from off-world, must get tiresome after a while.

"Now"—I spoke to the rest—"suppose we set this all to rights again."

Camp discipline held, though I knew they were impatient to go exploring. I had noted that the grav door was shut, and for that I was thankful. They would obey rules, I knew—no opening shut doors.

I was deswitching the heating units when something made me count heads and find two missing, Thad and Ifors. I repeated their names. Annet turned to count, but Dinan had an answer for us.

"They went out—after they packed the mess kits, Vere."

The com room? It would be just like Thad to experiment there, though I thought that the activation of the screens would be something even Thad could not do. But I started down the hall in swift strides, aware that Thad was becoming more the rebel—and I did not want the facedown to come between us here and now.

"—Griss Lugard!"

The volume was up, loud enough so that those words bellowed down the hall, echoing a little. I came into the room just as Thad's hand shot out to the button he had pushed a moment earlier. But, though he was apparently exerting pressure on it, the old fittings were now jammed, and the sound continued to roar.

"That is the situation, Gentle Homos." It was Lugard's voice now with a rasping, grating tone increased by the broadcast. "You cannot trust such treaties—"

"Perhaps you cannot, Sector-Captain." That was Scyld Drax. "The military mind is apt to foresee difficulties—"

"The military mind!" Lugard's interruption came clearly. "I thought I made it simple—the situation is as plain as the sun over you, man! You say you want peace, that you think the war is over. Maybe the war is, the kind we have been fighting, but you don't have peace now—you have a vacuum out of which law, and what little protection any world can depend upon, has been drained. And into this is going to spread, just like one of your pet viruses, anarchy. A planet not prepared to defend itself is going to be a target for raiders. There were fleets wrecked out there, worlds destroyed. The survivors of those battles are men who have been living by creating death around them for almost half a generation, planet time. It has become their familiar way of life—kill or be killed, take or perish. They have no home bases to return to; their ships are now their homes. And they no longer have any central controls, no fears of the consequences if they take what they want from the weaker, from those who cannot or will not make the effort to stand them off. You let this ship land—only one ship, you say, poor lost people; give them living room as we have a sparsely settled world—there is one chance in a hundred you read them aright.

"But there are ninety-nine other chances that you have thrown open the door to your own destruction. One ship, two, three—a home port, a safe den from which to go raiding. And I ask you this, Corson, Drax, Ahren, the rest of you. This was a government experimental station. What secrets did you develop here that could be ferreted out, to be used as weapons to arm the unscrupulous?"

There was a moment of silence. He had asked that as a man might deliver a challenge.

Then we heard Corson. "We have nothing that would serve as such—not now. When the authorities forced certain of us to such experimentation, we refused—and when that authority left, we destroyed all that had been done."

"Everything?" Lugard asked. "Your tapes, your supplies, perhaps, but not your memories. And as long as a man's memory remains, there are ways of using it."

There was a sharp sound, as if a palm had been slapped down hard on some surface.

"There is no need to anticipate or suggest such violence, Sector-Captain Lugard. I—we must believe that your recent service has conditioned you to see always some dark design behind each action. There is not one reason to believe that these people are not what they have declared themselves to be, refugees seeking a new life. They have freely offered to let any one of us come aboard while they are still in off-orbit—to inspect their ship and make sure they come in peace. We would not turn a starving man from our doors; we cannot turn away these people and dare still to call ourselves a peaceful-minded community. I suggest we put it to the vote. Nor do I consider that you, Sector-Captain, are so much one of us as to have a vote."

"So be it—" That was Lugard once more, but he sounded very tired. "'And when Yamar lifted up his voice, they did not listen. And when he cried aloud, they put their hands to their ears, laughing. And when he showed them the cloud upon the mountains, they said it was afar and would come not nigh. And when a sword glinted in the hills and he pointed to it, they said it was but the dancing of a brook in the sun.'"

The Cry of Yamar! How long had it been since anyone had quoted that in my hearing? Why should anyone on Beltane? Yamar was a prophet of soldiers; his saga was one learned by recruits to point the difference between civilian and fighting man.

There was another faint sound that might have been boot heels on a floor. Then a murmur and Ahren's voice rising above that.

"Now—if there are no further interruptions, shall we vote?"

As if Thad had at last loosed the button, though he had ceased to struggle with it some time ago, there was silence in the com room. Thad pushed the button again, as determined now to have it open as he had been earlier to close the channel. But there was no response.

"Vere?" Gytha stood a little behind me. "What was Griss Lugard talking about? Why didn't he want the refugees to land?"

"He was—is—afraid that they may want to turn pirate—or to raid here." Without thinking of my listeners, I gave her the truth.

"Which is simply stupid!" Annet said. "But we must not blame the Sector-Captain. He is a soldier, and he does not understand the kind of life we have here. He will learn. Thad, you should not have listened in on the Committee meeting—"

He looked a little guilty. "I didn't mean to—we were trying to see how many of the stations were still open. I hit that button by mistake, and it stuck there. Truly that is what happened."

"Now"—Annet glanced around the room as if she disliked what she saw—"I think we had better go. We had no right to come here—"

"He said we could go in any room where the door was open," Gytha promptly reminded her. "And this one was. Vere"—she spoke to me—"could we go up in the watchtower and look at the lava lands, even if we can't go out there?"

To me that seemed a reasonable request, and when we found that the door to the upper reaches of the Butte was one of the open ones, we went. There was a short climb and for the last part a steep one. Annet chose to remain below with the Norkot twins and Pritha, who disliked heights. We came out on a windswept sentry go. I unslung my distance lenses to turn them north and west.

Here and there were splotches of green vegetation native to Beltane, not the lighter, cultivated mutant off-world growth that lay about the settlements. In some places it formed odd shadows that seemed almost black. But the stretches of bare lava ran and puddled out in vast rough pockets. There were other runnels of the stuff, and I had never seen a land so forbidding and forsaken. Even if it had any life hiding there, a man could search for a year and perhaps never uncover so much as a trail.

"Yah—" Thad focused his own lenses. "Looks as if someone stuck a paddle down in seal-cor and turned it around a couple of times and then just let it cool. Where are the caves?"

"Your guess is as good as mine," I told him. When I visited the Butte in the old days, I had been too young to go exploring. I could not remember having seen this before, though I had probably been brought up to the lookout.

"Vere, how old is it—the lava flows, I mean?" Gytha asked thoughtfully.

"Read your geology tapes. I wouldn't know that either."

I unslung my lenses and passed them to Ifors, who would hand them in turn to Sabian and Emrys.

"But old—very old—" she persisted.

"Undoubtedly that."

"Then the lava caves might have been here a long time, too—as long as Forerunner times?"

"Who knows when those were? And there were more than one lot of Forerunners." I was evasive, trying to catch Gytha's eye and warn her against the treasure-hunting story. But she had leaned both elbows on the parapet and was holding Thad's lenses, giving a searching survey to the wild lands.

"Forerunners?" Unfortunately Thad had heard. "Why worry about Forerunners? There weren't any ruins here—"

Before I could stop her, Gytha answered. "That's all you know! Griss Lugard found Forerunner relics back in a lava cave before the war. If you'd read Beltane history tapes, you'd know a lot more, Thad Maky. There were men coming from off-world to explore—then the war broke out and nobody did any more about it."

"Is that so, Vere?" Thad demanded of me. "Forerunners—here! Is that why Griss Lugard really came back? My father said he was getting the Butte ready for a new garrison and the Committee wouldn't let them in. They'd put the repel rays on at the port if they tried it. Lugard landed before they knew it, but they aren't going to let any more of his kind in. But if he came back just on his own after Forerunner treasure—Maybe he'd let us help him—or the Committee could make him—"

"Thad! Gytha read a rumor in an old news tape. That is all there is to it. We are not going to mention this to Griss Lugard or at home—understand? This is a *hold*—" I appealed to one of their own private rules. "Holds" were just that, information they kept to themselves, some even secret from me. And I had always respected their reticence. But this was important.

Thad looked steadily back, but there were no reservations and no hint of mutiny in his answer. "Agreed." He used their regular formula.

Then I turned to Gytha. "Hold?"

She nodded violently. "Hold!" And the others followed her.

"Vere." Emrys had aimed the lenses east. "There is something coming—a hopper, I think. And it must be on top circle speed—it's really shooting."

I took back the lenses and followed the pointing of his finger. Our hopper—with Lugard. Perhaps it would be better to make ourselves scarce as soon as we could, so I headed my crew down to the lower levels.

Four

IF WE HAD expected to see in Griss Lugard some reaction to the dispute at the port, we were to be disappointed. Outwardly, he was one on a holiday now. He limped toward us as we waited by the door of the Butte, a smile on his face, though that was pulled slightly awry by the reconstruction flesh on his left cheek and jaw.

"My pardon, Gentle Fem." He spoke first to Annet, using the courtly off-world address and sketching with his free hand a half salute of courtesy. In the other one he carried the basket of food she had packed that morning. "It would seem that in my haste I carried off your nooning. I trust you found enough to make up for it—"

"We did," she returned tartly. But then she, too, smiled and added, "Better fare than was in that, Sector-Captain."

"No." He corrected her. "Not Sector-Captain. I have retired—there is no one here to command, nor will there be. I am Griss Lugard, and I own Butte Hold. But I am no commandant of any new Security force. That will not be seen again on Beltane." His tone, so light at first hail, was now serious, as if he uttered a warning rather than gave an explanation of his presence. Then his mood changed again, and his smile returned. "What think you of my hold?" The question was not asked alone of Annet but of all of us.

"I am afraid that we made too free, though you did say that the open rooms were for exploration," I spoke up. Best to have it clear that we had lighted on one of his possessions that he might not want to have common knowledge—the com system. "We activated the calls—"

But he did not lose his smile. "Did you now? And they worked? How well?"

Could it be true that he had not tried out the system for himself, that he had no curiosity about what could be a spy network across the sectors, did he want or need one?

"It worked. We got a little of your meeting with the Committee." Let him know the worst at once. If he then wanted to fire us out for meddling, well, we perhaps had that coming to us.

"My eloquence, which did not move mountains of pre-judgment, eh?" Again he did not seem disturbed but rather as if he had known all along about our eavesdropping, though I did not see how that could be possible.

Unless—could he have wanted us to do just as we had done? Again—for what purpose? I guessed, however, that would be one question he did not want asked or answered.

Then Pritha stood a step or two nearer to him and looked directly up into his repaired face.

"We saw something too—"

"In the Committee room?" Still in that undisturbed voice.

"No. Vere said it was in one of the old security posts. There was a wart-horn sitting in a chair—acting—acting as if it were a man!"

"What!" For the first time his serenity was ruffled. "What do you mean?"

"We got the visa-screen working," I explained. "Picked up Reef Rough post. The thing was crouched in a chair in the com room, looking straight at the screen. It was just a co-incidence, but a rather startling one."

"It must have been," he agreed. "But if the screen worked at its end, too, it must have been just as astounded, don't you think, Pritha?" He had remembered her name out of the mass introduction of the morning. "I don't believe we need fear an invasion of wart-horns—not wart-horns."

But refugees were different, I thought to myself. For all

44

his surface unconcern, Griss Lugard was inwardly uncommitted to Beltane ways.

For the rest of that day, though, one would not have believed so. Annet was won over as easily as the rest of the Rovers. I think even Gytha's curiosity about the Forerunners was appeased by Lugard's flow of talk. He spoke freely of setting up a new type of Reserve wherein he intended to study native wild life, applying certain techniques he had learned off-world. He would not be working with mutant animals but with norms. And the stories and projects he talked of were engrossing ∩nough so that we could believe he intended just such a life as he outlined.

He brought out his pipe once more, and the notes he drew from it, if they enchanted birds and beasts, could enthrall men also, for while he piped, we listened, and there was no idea of the passing of time until he put it aside with a laugh.

"You pay my poor music high honor, friends. But night comes with lengthening shadows, and I believe questions will be asked if you continue to linger here—"

"Vere!" Annet jumped to her feet. "It's almost sunset! Why, we've been here hours! I am sorry, Griss Lugard." She stumbled a little over saying his name. "We have imposed upon you far too long."

"But, Gentle Fem, it has not been any imposition. The Butte is lonely. A welcome for your guesting here, all of you, is ever ready. There will be no private latch upon this door." He reached one hand to his right and touched the portal with his fingertips, as if so to impress upon us his invitation.

"We can truly come again?" Gytha demanded. "When?"

He laughed. "Whenever you like, Gytha. All and any—whenever you like."

We said our good-bys and thanks. But I wondered as I set the hopper toward Kynvet if we would ever return to the Butte. Lugard's stand before the Committee would give them no good opinion of him, and Ahren and his colleagues would perhaps be now of the belief that close association with an ex-officer would corrupt their youth.

To my surprise, however, there were no comments made on Lugard's argument with the now rulers of Beltane. Some questions were asked concerning the day's activities. I did not think it was deception not to mention our inadvertent eavesdropping. And for once the unity of the Rovers was an aid, since they seemed to have decided among themselves that this was to be a *hold* as far as the adults were concerned. They were free enough on all else, talking a lot of Lugard's project on studying the wildlife of the waste. My own instinct was to question this, but he had already given it as the reason for wanting the Butte.

"So he asked you to return," Ahren commented when Gytha was done. "But you must not take advantage of his courtesy, daughter. He is here on a special grant—"

"Special grant!" I could not suppress that exclamation.

"Oh, yes. It is not at all what we suspicioned. He is, of course and unfortunately, apt to look at matters from the point of view of the Services, but he has severed all relationship with the forces. I gather his injuries made such severance mandatory. Now he is an accredited settler-ranger— with an archaeology grant into the bargain!"

"Forerunners!" Gytha cried with a triumphant glance at me. "I was right—"

But her father shook his head. "Not Forerunners, no. There was never any trace of such here. But before the war Lugard did find some odd remains in one of the old lava caves. There was no time for investigation thereafter—the universal madness had already burst. So the find remained unexamined since Lugard himself was drafted off-world before he could make any concise explorations. There had been a collapse of a cave roof that sealed off the portion he was interested in. Now that he is free, he has returned. Since we will no longer have a garrison here, he claimed Butte Hold and a section of lava lands for pay due him and was given the grant. He has entered that in the port records. I gather that it will take him some time to locate the portion he is eager to find. There have been further subsidences of the land thereabouts, and it may be he will never be able to uncover it again. Now, Vere"—he spoke directly to me—"I do not want the children to be a disturbance to Lugard. Poor man, he has had much to suffer. We cannot be impatient with his views. He has lived with violence so long that he expects to find it everywhere. If he wishes for company—perhaps that of younger people—" Now he looked thoughtful and added, "Did he say aught of what was done before the Committee this afternoon? Make some comment on the decision?"

"What decision, Father?" asked Annet, though I think she guessed the answer as quickly as I did—perhaps because it was more in keeping with her own views.

"It has been decided to extend the offer of friendship and homeland to the refugees," Ahren said a little impatiently before he returned to his main interest. "Lugard said nothing of this? Made no comments?"

I was able to answer no truthfully, for he had not to us.

"I told you." Gytha was inclined to be impatient when she was caught up in some idea of her own. "He talked about animals, and he said we could come again. And he piped—"

"Well enough. Yes, I see no harm in your going to the Butte again, but you will await some specific invitation from Lugard. On the other hand, Vere, you will go there tomorrow with a message from the Committee. We wish to affirm certain matters so there may be no misunderstandings later."

What the message was, I was not told. But I thought perhaps I knew part of what must be on the tape I took to the Butte the next morning. And when I handed it to Griss Lugard, the eyebrow on the normal side of his face twitched up and his wry smile curled.

He had crawled out from under a complicated piece of machinery I did not recognize, though it bore a small resemblance to a cultivator, save that where it should have sprouted a plow nose, this had an arm, now folded under, with a sharp point at its apex. And there were moving belts along its left side with bucket-shaped pockets.

Lugard flipped the roll of tape from one hand to the other, still smiling. "Official ease and desist?" But it seemed he asked that question more of himself than of me. "Or official grants to do as I will? Well, I suppose I better read so I can answer. What do you think of my monster here, Vere?" He seemed in no hurry to read his tape but now held it in one hand while, with the other, he traced along that belt of buckets, some upright, others reversed where the belt turned under. "Excavator." He answered my unasked question. "Made for this country—see her creep-treads? But still anyone mounting her is going to have a rough ride back there." He nodded to the lava lands.

"Then you *are* going to dig out a cave?" I do not know why I had continued to believe that Gytha's story of Forerunner treasure and Ahren's of archaeological exploration had seemed to me a screen. Had there really been a find of artifacts of some race preceding us on Beltane?

"Dig out a cave? But of course, probably more than one. It's all in my charter, boy." But I thought he gave me a quick, measuring glance as if he wondered now about me as I did about him. "She needs a good overhaul—has been laid up too long, though this was meant for hard labor under difficult conditions. Look her over, if you wish." He went into the hold with the tape.

Though I had never seen an excavator of this type before, I could understand most of the functions of the machine. The spearpoint on the now folded arm must be used to chip away at obstructions, the bucket band carrying the debris away from the work area. There were also two more attachments laid out on a plasta sheet, both smeared with preservative. One was a borer, the other a blower, both intended, I deduced, to fit on the end of the arm now carrying the pick.

It was a relatively small machine, meant to be handled by one man, mounted on elastic treads that should see it through the lava country. And it should be a very efficient tool. I wondered what other machines had been stored at the Butte. Lugard must have been owed a vast amount of back pay to gain all this. Or else there was another answer. If conditions off-world were as chaotic as he described, perhaps somewhere a bureaucrat saw no reason to keep on his books a hold on Beltane and had been ready to sign it away—perhaps even for some private consideration Lugard could offer him?

"So they did it, made their stupidly blind choice." Lugard came up behind me as I surveyed the excavator.

"You mean let the refugees in? But they may not be the menace you think them."

Lugard shrugged. "Let us hope so. Meanwhile, I shall make no attempt to corrupt innocent young minds with my off-world pessimism."

"Ahren gave you that warning?"

He smiled but with little humor. "Not in so many words, no, but it is implied. I am to be a responsible citizen, well aware of my duties as well as my privileges. Was there anything said about the children not coming again?"

"Just a warning to Gytha not to intrude if you were busied with your own affairs."

Now his smile was less of a grimace. "Good enough! And I'll play fair in return—no more warnings. I could not convince them even if I used a ply drug probably. They're as set in their own processes as that lava flow is glued to the mountain over there."

"They think the same of you," I commented.

"Which they would. But bring the children, Vere, if they want to come. The Butte is lonely sometimes. And they have quick minds. They might be far more of an aid than a hindrance."

"What are you hunting for?" I dared to ask then.

"I suppose some would say treasure."

"Forerunners really?" My disbelief must have shown. He laughed.

"No, I don't think Forerunners, though we cannot rule out any possibility until we uncover the ice cave—always supposing I can locate it again. Ten years—such as I have spent—is a long time, and there have been changes in the land, too—several landslips and cave-ins."

"What about this ice cave?" I persisted.

"We were exploring with the idea of developing storage centers," he said. "Time was running out. We knew we might be at war shortly. And then there was always a chance that Beltane would not be safely behind any so-called battle lines but right out in a fleet blast. We needed hidey holes then, or thought we did. Lava caves run like tunnels. We opened several new ones and were exploring them. The squad I commanded found ice and things in it, enough to show that we weren't the first to think of storing down there. There were supplies frozen in. But we had to close it off in a hurry. Security wanted no poking around at a critical time."

"Gytha found the story in an old news tape."

Lugard nodded. "Yes—men talk. Rumor got out. So your father decided to make as innocuous a tale as he could. We admitted a find and said it was sealed pending the arrival of off-world experts. Then we really sealed the whole section. I figure it will take some work to open it up now, perhaps more than is feasible."

"But if conditions now off-world are so bad—"

"Why do I want to go treasure hunting? Well, I have all the time in the world now, Vere. And I have no occupation. There is this equipment waiting to be used, and curiosity is nibbling at me, biting pretty sharply at times. Why not? Even if I am never able to find that cave again, or if I do, no one is going to be interested in my discovery except myself—but that is enough. Unless you and the children will—"

I was. There was no denying the surge of excitement in response to Lugard's story. And if he told the Rovers, there would be no holding them back. Help or hindrance, they would swarm to the Butte.

"So, let me get this old pick-rock to working and we're off—" He went to his knees and then lay flat to crawl under the excavator. "Meanwhile, if the children want to come, bring them, any time."

I repeated that invitation to Ahren when I returned to Kynvet, and to my surprise, he was receptive to the idea that the Rovers might visit the Butte and take part in Lugard's search. So in the weeks that followed, we did that several times. Once or twice Annet also joined us, always bringing food of her own to trade with Lugard for off-world supplies, an exchange that satisfied them both.

In those weeks the refugees, having landed their ship, not at the port but well to the north in a spot they selected, settled quietly to their own affairs. Since most of our people were long conditioned to be concerned only with their work, there was little visiting between any of the settlements and the refugee camp. They came into port now and then, made requests for medical aid or supplies, and tendered in turn off-world products, some of which were eagerly welcomed by the sector people. It would seem that Lugard had been indeed wrong.

That Lugard himself would have some contact with the off-worlders I should have foreseen, though knowing his estimation of them, I was surprised to find a flitter, definitely not one from the port, on the landing space by the Butte when I brought the hopper in one morning. As it happened I was alone, for which I was glad, since, had there been any witnesses to carry the tale of what happened—

Lugard was at the door of the Butte, but he held no pipe in his hands. One hand swung idly at his side as he faced the two men standing before him; the other rested only inches away from a weapon leaning against the door, one that was not a conventional stunner.

The men both wore shabby tunics that had been part of uniforms, and their deep tans said they were out of space. They kept empty hands ostentatiously in sight, as if in no way wishing to alert Lugard.

I felt in the side rack of the hopper and loosed the stunner. Holding it in hand, I dropped out, to walk across the sand, my soft woods boots making no sound. But Lugard saw my coming.

"Good guesting—" He raised his voice in the Beltane greeting.

"High sun and a fair day," I returned. The men turned in a swift movement, as if they had been drilled. I fully expected to see weapons facing me, but their hands were still empty. They stared at me blank-eyed. I was sure that neither would forget me and that they had quickly summed up my potential in relation to the scene.

"The answer is no, Gentle Homos." Lugard spoke now to them. "I have no need for aid in my work here—save what is offered by the settlers. And I have no wish to be overlooked while I work either."

The taller of the two shrugged. "It was only a thought," he said. "We believed we might help a fellow veteran—a mutual-aid pact—"

"Sorry—no!" Lugard's voice was cool and final.

They turned and went, without a backward look. But still I felt a need to hold the stunner ready. I had never used even that defense save to control a man in such a temper as to unleash violence. But what I sensed emanating from the two now climbing into the flitter made a chill crawl between my shoulders. If I had been conditioned to nonviolence by my childhood training, then in that moment the conditioning cracked under an inheritance from generations of fighting ancestors. I could smell the cold promise of trouble.

"What did they want?" I asked when the flitter lifted in an upsurge that blew sand spitefully around us and into the half-open door to the hold.

"According to their story, employment." Lugard's fingers closed about the weapon he had had on display. He looked down at it, and his mouth was set. "We could not have expected they would not hear the treasure story—"

"And they may be back, with reinforcements?" I asked. "With you alone here—"

But at that Lugard laughed. "This is a Security hold, remember? I have devices to activate, if I wish, that will close this tight against anything they can bring up. No, this was just a try-on. But I tell you, Vere, when the Committee invited them in, they opened the door to night, whether they believe it or not. Now, what can I do for you?"

I remembered my own news. "They're going to give me a post—in the Anlav Reserve."

"How soon?"

"Next month." It seemed to me that he had gone tense when I had told him of my luck, almost as if he feared to hear it. But why? This was, as he had known from all the talking I had done, the only future I had on Beltane. And to get the appointment now, with no more putting off because I had no formal schooling, was a triumph due to my continued persistence.

"Next month," he repeated. "Well, this is next to second

Twelfth Day. Suppose on third Twelfth Day we do a little celebrating out here? The whole of the Rovers, plus Annet, if she can come, and urge her to it, Vere. I'm getting close to a find. Maybe we'll break through in time to make a double occasion of it."

I was distracted by his mention of a breakthrough. He would not say that unless he was sure of success, and again the excitement of a treasure hunt tingled in me. I agreed and spent some time working with him on a new machine, one meant to carry supplies but which he thought could be used to transport debris away from the promising cave he had just opened.

When I returned to Kynvet, I found again a convocation of transportation in the yard. But the drivers were already taking off, and Ahren waved me out of the hopper with haste, almost climbing over me to take his seat at the controls. I went in and looked to Annet for an explanation. For once she was not busy at any household task but stood at the window watching her father away, a worried look on her face.

"What has happened?"

"There are two more ships in orbit. They say they want to join the refugees—that they were promised a place here."

"I thought there was a treaty for one ship only."

"They say that is a mistake, that the first ship meant to treat for them all. The Committee is going to talk with their representatives. They came down in a lifeboat."

I thought of Lugard's disregarded warning, of the type of men who had visited the Butte, and of the undefended and now undefendable port. That sensation of danger I had had at Butte Hold was again cold in me. But did Lugard know? And knowing, what could he do to defend people who would make no move to help themselves?

"Dr. Corson says they seem very reasonable," Annet continued. "After all, it is only just that they should want to be with their friends, and it could all be a misunderstanding. But they will have to put it to the full vote. Vere, what did Griss think of your news?"

I told her of the invitation, and she nodded. "I think we could go. If they have a full vote, all the sectors combining, it will come about then, so they won't mind what we do. It would be wonderful if he did find something and we had a chance to see it first!"

She did not mention the refugees again. It was as if she purposely avoided a subject too indelicate or unpleasant to discuss. But I knew that from that hour it was always in our minds.

Five

FULL VOTE was decided upon we learned, which meant that all the adults at Kynvet, as well as those of the other settlements, would gather at the port. And the Ahrens, as well as the parents of the other Rovers, welcomed our plan for going to the Butte. I gathered that this time there was divided sentiment over allowing the landing of new ships, and there might be protracted argument. Perhaps some of Lugard's warnings were beginning to make sense to the more suspicious members of the Committee. There were defenses at the port, but how much these had suffered from years of neglect no one really knew. And whether the handful of veterans who had returned could successfully activate them was also a question, not apparently that any move had been made to do this.

We left early in the morning of the third Twelfth Day—the whole of the Rover crew: Dagny and Dinan Norkot, Gytha, Sabian Drax, Emrys Jesom, Ifors Juhlan, Pritha, and Thad, as well as Annet. We carried our field kits since this was to be a real trip into the lava country; the hopper was loaded to the point that we had to make a low flight with many rest runs on the ground. Thus, it was past the ninth hour when we set down at the Butte. Lugard was waiting, sitting at the controls of what had once been a squad troop carrier. He was impatient, but he left the loading of our kits to us, going back to the hold himself for a long moment just

55

before we pulled out. When he returned, the leaves of the door clicked to behind him with so sharp a note that I turned my head just in time to see him slip the metal plate that locked them into the front of his coverall. So, did he fear that there might be visitors during our absence? I did not wonder at his precautions.

It might have been a tight fit in the squad carrier had we all been adults, but the children were reasonably comfortable as Lugard put it into gear and we rumbled out, Annet sharing the driver's seat with him. The rest of us were wedged in against too much jouncing by our kits and bundles already there. I looked among those and in the sling behind his seat for the weapon he had had. But the arms slings were all empty, and if he carried any such, they were hidden.

We all snapped on dark goggles as we crawled deeper into the knife-ridged land under the baking of the sun, which was reflected from the congealed flows. There was a crunched trail ahead twisting and turning upon itself, seeking the best passage. I thought that Lugard must have been this way many times before, though this was the first time he had taken us farther than past the first barriers of the forbidding territory.

Scrapes along outcrops suggested that some of those trips had been made in vehicles larger than the troop carrier in which we now rode or the excavator he had first put into working order, and I wondered what other types of machines he had brought into use. His determination suggested that, though he made his reports in an either-or manner, saying he thought he could find again his ice cave but was not entirely sure, he inwardly was more certain and was set upon proving it.

Now he took us along this very rough road at a pace that was the best a man might dare to hold in such broken terrain, as if there were a set hour for our arrival at the diggings and that it was important we not be late.

As he had earlier explained, and we knew, the lava caves were tubes that one could enter only through the collapse of some roof section. We passed now more than one promising hole. Twice we crossed a "bridge" spanning such a drop. There were bright lichens and a fringing of moss here and there. We had made so many turns in our trail that, had there not been a compass on the board, I could not have truly said that the Butte now lay either behind or before us, for there was a deceptiveness to this land that I had never experienced before in the wilds of Beltane—as if the many frozen flows, cones, craters, and the like had been deliberately formed to confuse the eye and sense of direction.

Time was also difficult to judge. Under the heat of the sun in this hot bowl country, it seemed very long since we had left the Butte. Yet when I looked at my watch, I discovered that we had been on our way less than an hour. We had seen no signs of life, but then the constant crunch-crunch made by our own progress would warn away any animals that chose such a waste for their homes or hunting grounds.

We rounded at last a broken cone, which had the height of a steep-sided hill, and saw that the tracks led straight to a gap, above which was the skeleton frame of a derrick. Lugard pulled up beside that opening.

He had a small platform to lower into the hole and suggested that I go down with Thad as the first to embark, while he worked the lift.

I was not a speleologist and took my place somewhat gingerly on that unsteady surface, Thad facing me, our fingers interlaced on the safety cords, a pile of kits and one of Lugard's bundles between our feet. We spun down, and it was a sensation I was glad lasted no longer than it did. The light was dim and not dark; yet the murk arose to engulf us as if we were being swallowed up by some great beast.

It was cooler, a welcome relief from the parching of the sun without. I remembered that air movement underground was slow, and within a few feet of the entrance of any cave the temperature falls to that of the walls. Lugard had suggested we bring overtunics for that very reason, and now, shivering, I could see why.

The platform made several trips, bringing two passengers and kits and supplies on each descent. I wondered at the number of boxes and bundles Lugard sent down, since there were not only those from the troop carrier, but also some from a pile waiting at the mouth of the cave.

At last he swung over and down by himself, not drawing up the platform but using a rope with such ease as showed he had done the same before, while the platform remained on the floor of the cave. I suspected he wanted it so as a means of protection. He had not mentioned any return of the refugee-ship people, but he might be taking precautions against surprise. However, I was also certain he would not have brought the children here had he believed there was any real danger. Only, what is danger? We were to learn the degrees of that without warning.

Once below, Lugard switched on a beamer to reveal the road for us. Caves acted as cold traps in winter. Air settled to the lowest levels there to leave unending frost upon rock surfaces. Lugard was searching for an ice cave, and our path grew colder as we drew away from the entrance.

We had gone only a few paces in when Lugard shot the beamer ray toward the roof. Untidy masses were plastered there against the walls only a handbreadth from the ceiling. We saw restless movement.

"Westerlings!" cried Gytha.

Long-billed avian heads swayed or bobbed up and down. Westerlings they were, in nests of bits of withered stuff and mud. They were night flyers, mainly noted for the action that gave them their name—their flocks flew almost always from east to west when aroused from feeding.

But their nest colony was set close to the door into the open, and we were soon past them in the long bore that was the cave. This descended, not abruptly but at an angle, which did not make walking too difficult. I looked around for some signs that Lugard's machines had been at work here. But there were no tread marks on the floor, no scrapes on the walls.

At his asking we made use of the only aid he seemed to have imported into this stone tunnel—a small, treaded traveling cart, loading it with all the bundles he had brought down. But our packs we backed ourselves. Again I wondered at the reason for the pile of supplies, if supplies these were.

We had journeyed for perhaps an hour when Lugard halted and suggested a rest. He himself pulled the bundles from the cart, piled them against the wall, and turned to face back as if it was now in his mind to return for those we had left. But he never had a chance.

There was a wave of vibration through the walls of the cave, in the solidified layer of lava under our boots, giving one the sickening sensation that the world one had always accepted as solid and secure was that no longer. I heard a shrill scream and saw in the glow of the beamer wide frightened eyes and mouths opening on more cries of alarm. A small body lurched against me, and I instinctively threw out my arm to draw Ifors closer, while his fists balled wads of my coverall and he clung to me as if I were his only hope of protection.

A second shock came, even worse than the first. Lava chunks broke loose, rattling and banging. I cowered, deafened by the sound, while dust arose about us in choking clouds.

"Out—" I saw Annet staggering for the way down which we had come. She pushed before her one of the children and dragged another. A taller figure, which was Lugard, tried to intercept her, but, intentionally or not, she eluded him and wavered on. "Out! This way, children!"

"Get her!" Lugard rounded on me with that order just as a third shock wave hit with force enough to send me crashing against one of the walls, Ifors still clutching me in a hold that could not be easily broken. I saw Lugard go down, while the beamer he must have put on the floor went into a weird dance as if the surface under it were rising and falling in quick, panting breaths. There were more falling chunks, some of them striking the supplies he had just unloaded.

With one hand I fumbled with the buckles of my pack and managed to jerk at it until I was free of its burden. I saw Thad sitting down, a stunned expression on his face.

"After her," Lugard panted. "The entrance—loose rocks—it may cave in—" He was struggling to get to his feet, but the last tremor had caused the bundles to land on top of him, and his lameness was to his disadvantage.

I pried Ifors' hold from my coverall, and the fabric tore as I tried to loose the shocked boy. "Thad! Take Ifors!" With a last rip I held him away from me and pushed him toward Thad, who was getting dazedly to his feet. The others were all there, Gytha, on her knees by the beamer, setting it steady again, Pritha in a small ball beside her, Emrys shaking his head and pawing at his eyes with both hands, Sabian—Only the twins and Annet were gone.

To be caught in a collapse of the roof! I could share Annet's fear, but if she were running straight into danger—and Lugard knew the ways of these burrows best—I could not run, not over this rough flooring, but using my belt torch, I went at the best pace I could manage, back along the trail, calling Annet's name as I hurried.

She had not gone so far that I could not overtake her. But what had halted her was a fall of rock that almost closed the tunnel. Far above we could see a small patch of sky. As I reached her side, she was pressed against the wall, looking up at the freedom out of her reach, the twins in her arms, their faces hidden against her.

"Back! Lugard says it is dangerous here—the roof may come down!" I took a good grip on her arm. She tried to twist away, but my strength was greater than hers, though I could not drag her more than a pace or two back. And I feared a second collapse might crush us before we were beyond that danger point.

"Out—" She tried to pull in the opposite direction, even though the way was blocked. "We have to get the children out!"

"Not that way." I pinned her to the wall with my shoulder, my face only inches from hers as I summoned her to reasoned thinking again. "Lugard says it is dangerous. He knows these caves, and there are other ways in and out—"

However, I wondered at that. If the tackle for the platform had fallen—and surely such shocks had unseated it—then how could we get out, even if the fall choking the tunnel was loose and easy to clear? Someone would have to climb that shaft and see about the lowering ropes. And I knew who, though the thought of it made me sick, as my head for climbing was not good. Best get back to Lugard now and discover if there was another exit, one less demanding.

"Lugard!" Annet almost spat the name at me. "He had no right to bring us here—to endanger the children!"

"I suppose he could foresee this quake?" I demanded. "But we must get back. It is deeper and so safer back there." But that was another bit of reasoning of which I was not sure.

Reluctantly, she started back. I picked up Dagny, whose small body was convulsed with shudders. She was not crying but breathing in gasps, her eyes wide in her small face, clearly so deep in fear that she was hardly conscious of her surroundings. Annet half supported, half led her brother.

We had not yet reached the others when there came another series of tremors. We crouched against the wall, the two children between us, sheltered by our bodies as much as possible. Rocks rolled, not only from overhead, but also down the slope of the cave. It was a miracle that none of them struck us. After a last jar there was again a period of quiet, and a new fear stirred in my mind. Once this had been volcanic country. Could such shocks as the earth had just suffered open some fissure on inner fires and set the cones to blazing again? Annet was so right in her instinctive flight for the surface, and the quicker we *were* out the better.

"Vere! Annet!" Our names echoed hollowly up the corridor of the cave, the sound distorted and booming.

I got cautiously to my feet, almost fearing that that small movement could bring a return of the tremors, so unsteady had our world suddenly become. "Here!" I answered, my voice hoarse from the dust drying my mouth and throat.

Under my urging Annet got up also. I once more held Dagny while she led the boy, and we took one cautious step after another on the down slope. Thus, we gained the halting place. Lugard sat on the cart, his right leg stretched out before him as he rubbed at it with both hands, working with a grim purpose and determination. He looked up as we came, and I saw a flash of relief in his eyes.

"Aid kit." He did not leave off rubbing his leg to point to where that lay in the tossed bundles and abandoned kits, but rather indicated it with his chin. "Give each of them one of the green tablets—they're in shock."

He must have already so aided the others who needed it, for Ifors sat relaxed with his back against a bale and Pritha drank quietly from a canteen, while Thad was at work straightening out the mess of tangled boxes, Emrys helping him and Sabian standing by. Gytha knelt by Lugard, holding another canteen ready for his use.

Annet crossed to stand directly before him. "How do we get out of here?" she demanded. "The children—"

"Are probably far safer right here than on the surface now—" he told her.

"In here?" she shot back incredulously. "With rocks coming down on their heads?"

"It's safer farther on. We'll move now," he said.

"A quake—or quakes such as these—" I knelt beside him to ask my own question in a whisper. "What about renewed volcanic action?"

"Quakes?" Lugard repeated. Then his mouth tightened in a grimace that might have been caused by pain in the limb he nursed. "You poor—" He checked himself and began again. "Those were not quakes."

"No?" Annet squatted on her heels, finding it too difficult to see eye to eye with Lugard since he did not rise. "Then what were they?"

"Distributors."

For a moment I groped in the dark, and I do not think that Annet understood at all. Then the years-old meaning of the term struck home, and I think I gasped. I could have shuddered as deeply as Dagny was still doing against my shoulder.

Distributors—an innocuous name for death and such destruction as Beltane had never seen, though such had made deserts of worlds as peaceful as this one.

"The refugees?" My mind leaped to the only explanation.

"Just so." Lugard paused in his rubbing. Now he flexed his knee slowly and carefully, and he could not conceal a catch of breath when he set foot to floor.

"What do you mean?" Annet's voice rose, and Gytha drew

closer. That stopped the work of his labor gang, and they all listened. "Distributors?"

"Bombs." Thad answered before Lugard could. I think that at that moment Lugard was angry with himself for revealing the truth, though it was indeed best that at least we older ones knew who and what we now faced.

"Bombs!" Annet was entirely incredulous now. "Bombs— here on Beltane? Why? Who would do such a thing?"

"The refugees," I told her. "What chance—?" I wanted to ask the rest of that badly but knew better than to blurt it out, though at least Thad, as I could read the expression on his face, was already close behind me in thought. No, it was best not to think now of what might be happening up there and to whom. This was the time to concentrate on those locked in with me and the responsibility I had to the group I had so trustingly led into peril.

I said directly to Lugard, "You knew—or suspected?"

Slowly, he nodded. "I suspected from the first. I was sure last night."

"The com link?"

Again he nodded. And the arm I held about Dagny tightened until she stirred and gave a soft cry, which was part moan. If Lugard had had warning of attack, then he had deliberately brought us here because—

He might have been reading my thoughts. "Because this is the safest place on Beltane—or in Beltane—here and now. I told you we opened passages for shelters here before the war. I've been reopening those. If I had had more time, if those poor benighted fools of the Committee had only believed me—we could all have been unharmed. As it is, *we* are safe—"

"No!" Annet's hands were at her mouth, smearing the dust across her chin and cheeks. "I don't believe it! Why would they do such a thing? We gave them a home—"

"They may have only wanted a base," Lugard replied. There was a weariness in his voice, as if he had been driving himself to this point and that now, when his worst fears had been realized, he could no longer hold to such determined energy. "Also—perhaps the vote went against the two new ships, and those refugees were prepared to take what was not given."

"Where do we go now?" I broke the silence that followed.

"On." Lugard nodded toward the passage. "There's a shelter base down there."

I expected Annet to protest, but she did not, only got slowly to her feet and went for the aid kit. Lugard held out his hand.

"Give me a boost," he ordered. "We can use the cart for quite a while yet. Then we'll have to pack in."

"These are supplies?"

"Yes."

I helped him up, and he leaned against me for a long second or two before he tried to put his weight on his leg. Apparently, he could do that, and he took a limping step or two onward. But that it cost him more than just effort I deduced by a jerk of muscle beside his mouth on the untreated side of his face.

While Annet tended the twins, we all set about loading the cart, though I thought that before long we would have to dump some of it and let Lugard, and perhaps the twins, ride.

Thad and I shared the pull rope, and Gytha moved forward quickly and took up Lugard's hand to settle it on her shoulder, providing him with a crutch of willing flesh and bone and redoubtable spirit. Annet carried Dagny, who lay against her shoulder with closed eyes as the sedative worked, while Emrys and Sabian between them guided Dinan along, and Ifors stumbled beside the cart, one hand on the lashings that fastened its cargo.

We proceeded with many halts, and at last I persuaded Annet to lay Dagny on the cart. But in turn she took one of the bundles from the top. She did not try to argue any more. However, I thought that she still did not believe Lugard, and she must be raging inside to be out of the caves to prove him wrong.

Twice we crossed mouths of other caves splitting from the road we had chosen, as if the long lava floods had divided. But Lugard always nodded to the main tunnel. He was sweating, the trickles of moisture down his face washing runnels through the dust. Now and then he breathed shallowly through his mouth. But it was I who called the halts, and he never made any complaint when we trudged on again.

My watch told me we had been two hours underground when we made a more lengthy pause and ate. I saw Annet stare down at the food she unwrapped and guessed at her thoughts. High among them must be disbelief that *this* could be happening, had happened since this morning, when she had set together those rounds of bread with a preserve of irkle fruit—fruit she had stewed herself and stored in the cupboard at Kynvet.

Did Kynvet exist now?

Lugard made only a pretense of eating, though the children were hungry and wolfed down all we gave them. I wondered if we should hold back a portion. How long must we stay in these caverns? Lugard had brought supplies—food, water—but—

And if we went out, what would we face? Suppose the refugees had finished off—though my mind shied from that, and I had to force myself to face a very grim guess—the sector people? Would we fare any better were we to turn up after the initial massacre? Yet Lugard must believe we had a chance for survival or he would never have labored so.

He was fumbling in the front of his tunic, having set aside most of his food untouched. Now he brought out his pipe. Beside me Annet moved and quickly checked. Perhaps she had been about to protest. But if so, she thought better of it.

So in the depths of that cave, with our world reft from us, Lugard played. And the magic he wove settled into us as a reassuring flood of promise. I could feel myself relaxing; my whirling thoughts began to still, and I believed again. In just what I could not have said, but I did believe in the rightness of right and that a man could hope and find in hope truth.

I shall always remember that hour, though I cannot now draw back into mind the song Lugard played. The feeling it left in me I do know, and regret I shall not have it to warm me again, for of all we lost on that day, we had still to face the greatest blow from what men call fate.

It began when Lugard put down his pipe and we awoke

out of the spell he had woven to soothe us. There was another sound, and it had nothing to do with music.

Lugard's head went up and he cried out, "Back against the walls!"

We moved as if his shout had been a blaster aimed at us. I hurled Annet, Dinan with her, back and swept up Gytha and Emrys to join them, while across I saw Thad, jerking Ifors and Pritha, stumble toward the opposite wall.

"Dagny!" Annet screamed.

She had been lying asleep on the roll of blankets by the cart, and now she was out of reach—out of ours, but not Lugard's. I saw him lurch forward and his arm crook about the little girl. He swept her back and away from himself. But when he would have followed, his leg gave way under him, and he sprawled on his face, while the glow of the beamer made it all clear. There was a rushing rock slide down the core of the cave, not directly from overhead. And before I could move to pull him free, that slide swept over and about him as might the flood of a river in high spate.

Six

THE SAME RIVER of rock had knocked out the beamer, and we were choking in the dark, coughing and hacking in the dust. For a moment I could do no more than lean against the wall and try to ease my tortured lungs. Then somehow I got my belt light on. In the place of the wide rays of the beamer, it was only a small thrust against the dark. And what it showed made me want to switch it off again.

Our cart, which had been left in the middle, must have acted in part as a dam, though the force of the sweep had carried it on. And in the debris that had piled up behind it—Lugard—he must be caught in that!

"Gytha! Dinan! Thad!" Annet's voice, so husky that the names could barely be distinguished, rang out from beside me. She was calling the roll.

One by one they answered. But I was already at the pile of rocks and Thad not long in joining me. We had to work with what seemed painful slowness since the stuff moved and we were afraid of starting a second slip. Then Gytha joined us, also lighting her belt torch, and Emrys. Lights flashed on, giving us a good sight. Annet took from me the stones I freed to put to one side, and I saw each of us had such a co-worker.

We made no sounds except the coughs that hurt the throat, and I knew that all were doing as I did, listening with both fear and hope gnawing at them. We had to go so slowly when there was such a need for speed.

It was part of the cargo of the cart that had protected him from an instant crushing death we discovered when we had him free. By some chance, two of the bundles had fallen on either side of his body, providing a part defense.

I hardly dared to move him from where he lay face down. He made no sound, and I was certain he was gone, but we cleared a space about him, and Annet quickly unrolled blankets, spreading them out as long as his dust-covered body. Somehow we got him over, face up, on that small easing.

His eyes were closed, and there was a dark trickle from the corner of his mouth. I am no medico, my knowledge being only enough to provide first aid in an accident. He had broken bones and, I was sure, internal injuries. Annet had the kit open. Luckily it lay close to the wall against which Lugard would have been safe had he not returned for Dagny. But there was little in that save what might alleviate pain for a short time. And to move him, even onto the cart, could kill him, but it could be our only chance to save him.

"Get the cart free," I ordered Thad. "Then strip it down."

He nodded and shooed the other boys before him to that task. Annet spilled some water to sponge Lugard's face from her canteen onto a strip of cloth she tore from an inner garment, and under her touch his eyes opened. I had hoped he would remain unconscious. Such hurts as he had taken must keep him in agony.

I saw his lips move and leaned over him. "Don't try to talk—"

"No—" He got that out as a whisper. "Map—inner seal pocket—get on—to safe quarters." Then his face went oddly slack, and his mouth fell loose, while the trickle from it became a dark froth, which Annet wiped away.

My hand felt for the pulse at his throat; I feared to try to touch his chest to hunt for heart beat. He was not gone—not yet.

Only I did not believe he could stand even lifting to the cart, and to carry him in a blanket would be worse. There were supplies ahead—he had mentioned that earlier. Suppose there were medical ones among those? Lugard had had all the stores of the Butte to plunder. In such there might be something—though one part of my mind told me that anything less than quick hospitalization at the port would not save him.

But you cannot sit and wait for death, not when there is the slimmest of fighting chances. Annet must have agreed with that, for she looked across to me.

"Take the map, go on. There may be things there—"

But to leave the rest—Again she read my indecision.

"It is the best. We cannot move him now. There may be a stretcher there—other things—"

"And if there is another rock fall?" I demanded.

"We can pull the blankets over there." She nodded to the side, her hands still busy with that patient washing away of the ever-gathering blood foam. "We shall have to do that much. And we shall stay there. We can't leave him here, and we can't wait forever. There has to be *something*—perhaps a better cart. You must try it, Vere."

We pulled Lugard a few inches at a time over to the wall. As gently as I could, I unsealed his stained tunic and took out a folded piece of plasta-mat. The lines on it caught fire from our lamps, and I saw it was drawn with cor-ink for use in limited light. But the branching passages on it were many, and it took me a moment's study to locate the tunnel that held us. Once I had traced that from our entrance point, I could see the path ahead running reasonably straight. And perhaps Lugard's secure place was not too far beyond.

Thad had found the beamer and set it up. It had been made for hard usage in the field, and after he had tightened a loose connection, it flashed on again. I took up one of the canteens, longing to drink but prudence warned me to endure the thirst as long as I could and conserve water, the more so as we found that the tank of liquid on the cart was leaking. Annet moved quickly to add what she could of its contents to all our canteens and began hunting around for other possible containers.

I stood for a long moment over Lugard before I left. He

was still breathing, and as long as a man lives, there is hope. I clung to that as I went.

The beamer provided a beacon behind me for a space, but I did not turn to look at it. Then I came to one of those divisions of ways, and this time my fire-drawn map said not to stay on the main course but to take a new. Within moments I was in the dark and flashed on my belt torch.

Caves have their inhabitants, which vary with the depth, moisture, content, and the like. I had seen in the labs some blind creatures taken out of this eternal dark. Beltane had once had a small biospeleology department, but when Yain Takuat had died, there had been no replacement for his specialty.

Only the creatures I had seen had come from the moist water-formed caves, while this was different country. I swept my light from side to side, hunting for any hint that this was not just dead rock. I would have welcomed a single slime trail, a single flatworm clinging to the roof overhead.

What my light did pick up was a curl of skin and bones rolled against the wall. I took a step closer. My first aversion was not justified—these were no human remains but the dried remnants of a wart-horn, one larger than I had seen before. But those lived in swamps. What was such doing here? Unless there was some outlet in the maze, leading to water, and the thing wandered in and became lost. That was reassuring in its way with the promise of water.

It was only a little way beyond that I came to where Lugard had said we could not take the cart, for here the floor of the tunnel, which had been sloping gradually all the way since we had left the surface, now gave way. There were a series of ledges—a giant staircase—to descend. I looked at it in despair. We could never get Lugard down unless we could find some aid—

I thought of a stretcher, even a section of crate or box. Could he be lashed tightly to that and lowered? When one is desperate, one can always improvise. Now I swung from one ledge to the next, my belt torch showing a wild scene of fallen rubble and bad footing below.

The air here was colder, far more so with every ledge I

passed. I found it hard to lay hand to the surfaces of the rock, for there was frost on some of them. Then I reached the bottom and picked a way among heaps of fallen scree. There was a path here. Heavy objects had been dragged along, leaving a road. I wondered at the energy Lugard had expended. Or were these signs left by those who had once thought to make an underground war retreat before Butte Hold had been closed?

This lower cave widened out from the narrow end where I entered. Then my light picked out what was there, and I was startled into a full stop. There were structures, three of them, though my light could barely reach the end of the farthest one. Between them were stockpiles of boxes and crates. Lugard certainly could not have done all this. It was the remains of the plan never carried through.

Each of the buildings was walled with cor-blocks, which had probably been fused together on the spot. They each possessed a single door in one wall but no other openings. And the roofs were half arcs made of sheets of cor that had been welded into solid masses.

If they had been locked, Lugard must have opened them. Perhaps the same master key that controlled the Butte door also worked here. The first I explored must have been intended for a headquarters, perhaps also a com center. The divisions in it did not reach the ceiling but arose about seven feet from the floor to make three rooms of the structure. One had two desks, a rank of files, and the board of a small computer. The next had banks of com boards almost as elaborate as those in the Butte. I tried to activate one. I do not know what I hoped for—perhaps to reach some answer on the surface—but here all was dead. The third and last "room" had four bunks and very simple living arrangements—by the look never put to use.

The next building held more bunks in one large room and at its end a smaller compartment with a cooking unit and water taps. I turned one, and there was a thin trickle from it, dripping down into a cor-basin. Water, anyway.

In the third building was a bewildering array of control boards, not coms I was sure. Perhaps they were meant to aim and fire missiles or destructs—weapons that might never have been installed on the surface at all, or if they were, had been dismantled when the last of the Security forces were ordered into space.

I went back to the bunkhouse. One of the light metal cot frames there was the only possible stretcher I could find. It took me some time to loosen it from the support stanchions. I looked at my watch. It must be well after nightfall now—not that day or night had any meaning here. At least the buildings had been insulated against the cold and could be made warmer if we could use the heating units. We had a far safer refuge here than I had hoped for.

The bunk frame made an awkward burden to pack, and I had found no rope we could use for making Lugard fast to it or for lowering it back down the cliff. Perhaps we could cut blankets into strips to serve. The climb up the ledges pulling the frame with me was a struggle that left me panting and ready to take a long rest when I at last reached the top. Only there was no time for that now.

At last I dragged it behind me, changing hands time and time again as my fingers cramped about the end rod. It scraped and banged along the rock, making enough din to give one an aching head. I had to stop again and again to flex my fingers free of cramp lest I lose the use of my hands. It was just too heavy to carry along and too large to drag well. Also it caught now and then on rough bits of rock, and I had to halt to free it, until the whole world shrank to my struggle with the stubborn thing and I could have gladly smashed it to bits with my bare hands.

I came out of the side tunnel and saw the light of the beamer. A black shadow ran toward me, and Thad came into the light of my own torch. He stared for a moment then hurried up to lay hands on the frame. I unhooked my fingers one by one and let him take it, and I staggered a little as I went.

"What's it like?" Thad asked.

"Good." I rasped hoarsely. "Lugard?"

"Still alive."

I had not dared to hope that would be the answer. But if

he continued to hold to life and we could get him down to the lower cave—I had not hunted for medical supplies, but surely there would be some.

It was all I could do to make the gathering by the cart. I went to my knees there, breathing heavily, while Thad thumped the bunk frame flat on the rock.

Annet had covered Lugard, all but his face. She no longer wiped the dribble from his lips. That had stopped, and I could not guess whether that was a good or bad sign.

"Tie him on that." I made my idea as simple as I could. "Take him on the cart. But we will have to lower him to another cave. They had a Security base down there—even houses—"

"Houses?" she echoed. She held out to me an E-ration can from which she had just twisted the self-heating top. The smell of it was so good that I stretched out my hands, but my fingers were so numb that I would have dropped it had her grasp not continued. She held it to my lips, and I drank the rich contents, their warmth and refreshment bringing me out of the fog of fatigue.

"Installations in them," I said between gulps. "But there is a bunkhouse. We can camp out there."

Annet glanced down at Lugard. "He is unconscious—"

"Better so." It was the truth. We must handle him to get him on the bunk frame and to secure him there. I did not want to think what that might do to his broken body. Only I—we—had no choice. To go on gave him a slim chance; to stay, that was to do nothing but wait for the inevitable end. And there might be a second rock fall, though Annet assured me that nothing had threatened while I was gone.

We worked as best we could, lifting Lugard in the blanket, settling him on the bed frame, then winding about it all the strips Gytha and Pritha cut from our blankets, rendering him as immovable as possible.

The supplies, except for our own kits, we stacked to one side of the cave, but our packs we took with us. The frame we had slung on blanket straps that went about my shoulders and Thad's so we could lift him to the cart.

So we transported him at a slow pace, Annet and the

children at the sides, the cart, with Thad and me to steady it, down the center. Gytha, with the beamer, was our forescout, and with such light it was easy to avoid the roughest bits. Yet all our straining could not make it really smooth going.

I was ridden by the need for haste; yet that we dared not attempt. The framework that held Lugard was balanced precariously on the cart, and the least shift, in spite of our efforts to steady it, might send it crashing to the rock.

We turned into the side that led to the lower cave. Annet came once to look into Lugard's face. There had been no sign he was conscious. I hoped he was not.

"We must get out. He needs help—Dr. Symonz at the port."

If there was still a Dr. Symonz and the port, I thought. But either she continued to hold stubbornly to the idea that Lugard was wrong in his story of bombing, or else she wanted to preserve hope for the children. I had no intention of trying to find out which. I was too busy trying to plan for that drop down the ledges.

"Look!" Emrys pointed to the withered carcass of the warthorn. "What's that?"

"A wart-horn, silly," Gytha answered. "Probably got in here and was lost. But then he must have come from water—"

She made the same deduction I had.

"There's water below," I returned, "but it's piped in." But those pipes came from somewhere. And water could be a guide to the outer world.

We came at last to the drop, and Gytha swung the beamer down the slope to pick up in bright light and dark shadow all the roughness of that descent. I heard an exclamation from Annet.

"Down there! But we'll never be able to lower him—"

"We have to. I didn't have any luck finding ropes, though." I stared dully down that stairway of ledges, and threatening slope of scree at its foot. To go down and return—I did not know whether I had the strength. But Thad had the answer.

"Emrys, Sabian, uncoil what we found!"

At his order the two younger boys began to pull lengths from beneath their tunics. What they had when they spread it on the floor was no conventional rope that could be trimmed or broken, but strands of tungfors—the same alloy that was used to coat rocket tubes. These had been fashioned as chains, and there were hooks of the same durable metal at either end.

"Found 'em in the supplies we had to dump," Thad reported. "They what we need now?"

I could not have done better had I been able to pick and choose from a variety of equipment, and I said so as we laid them straight. They would reach from one ledge to the next, but whether we could take the strain of Lugard's weight for lowering I did not know.

"You go ahead with the children," I told Annet. "Thad Emrys, Sabian, and I, we'll try to manage it. But I want you all safely down and out of the way first."

I could foresee that a single slip might rake us all from our feet and send us crashing, not only to our own peril, but also to that of anyone ahead. She might have protested, but then she looked at Dagny, whom she had carried most of that weary way.

"How? Yes, the pack harness!" She laid the little girl on the floor and began to shuck her own burden.

"I don't believe that—"

"I can do it!" She turned on me with some of the same fierceness she had shown when she tried to reach the surface after the bombing. And I could not deny her the effort. What strength I had left I must use for Lugard.

So we watched as they went over one by one—Gytha first, having shored up the beamer on the lip of the cliff to give light, taking Pritha's hand, cautioning her not to look down but only immediately before her; then Ifors; and last and very slowly, with Dinan between her and Ifors, Annet, Dagny made fast to her in the pack harness. Luckily, the ledges made a fairly easy descent, but the treacherous pile below troubled me more. I shivered with far more than the outer cold of that place as I watched them win, shelf by shelf, to the floor below.

Gytha was down, then the others—all but Annet, who moved slower and slower. By my own experiences in dragging the bunk frame, I could understand what wearied her. She rested for what seemed to me a very long time before she made the final drop into the scree.

Then they were all crawling through that. Emrys moved to loose the beamer. I shook my head.

"Leave that! We shall need all the light we can get."

"How do we go now?" Thad wanted to know.

I could see only one way—perhaps not the best, but the only one visible to me.

"Hook these, one end up here." I picked up one of the chains. "Other on the stretcher. One of us gets down to the ledge to steady it. I lower one line—you two the other."

Thad nodded. "Sabian to do the steadying."

Sabian was the smallest. We would need our major strength on the lowering. I looked to him.

"Think you can do it?"

"I don't know," he answered honestly. "Can't tell till I try, can I?" With that he slipped over to reach the surface of the first ledge and stood there, looking up, his eyes large and dark in a face that seemed unusually pallid by the beamer's glare.

We set the hooks in the frame at either end and tested their hold. The others we pounded into the rock beyond the lip and again tested. Then we slid the frame and its silent burden toward the lip and began what were the worst hours of my life.

It took us more than two hours to make that slow crawl down since we paused on each ledge to test, to rest the strain in our shoulders and arms, to bend over Lugard and hear those painful bubbling breaths and know that we still dealt with the living and not the dead. I lost all measure of time as I had known it in a sane and normal world. This was time as some evil being might have conceived it as a special torture. During the last part I moved in a kind of thick fog, so that when we came to stable footing I collapsed, unable to do more than breathe shallowly. Nor were the other boys any better. Emrys lay limp at the side of the frame; Thad hunched at its other end. I heard a shuffle and then a thin cry of welcome.

"Annet!"

Something was pushed into my hands and, when I could not hold it, held then to my mouth. Again I sucked feebly, rather than drank, a hot mouthful of ration. I knew that such emergency food was laced with restoratives, but whether that could get me on my feet again now, I doubted.

In the end we staggered along while Annet, Gytha, Pritha, and Ifors made use of the blanket shoulder straps and carried the frame and Lugard ahead of us. I roused enough to put an arm about Emrys' shoulders and pull him up and to give some support to Thad. My shoulders and arms had gone numb. Now they began to ache, first dully and then with increasing pain.

We slipped and slid, though we never did quite fall, until we were past that treacherous pile and in the wider part of the cave. There was a blaze of light streaming from the door of the barracks, and to that we were drawn. I remember crossing its threshold, looking dully at the room—for the rest nothing at all.

When I awoke, I was lying on the floor, under me a pad that I had stripped from the bunk I had earlier dismantled. And I ached—how I ached!—as if my arms had been pulled from shoulder sockets, the bones of my spine put to such strain as no man could be expected to take.

Perhaps I made some sound. Even turning my head required painful effort. Annet's face hung over me, a face drawn with dark shadows beneath the eyes and a set to the lips I had never seen before.

"So, you're awake—" Her voice was sharp, and something in the tone brought the immediate past into focus.

I tried to sit up and found it an effort. She made no gesture to aid but sat back on her heels watching me with a kind of impatience in her tense position, as if she had been waiting too long for me to move.

I rubbed my hands across my face, felt the grit of rock dust between palm and cheek, and blinked.

"Lugard?"

"Is dead." She answered me flatly.

I think my first reaction was a kind of anger that all our

struggle had been for nothing, almost anger at Griss that he should have slipped away when we had done what we could to keep him with us. And after that another thought grew. With Lugard gone, who did we have to turn to? As long as I had had the problem of getting him to this shelter, I had never looked beyond. There had been a kind of completion when we reached the foot of the cliff, as if our greatest struggle now lay behind. But that was not the truth.

Somehow I wobbled to my feet. Thad lay in a bunk to my left; beyond him, sharing another, were the two others who had aided in our ordeal on the ledges. From the back room where the cooking unit was installed, I heard the murmur of voices.

"Vere, you're awake!" I turned my head slowly. There was a feeling that if I tried any swift movement, I might fall apart. Gytha came out of the mess room.

She caught me by the arm. "Come on—supper is ready. You slept most of the day."

I yielded to her pull. Annet was on her feet, too, and when I staggered, she suddenly put out her hand to steady me.

"There is plenty of food anyway," she said, as much to reassure herself, I thought, as me. "And the cook unit runs."

Perhaps the smells were not as enticing as the ones back in a Kynvet kitchen, but they seemed to me to be so at that moment.

Seven

I HAD TO PROP both elbows on the narrow table to steady my hands in order to raise a mug of steaming caff to my lips. As its warmth flowed down my throat, I awakened out of the daze of fatigue and not caring that had fallen on me at the bottom of the cliff. Annet sat down opposite me, her hands resting on the table top—lying I should have said, not resting, for there was such an aura of tension about her that her unease flowed across the surface dividing us.

"He was mad—he must have been—" she said flatly.

"You felt the tremors." I would not let her build vain hopes. I had seen the two refugees at the Butte, and I could and did believe that Lugard had overheard something on the com, enough to let him think we were fleeing actual danger. Far from being mad, I had come to suspect he had been perhaps the sanest man on Beltane when it came to foreseeing and assessing the future. But now—

"Did he regain consciousness before he—went?" I asked. If there were only something I—we—could use as a guide!

She shook her head. "He was breathing heavily. Then—all at once—that stopped. Vere, what are we going to do—if we can't get back the way we came?"

I put down the mug to bring out the map. Now I spread it flat on the table. In the steady light of the barracks, I was not so fully aware of the phosphorescence of its markings but they remained plain without that addition. From the entrance Lugard had found, I traced with a forefinger the path to our present camp, the huge lower cave. From that three passages spread. Two of them seemed to lead to surface outlets. But I remembered Lugard's saying that this whole section had been sealed by Security in the days before Butte Hold was closed. He had opened this way with hard labor— but he had not had time, I believed, to so deal with the others, even if he had wanted to.

There was no use in expecting the worst before it was proven, as I now said to Annet. She wanted us all to go as soon as we could. But I argued against further disappointment and perhaps shock for the younger children. Finally, it was agreed that I could try by the map both those passages.

But before I left, there was one more duty, and it was a hard one, perhaps more so for some of us than others. Ideally, one does not bear resentment for the dead, but I think Annet looked upon Lugard as a madman whose twisted fears had involved us in disaster. She would not have wished him dead, but she had no tears for him now. However, she shared with me the covering of his body by a plasta-sheet out of the stores. While we did so, something slipped from the blanket strips that had kept him secure during that dark journey I did not want to remember.

It crunched under my boot, and I picked up a shard of the pipe with which he had wrought his magic. It must have broken when he took his hurt. Now I searched and gathered up all the bits from the rock and tucked them carefully back under the edge of his tunic.

"Not Dagny," Annet said abruptly when we had it done. "Nor Pritha, nor—"

"Yes, Pritha." She spoke for herself. "And all of us, Annet, yes!" So in the end, Thad and I carried the stretcher back into the rubble by the descent. And the rest of them, save Dagny who still slept under sedatives, followed.

We could not dig in the rock, but we fitted the frame into a crevice and with our hands covered it, first with gravel we scooped up, and then with rocks, until we had built a recognizable mound. I wished for a laser so that I could mark the wall beyond. But, in spite of all that had been left here, we had found no weapons. We had only the stunners worn by Annet, Thad, and me.

Gytha dragged one last rock up and, with an effort, set it atop. I saw the shine of tear tracks on her cheek. "I wish— I wish we could have played the pipe. He—he was a gentle man, Vere."

Gentle was not an adjective I myself would have applied to Griss Lugard, but I remembered his ways with the children and knew that she saw him aright from her point of view. Suddenly, I was glad that this could be remembered of him, along with his courage and his belief that he must do what was to be done. That he did believe he had saved us, I had not the smallest doubt, let Annet think as she would.

Yet she, too, could not leave him so. She clasped one hand with Gytha, held the other to me, while I took one of Thad's, and he Emrys'—and we made a linked circle about that grave of a starman who would never see the stars again. And she began to chant the "Go with Good Will," we picking up the words after her until the song arose and awoke eerie echoes. We cared not for those but sang on to the end.

I decided it was best to wait for morning before I set out on my exploration of the other ways, though night, day, morning, noon, and evening were all relative here, marked only by the hours of my watch. Meanwhile, we opened more of the stock-piled supplies, finding blankets to replace those we had cut apart, food in concentrated rations—enough to last for a long time—and some digging equipment. However, there were no weapons, and the coms in the headquarters structure remained obstinately silent, though we tried them at intervals. Perhaps Lugard had activated only part of the installations here. We had heat in the barracks and a workable cook unit—which was a blessing, since the chill of the cave was biting.

There was some additional clothing, all Security uniform issue, so too large for any of us save Annet and me. There were several beamers, all in working order, and more of the climbing ropes such as Thad had found in the other supplies.

The children worked eagerly sorting out what we could use. But as I was dragging along a box of concentrated fruit paste, I saw Thad standing apart at the door of the structure I thought might be a missile control. I dumped the box by the workers and went to him.

"What is it?"

He started at the sound of my question and turned his head a little. He did not meet me eye to eye, his attitude evasive.

"This is a weapons control, isn't it, Vere?"

"I think so."

"Then, if one could use it, one might blow those—those devils right off Beltane—"

"You believe then that Griss Lugard was right?" I counter-questioned. Having been faced so long with Annet's stubborn contention that we were victims of one man's obsession, I was almost surprised to hear this acceptance.

"Yes. Vere, could we activate this?"

"No. The missiles it was meant to fire are either long dismounted or missing. When this base was closed down, it was stripped of arms, and they wouldn't leave the most important behind. Also, even if it were activated and ready, we could not just use it blindly."

"I suppose so. But, Vere, what if we get out to find they have taken over? Then what do we do?"

He brought into the open the question that had been plaguing me. Lugard, judging by the preparations he had made, must have planned a stay here for some time. But I knew that Annet, unless it was proved to her that there was greater danger on the surface, was not going to agree to any such thing. She had will and determination enough that if I did not try to find a way out, she would leave on her own. But if we went, I was also determined to make every move slowly and not run blindly into the very danger Lugard had died to save us from.

"We can scout. I don't think anyone will be interested in the wastelands," I began and then wondered. The rumor of Forerunner treasure, would that attract the attention of the refugees if they were now in command up there?

However, the waste might have been designed for hiding.

And if we were up with a clear road of retreat back to this base, then—

"Guerrilla warfare?" Thad demanded.

"Warfare? With the Rovers? Be sensible, Thad. We can hide out if need be, for years. We'll just take it slowly until we can find out what happened."

He was not satisfied as I could see, but for the present I would not have to fear any rash action on his part. And of that I made doubly sure by appealing to his sense of responsibility and putting him in charge during my absence.

We slept away the rest of the period marked by the watches as "night." It was about eight o'clock the following morning, our third underground by such reckoning, that I set off on my exploration. I wished that I had a hand com with which to keep in touch with the base, but all such devices were as lacking as weapons. In fact, there were odd gaps in the supplies, and I wondered whether Lugard was responsible for the selection. Were coms missing so we could not attempt to signal the surface and so attract the very attention we had the most to fear by his belief?

I copied the map on a sheet of plasta, leaving that with Annet. Also I made her promise not to stir until my return and told Thad privately to make sure of that. Then, with a light pack, I walked resolutely away from the spot of light that was the camp. I glanced back once to see them lined up as dark shadows against that light. Someone, I thought by the size Gytha, raised a hand in salute, which I answered with a wave.

The left-hand passage was my first choice since it appeared to be the larger of the two possibles, though it was only a tunnel compared to the cave behind. I was heartened into believing I had chosen right when the rays of my belt torch picked up scrapings on the wall showing this way had been enlarged. It did not slope downward, as had the original one we had followed, but ran on a fairly level line. But within an hour I came to the cork that had painstakingly been put into it.

Someone had used a laser to good purpose. I could make out in the stiff mass that sealed the tunnel the half-melted bulk of work machines, mingled with rock that must have gone molten under the rays. They had driven their construction vehicles in here, piled rock about them, and used a high-voltage laser to convert the mass into a plug we had no hope of shifting.

That Lugard had done this was not possible. It had been a Security operation. I was puzzled. Why had they worked so to close off this underground retreat, as if they had some treasure to hide? Unless, of course, it was that control building—And if they *had* been forced to leave missiles in place here—

I considered that. Thad might have the right of it after all. We could hold under our hands an answer to any attempt to take over Beltane. Only I had not the least idea how we could put such a system to work, nor dared we try any experiments without knowing what was going on on the surface. No, that was out of the question. Only it was plain that great efforts had gone into the concealing of this base in the past.

If Lugard had known, then perhaps he had intended eventually to put it to our defense. Just another of the secrets he had not shared with us, and now it was too late.

I examined that congealed mass section by section, hoping to uncover some weak point, perhaps near the ceiling where the lava caves were the easiest to force. But there was no hope of that here. So I turned back, to seek the other passage on the map. When I came from the mouth of the first tunnel, I looked toward the camp. They had closed the door of the barracks. There was no longer any light since the huts lacked windows. Should I report my first failure? But that was a waste of time. Better be sure of the second now.

The second tunnel wound on and on, and there were no marks on its walls to suggest it had been in use until my torch picked out, canted to one side, its roll tread caught in a fall of rock, another of those carts like the one Lugard had used. Somehow it gave the impression that those who had left it so had been in haste—to get out? Was there an opening just ahead?

My deliberate pace quickened to a trot, always allowing

for the rough footing, as I pushed past the derelict. The tunnel-cave was angling to the right even more and sloping down, which was a disappointment, though good sense told me that no opening formed by a lava flow could have gone up. So I came to the second disappointment, a fall of rock, again fused into an impassable wall. But there was something different about this one. I was not sure—I could not be—only I thought it was not ten years old but only days. Had this been done by Lugard?

It seemed less cold here. There was no frost pattern on the walls. Then I caught the gleam of metal and went down on one knee by a weapon—the very one, or its twin, that I had seen beside the door of the Butte when Lugard had faced the refugees. It was as new as it had looked then. I did not think it had lain here for long.

I picked it up with a rush of excitement and pointed it at the top of that fused pile with some idea of burning through. But when I pressed the firing button, there was no answer. The charge it had carried must have been exhausted in the making of the barrier. Now I was sure Lugard had closed this door.

But why? Why had he wanted to seal us in? The preparations for a long siege and now this—What had he so feared might lie upon the surface that he took such drastic precautions? Was it only to save our lives, or was there some secret here that must be guarded—so his move would serve two purposes?

I sat down on the floor, holding the laser, and tried to think. Not that any guess of mine might even come near the fringe of fact. All I could light upon was that I might find some clue back at the camp—either left by Lugard or those who had first built and then left that base. For our own protection, we should have as much of the truth as we could uncover.

There was the third passage, the one I had not believed worth exploring. Should I attempt that before I returned—or get back for a more intensive search of the headquarters structure or the silent missile control? In the end, I decided in favor of return, and I took Lugard's discarded weapon with me. There was a small chance that I might discover a charge for it and could then use it to burn us through one of those plugs.

It was past noon, and I was hungry, so I ate before I began my retreat up the tunnel. And it was as I was idly surveying the walls about me that I saw, in the smooth dust of the floor by one, a line of prints.

Much as I knew of the creatures of the Reserves, this was no track I had seen before. The prints were as long as my hand, which certainly argued for a creature of some size, and they were marked by three long toe lines, so thin as to suggest a foot near to skeleton. Had some other thing been lost like the wart-horn, to drag its starving body along?

And these had been made since Lugard had set this barrier! I had not noted them coming down the tunnel, and there had been no places along it where any large thing could hide. More than ever now I wished that the biospeleology lab had not closed and that I had some reference to what lived naturally in these underground regions. Of course, life that sought out the lava caves for a refuge would not be like that found in the moisture dripping, water-cut caves.

I hunched forward to measure my hand to the print. The fine sand and grit gave no impression of depth, so that one could not guess at the weight of the creature. But I did not like the looks of it in the least. And the three-toed structure was that, I believed, of some reptilian form of life.

It had, I decided after closer study, come down the cave tunnel on one side, been stopped by the barrier, and crossed over to retrace its way up the other. Apparently, it had an affinity for walls, since the marks kept close to them.

I stowed away my empty ration tube and arose, playing the torch down on the tracks that led back toward the big cave. They could have been made an hour before I came this way—or a day or a week—whenever Lugard had put that seal here. But I disliked the thought that an unknown thing might be lurking near the base camp.

If it were carnivorous and starving—why, it might charge anyone in sight. A stunner will act quickly on any warm-blooded creature, but its effect, unless on high beam, was

86

much slower for a reptile, and we kept our weapons on low beam.

So I scrambled along the tunnel at a faster pace than I had so far used that day. When I came to the cart, the prints moved out from the wall and were lost in the central rock. As I played my torch closer over the transport, I saw a ragged tear in one of the treads. Such clean-cut edges could not have come from rocks. They looked far more to me like rents left by claws. And claws able to break the tough substance of those treads were—I clutched tighter the weapon I had found. If I could only discover a fresh charge for that, we would have no worries. A laser with power enough to melt a rock plug would stop even a bear-bison, the most dangerous beast I knew—one never approached by a Ranger unless it was first stunned.

I came back into the large cave. There the prints turned sharply to my left, again along the wall. And for that I was thankful, for if the thing did not like open space, it would have to face crossing a wide stretch of it in order to reach our camp, while the shelters had been built sturdily enough to withstand any clawed attack. We would merely have to be alert when outside their walls.

I continued to follow the tracks until they vanished into a crevice, which, after a moment's comparison with my map, I thought must be the entrance to the third passage. There in the dust were several lines of three toes coming and going, which looked suspiciously as if this third way was a regular route for the thing. Also, from the mouth of that ragged opening came such a chill that I was astounded. If the thing was reptilian, then how could it face that cold? While reptiles could not take direct sun or baking heat, yet chill made them torpid and forced some into a state approaching hibernation. It had been the study of such animals, along with other creatures, that had first given my species the "cold sleep" that, before the discovery of hyperjump, had carried cargoes of mankind in coffin-like boxes across the vast distances between one solar system and another.

Here was a thing that left a reptilian track, yet seemed deliberately to choose a passage even colder than the chill cave. The latest prints, which overlaid the others, led into and not out, and I was content not to trail any farther.

Instead, I went to the camp. The door of the missile control was half ajar, the interior dark, and the com-headquarters building the same. On impulse, I did not go directly to the barracks. After all, I had set no time limit on my return, and I wanted, very badly indeed, a charge for Lugard's laser. Such might be found in headquarters. Had it been in the barracks or among the supplies, I would already have known it.

I stood in the stark office room. As I closed the door behind me, the light went on as it did in the barracks. It had not in the missile station. Could I deduce from that small fact that Lugard had reason to activate part of the equipment here? We knew that the com did not work, but what else was there?

I crossed to the files. They had security locks set to fingerprint release. But when I touched the first, it came open easily enough—to show an empty interior. There were sections for micro-tape and reading tape but no rolls. Thus it was with every one of them. Then I began to search the surface of the walls, looking for a slight depression that could mark another finger lock. I found four such. But if they held any secrets, they continued to guard them well. No pressure of my fingertip freed them. Perhaps they had been set to Lugard's pattern, or even my father's, if they had not been opened since the war began.

I sat down behind the desk, laying the weapon on it. There were three drawers, all as empty as the files. Then I noted a fourth, which was a very narrow slit set in the edge of the desk top. It could be seen only when the belt torch I had neglected to switch off flashed across it endwise as I moved.

There appeared to be no way of opening it, no releasing catch or button. I brought out the long iridium hunting knife that rode in my boot top and picked, with its unbreakable point, at that faint join line. It required a lot of patience, that struggle between knife point and the desk, but finally the less hard substance of the latter chipped, and I pried out a very shallow drawer.

It was so shallow that it held only a single sheet of the same plasta as my map, and it was also a map. I spread it out on the desk to compare it with the one Lugard had given me. A section of it was the same, but reduced to a miniature, so that the old only formed about a quarter of my new find. Again I saw a spread of passages ahead. In each case, beyond the stoppers I had come against, were sections that extended beyond dots indicating passage walls, as if there were rooms or installations of some sort built into and outward through those.

Missile pits? Or their equivalents? There were numbers so small that I found them difficult to read, which I thought were code. But since those ways were now sealed to us, it did not greatly matter what lay there. It was the chill third passage I wanted to trace. On Lugard's map it was only slightly indicated; here it was in far greater detail.

It led, according to this map, to a cave, which might be as large as the one we were now in, or perhaps two caves with a wide entrance between them. And the far side was left open as if it had not been fully explored by the map maker, so he did not know the exact perimeter. Also this space was given an added significance with a shading in print that glistened with the lettering of code.

I remembered Lugard's story of the ice cave where he had found the alien remains. The cold coming from the crevice could mean ice. And the special marking on this map suggested importance. But nowhere was there any sign of an exit to the surface. The fact remained that two were sealed, and we might have to return the way we came.

Doing that, we must clear the fall Annet had encountered. And beyond—I flinched from visualizing the climb back if the crane no longer worked.

I folded the new map with the old and stowed both in my tunic. A survey of the com room, and then of the stark living quarters, brought me nothing more. But I took the weapon with me when I left, determined to search carefully through all the supply boxes before giving up hope of finding a fresh charge for it. I wanted that fiercely. We needed it.

It was when I came out of the door of headquarters that I heard the calling.

"Dagny! Dinan!" A shout and the echoes of it rolled around the walls. "Dagny! Dinan!"

The door of the barracks stood open, the light streaming out. Annet was at the narrow tip of its radiance, calling. I saw a figure that could only be Thad moving farther out into the shadows, and one that was perhaps Gytha heading in the other direction, back toward the ledges. And I ran—remembering those three-toed tracks and fearing a scattering of our party that might lead to danger yet unknown.

"What is it?" I came up beside Annet as she voiced another of those echoing shouts.

She swung around, her both hands out, to clutch me by the upper arms.

"Vere, the children—they've gone!" Then she turned her head, still holding onto me, to call, "Dagny, Dagny! Dinan!"

Someone to my other side flashed a light ahead from one of the beamers. That reached to the wall of the cave, and the edge of it touched the crevice down which those sinister tracks had led.

"Home—" Under the echoes of Annet's call, I heard that other word and looked at Pritha. Meeting my gaze, she nodded as if to emphasize what she would say.

"Dagny wanted her mother; she wanted to go home. She didn't understand what happened. When Annet went to get her some food—she was asleep we thought—she ran away. And Dinan—he would never let her go alone."

That was true. Where one of the twins went, the other followed, though Dinan was usually the leader of the pair. He would not have allowed his sister to go into the dark alone.

But the tracks were so to the fore of my mind, I twisted up my hand and caught Annet's wrist.

"Be quiet!" I put into that order what force I could. "Get them back—all of them!"

She stared at me, but she did not call again.

"We may not be alone here." I gave her the best explanation I had ready. "All of you—get in there and stay, and put your stunners on high."

Thad came running out of the dark. "They left a trail," he

reported and then interrupted himself. "Vere! Is there a way—"

I shook my head. "There is no way out. And where are those tracks?" I had hoped against hope, but my fears were realized when he waved to the cold crevice.

"Annet, Thad, get the rest of the children in—and keep them so! And here—" I thrust the useless laser at Thad. "Scout through the supplies and see if you can find a charge for this. Shoot at anything that does not signal with a torch."

He nodded, asking no questions. Annet might have, but I gave her a push. "Get them in!"

"Where are you going?"

"After them—" I was already two strides nearer to the crevice. "And," I added a last caution, "keep that beamer on—pointed this way."

Light might not be any deterrent to a menace, but if it were a creature of the dark, it could help.

Eight

I FOUND THE TRACKS Thad had seen. There was no mistaking the small boot-pack prints. And they lay over mine where I had halted to study that other trail. Seeing that, I winced. Had I returned at once to the barracks instead of going to search the headquarters, I might have prevented this. But there was no time to waste on might-have-beens.

For a moment or two, I debated the wisdom of using my belt torch. While the light was needed, it could also attract unwelcome attention, but the advantages outweighed the disadvantages. I would not call as they had been doing, though.

The cold grew worse. The walls of this tunnel were covered with frost crystals, which sparkled in the light. What had drawn the children into taking such a forbidding way, I could not understand—unless, knowing I was exploring the other two outlets, they had determined to avoid me.

That was not like the twins. And I could only believe that the shock that had gripped Dagny had unsettled her usual rather timid nature. She had seemed half dazed when she had not been sleeping.

As I went, I listened for sounds of the children, for they could not be too far ahead, and, I will freely admit, with a pumping heart, for anything else that would suggest alien life in this hole.

Once again, after passing the rough entrance, I saw signs

that this had been a used way. Projections had been lasered off; there were scrapes along the wall and a few marks of crawl treads, all signifying that not only men but perhaps one of the carts had traveled here. It was sloping down again as the cold grew. All I heard was the soft pad of my own boot soles. I saw nothing within range of the torch beam. I went with my stunner in my hand. And, as I had warned the others to do, I had turned it to the highest force, although to use that long would exhaust the charge. I tried now to remember how many extra charges I had. There were two in my belt loops, some in my pack—but those I had left behind. How many did the others have? I should have checked that last night when we were examining the other supplies, though at that time food and water had seemed all important.

I glanced at my watch. Four—in the afternoon where the sun still shone and it was day. But here such reckoning had no meaning. The children could not be very far ahead. Yet I dared not risk too quick a pace over rough surfaces. A twisted ankle could mean disaster for us all. If they could see my torch, would that make them hurry on? Or would they have had enough of the cold and dark and be ready to turn back? I longed to call, but the memory of the tracks kept me quiet.

It was now a smaller replica of the road we had traveled before, for the cave passage again ended in a drop, a rough one descending not by ledges this time but by handholds. I was surprised that the twins had gone down—but they must have, or I would have overtaken them.

I heard it then, muffled but still audible, a desolate crying, coming from down there. And I saw a faint glow that could only be a belt torch. Heartened, I swung over, into a cold so intense my fingers flinched from the stone. How *had* they come here?

Luckily, the descent was not as great as the place of ledges. Part way down, I let go, to drop, lest the cold destroy all feeling in my hands, my feet plowing into loose gravel, which was a sharp way to cushion any fall. But I was up again, having suffered only minor scraping.

"Dagny—Dinan?" I dared to call now.

There was no halt to that minor plaint, which somehow hurt the ears and made one's mind flinch. But I was answered; only the voice did not come from where the light glowed.

"Vere, please—Vere, come and get us—" That was Dinan.

"Where?" I still looked toward the torch, unable to believe that did not mark my quarry.

"Here!"

Here was farther to the left and higher, if the echoes did not utterly mislead me. I waded through the scree in that direction.

"Vere—" Dinan again, his voice very thin and weak. "Look out—for the thing. It went away when I threw the light. But it bit the torch and jumped on it—and maybe it will come back. Vere, get us out of here!"

I shone my own torch in the general direction of the voice, and there they were. It was a ledge of sorts but a shallow one. Dagny was crowded to the back, Dinan before her as if to serve as a buffer. She was crying, her eyes staring straight before her, no tears running from them, only the moaning from a mouth that hung loose, a dribble of saliva issuing from one corner to cover her chin. Her lack of expression frightened me, for all I could think of was that she had retreated into idiocy from which we could perhaps never draw her again.

There was fear in Dinan's face also, but it was a fear that was turned outward, not bottled within him. He reached down his hand to me, grasping my fingers in his cold small ones, in that moment giving a vast sigh as if an intolerable burden had rolled from his shoulders when he was able to touch me.

The perch on which they were crowded was too small for me to join them. And getting Dagny down, unless she became more aware of her surroundings and able to help somewhat, presented a problem.

"Dagny." I pulled myself up on a pile of rubble until I was able to take both her hands in mine. They lay limp in my grasp, as if she was not conscious of my touch. She continued to stare straight ahead, and that moaning never ceased.

In cases of hysteria, I knew, sometimes a sharp slap might bring the victim out of such a state. But that this was worse than any hysteria I was now certain.

"How long has she been like this?" I asked Dinan. Surely, she had not made all this journey down the icy tunnel in this state.

"Since—since the thing tried to get us." His voice quavered. "She—she won't listen to me, Vere. She just cries and cries. Vere, can you make her listen to us?"

"I don't know, Dinan. Can you get down and let me reach her?"

He edged along obediently and swung down, giving me room to put an arm around his sister. Again she showed no sign that she knew of my presence. I feared she had entered an enclosure for which none of us had the key. Like Lugard, she needed professional help, which could only be found on the world we were far from reaching.

Somehow I got her off the shelf; then she lay limp across my shoulder, still moaning and drooling. And I must get her back up that climb—

"Vere! Listen!"

I had been hearing only Dagny's moaning. But when Dinan pulled at my arm, I did listen. And there was another sound—a rattle, which could come from a stone dislodged to click against another. The direction was deceiving, though, because of the echoes. I thought it did not come from above but from the space beyond.

"Vere—the *thing!*"

"What is it?" Best be prepared with at least a partial description of what I might have to face.

"It's big—as big as you—and it walks on its hind legs. But it's worse than a wart-horn—all scaly and bad, bad!" Dinan's voice grew shriller with every word, as if he could no longer control his fear.

"All right. Now Listen, Dinan. You said it came for your torch—"

"I don't know—Vere, it hasn't any eyes—any eyes at all!" Again terror spoke through him. "But it didn't like the light. I threw the torch at it, and then it didn't follow us. It jumped on the torch and bit it and threw it—and then—it went away."

Attracted by heat radiation I wondered? Perhaps this stalker in the dark had no need for eyes, but heat it could sense. Yes, small patches of knowledge came back to me. That was how the minute creatures found in the water caves tracked their prey, by sensors that picked up an awareness of body heat. Some of them, it was said, could be drawn from the crevices in which they dwelt by the warmth of one's skin if you set your bare hand against the rock near their holes. If this creature hunted by heat, then it would be drawn first to the torch—and it could now be attracted by the one on my own belt.

So perhaps I could use that as Dinan had luckily done with his were we caught in a tight place, though I feared trying to make the climb back without light and the helpless girl.

Dinan's torch still blazed, though now it flickered. These were stoutly made, and the beating he said it had taken might have battered it but had not extinguished its rays. Also, the sounds we heard now were from that direction.

I saw no way of getting Dagny up that climb without rendering myself almost defenseless under attack. That I dared not risk. There was one other choice—lure the beast into the open and stun it. And I could not be sure of that either, even with the stunner set on high.

Now I examined Dagny's belt as she lay against me, her face turned to the rocky wall, her eyes wide and seeing nothing. Yes, she still had her torch. I unhooked it, she limp and passive under my handling as if she were a toy.

"Listen, Dinan." So much depended now on what we could do. If I were to face this thing, I must do it on ground I could pick, well away from the children. I turned my torch up the wall we must go. Well above my head was the widest of the rest places I had found during my descent, one as good if not better than that on which the children had earlier taken refuge. "This is what we must do. I cannot risk climbing with Dagny while she is—ill—not with that thing able to attack. So, I am going to get you both up there. Then I will leave you this torch. Keep it safe. I'll come down here again and set up my belt torch as bait. When the thing comes at it—"

"But you don't have a blaster or a laser!" His voice trembled, but he was thinking clearly.

"No. But my stunner is on full ray. If I am careful—and I will be—that ought to work. It is just that we cannot climb when there is the threat of that overtaking us."

I saw him nod, and his hands closed so tightly about the torch from Dagny's belt that his knuckles were sharp knobs peaked in his cold-blued skin. The torch he had thrown away was flickering faster, weakly, on and off. I listened, but the sounds had ceased, and I could only hope that did not mean the creature was using some natural cunning to creep through a terrain native to it.

The struggle to get Dagny to the ledge I had selected for a temporary refuge confirmed my belief that it would be a long, hard pull to the top and one I dared not take with a threat of attack from behind. I must settle Dinan's "thing" before I took the road back.

Once I had Dagny wedged with her back to the cliff wall, Dinan before her to keep her there, I rested a moment, giving the boy my last orders.

"I'll go down near that torch you threw. And I'll switch mine on and wedge it between the rocks. I'll still be between you and the thing. Don't switch on your light. That is very important. If it does hunt by heat, it will be drawn to my torch first, and that radiance may block out the emanations from our bodies."

"Yes, Vere."

I handed him my canteen and supplies.

"Give Dagny some water if you can get her to drink. And there are E-bars in this bag. See if she will eat. She and you both need energy to combat this cold. Now, if you don't hear anything for a while, Dinan, don't worry. It may be that we shall have to wait."

But not too long, I hoped silently as I swung over and down. The cold here was such that the children certainly could not resist it for long. And my own reflexes were so stiff that I feared to depend too much on any agility in battle.

The periods of dark between light as the other torch flickered on and off grew longer. Its glow when on was quite feeble. I worked my way near it with all the care of one on a hunting stalk, though I was not prepared here to use the terrain to the same advantage as I could have on the surface. The continued quiet bothered me, for my imagination painted a picture of Dinan's thing crouched in some crevice, very well aware of my every movement, ready at any second to charge before I could bring my perhaps useless weapon to bear.

I wedged my torch between two rocks, switched it on, and hunkered down to wait. The cold crept upon me, dulling my senses, or I feared that it did. And I had to move now and then or I would have cramped, unable to move at all. The watch on my wrist I could no longer see, and time became a long stretch of discomfort and tension.

There was no sound to herald its coming—it was suddenly *there!* It stood, with its head a little to one side, its snout pointed at the torch, its shoulders hunched, while above frond-like strips of skin fluttered and then stiffened, pointing to the light—or perhaps to me behind that beacon.

It was a dead gray-white, and Dinan was right. There were two small swellings on the head that might mark the place of eyes it had surrendered for lack of use eons back in evolutionary time. How so great a creature could find enough here to sustain life I could not guess. My understanding had always been that cave life tended to be minute, the largest being the blind fish. But this thing was as tall as I as it stood on its hind legs. In addition, it was apparent that the bipedal form of locomotion was normal to it, for the front limbs were much shorter and weaker seeming, and it carried them curled close to its belly.

Skeleton proportions added to its eerie appearance. All four limbs looked to be only scaled skin stretched tightly over angular bones. The head was a skull hardly clothed with flesh, except for its antennae, and its body as lean as if it were in the last stages of starvation. Yet it moved alertly with no sign of weakness, so that the excessive leanness must have been its natural state.

As a biped, it was somehow more alarming than if it had

run on four feet. We are conditioned to associate an upright stance with intelligence, though that can be far from the truth. I had the impression that I was confronted by no mindless beast but rather by something that ruled this dark underground world as much as my kind ruled the surface over its head.

But there was little time for such impressions. The blind head moved in sharp jerks right and left, always centering in a point at the torch. It was a long, narrow skull with a small mouth, which was surrounded by the only excess flesh on the creature, a puckered protuberance, as if the thing got most of its nourishment by sucking rather than biting and chewing. All in all, it was something out of a nightmare.

Now, without any warning, it charged. I was a second or two late in my reaction. Perhaps I had been so startled by its alien appearance that I had gone off guard. It was to cost me dear. I did swing up the stunner and press the button, aiming for its head, long since known to be the most vulnerable point of contact for that weapon.

Though known to be for most living things, it would seem that now I dealt with one not to be so judged. I did not even see how it altered course in the middle of a spring. But now it headed not for the lamp but directly for me. And those arms, which had looked weak when compared to the more powerful legs, snapped up and out, the clawed paws making ready to take me.

I beamed again at the head, but the ray did not slow it. Then it gave a leap that raised it to the top of the rocks behind which I crouched, and it aimed a blow at me in return. Its blindness did not appear to limit its capacity to know where I was.

The raking claws tore, but not across my head by the one scrap of fortune I had. Instead, those claws peeled tunic and coverall from my shoulder halfway across my chest on the left side, leaving bleeding gashes. All that saved me was that its rock perch moved under its weight, and it had to balance.

I threw myself to the right and rolled behind a rock, but now it was between me and the children. And, having made sure of me with a second blow or a third, it could take them at its leisure. So I must keep its attention and try to pull it away from the ledge, though how long I could continue such a desperate game I did not want to think.

It would seem that the stunner was useless. Two full head shots it had taken—which should have been enough to addle any brains it had. But they had not even seemed to slow it. My roll brought me closer to the lamp, and I surrendered a precious moment to loosen that for a lure. Not that I needed one now. It was thoroughly aroused, wanting nothing more than to get claws on me. But still the direct rays of the lamp appeared to bother it. To my relief it did not try another of those lightning charges but gave me a small breathing space in which to pull myself together, while it squatted on the top of the unsteady rock, its head turned at a sharp angle on its narrow shoulders to follow the light it could not see but sensed in some other fashion.

I wondered if it were a creature of the extreme cold so that even the limited radiance of the light was both an attraction and a source of discomfort to it. If so—if I only had a laser! But I might as well wish for a distributor to make entirely sure of it.

However, as I worked myself back, away from the cliff and the children, it leaped from the rock and followed, much as if I were piping it with Lugard's pipe. Only it came warily.

So tailed by the hunter, I came into a strange place. There were stalagmites of ice, like huge teeth, awakening in frozen glory and glitter when the lamp touched them. Parts of the floor were coated with transparent sheets of ice made up of hexagonal prisms standing vertically, their honey-combed divisions clearly visible on the surface. And, on the one portion of wall we passed where my light reached, I saw more, greater crystals with well-developed facets. At another time the wonder of it would have amazed me. Now I only tensed and feared, lest my boots slip on one of those patches and bring me down, easy meat for the stalker.

The creature showed no discomfort from the cold, and I believed that this was its native habitat, though it went against all we knew of such life. My shoulder and chest were bleeding, and the chill struck through the rags it had made of my clothing. If I let it herd me in too far, then the cold might be its aid in our final battle. I raised the stunner for the third time and fired, this time not at its head but at its middle section—with surprising results!

It shivered in the light of the lamp and threw up its head. Then from that puckered mouth burst an odd quaver of sound, which was answered—from behind me!

I swerved in my horror, brought up against one of those ice pillars, and fell, skidding across the floor. The stunner was gone, but somehow I clung to the lamp. My body whirled around, so that I hit with my good shoulder against a broken surface. And I was looking—looking straight at objects that were certainly not native to that place.

They must have been deeply encased in ice earlier, but something or someone had begun the process of melting them free. I could see shadows, shapes, all ice-covered. But what was directly before me was a rod projecting from a chest or container in which lay others like it. I seized upon that as my only hope of a weapon, though to swing it one-handed might be more than I could do.

That sucking hoot was louder. I did not waste time getting to my feet, rather pulled myself around on my knees and swung up the rod. There were depressions on the surface I gripped, into which my fingers sank as I tightened hold.

From the tip of the rod shot a coruscating ray of light. It struck one of the ice pillars. There was a hissing, a clouding of steam. Heat beat back at me; water boiled away. Again I swung the rod, this time with intent, pressing my fingers, and that thing that wobbled toward me across the floor was headless. But still it kept its feet! And it came on! Until I blasted it past its chest, it came.

Out from between the forest of ice pillars came another. But at the sight, or sensing of light, it became more wary, circling, moving with a speed that frightened me, for my own reactions were so hindered by the cold and my wounds that I could not match it. At last I simply did not aim the rod but whipped it about, unleashing it in a sweep across the whole sector where the monster bounded.

It went down, but so did other things. Pillars crashed in great knife splinters of ice, and there was a giving beyond those. It was as if the wall melted. A black hole opened there, and from it issued a rushing, roaring sound.

For a time I lay where I was, unable to find the strength to get to my feet. At last, upending that miraculous rod and using it as a support, I managed to stand up. Halting and wavering, I came to the black hole the ray had cut and shone my lamp through. The light was reflected from the surface of water, a river of it, moving from dark to dark again.

I began a slow progress back to the cliff, shining my lamp ahead so that Dinan would know it was I who came.

"Vere! Vere!" Again I heard his call and leaned against a rock to consider what must be done. I had pressed the rags of my clothing as tightly against my wounds as I could. But blood still welled there. And the cold had eaten me, too. I dared not make that climb carrying Dagny with no more help than Dinan could give. Nor could I leave the girl and go for help.

"Dinan—"

"Yes, Vere?" he responded eagerly.

"Do you think you can climb to the top and get back to the camp?" It was a lot I was asking of him. Had the two monsters I had killed in the ice been the only representatives of their kind hereabouts? And would he be able to walk the distance unaided now?

"I can try, Vere."

"It will have to be better than try, Dinan." I dared not show concern; my firmness might be the one prod that would give him the will and grit to keep moving. "Now listen. I have here a weapon. I don't know what it is—I found it back there. You point it, you press your fingers in places in its surface, and it shoots a very hot ray. I am going to give this to you. If you meet one of those things, fire at the middle of its body—understand?"

"Yes, Vere." His voice sounded steadier. Was it because I could put into his hands some defense? One of our species always feels more secure with a weapon to hand, which may be why we have clung to such for all these generations, turning first to might of body rather than might of mind as those on Beltane argued should be done.

But to disarm myself—I faced around, pulling along by hand holds on the rocks about me, very unsure at that moment whether I could make the trip I must for the small margin of safety for Dagny and me.

"Wait, Dinan. I must get another weapon." I lurched forward, fearing to pause lest I fall and be unable to get to my feet again. The claw wounds burned with a fiery agony. I thought of poison and then pushed that thought resolutely from me, concentrating only on reaching the ice-bound storehouse and another of the rods.

I crept past the charred remains of a monster, and my torch picked out the half-thawed wall and the box projecting, its lid thrown back.

Now I stooped and picked a second rod from the chest. There were two more there. But these, my lamp told me, were different. The one I had just taken up was a steely blue, like the first I had found, the last two dull silver. I pointed the one I now held at an ice pillar and fired. Again the swift melting, the backwash of heat.

Only that one chest was free. I was able to see dimly behind it massive boxes, shadows I could not be sure of. Was this Lugard's alien treasure? If so, who had left it here and how long ago? And Lugard, had it been his efforts that had freed the one chest from the grip of the ice?

A momentary dizziness nearly sent me reeling. My shin rapped painfully against the edge of the chest as I strove to retain my balance, and my torch swung close to its surface. It bore a pattern, not incised deeply, but lines to be seen under the direct light. A head formed out of those lines. The monster! No, this one had eyes, but the general shape of the skull was the same, if not so emaciated. Could—could the hunter and its companion have been left here, too, eons ago? No space traveling man says aught is impossible. We have seen too much on too many worlds that we cannot explain satisfactorily. But that picture was allied to the monsters—there was no doubt in my mind.

I had no time for speculation or exploration now. I must start Dinan on his way for help. Holding tightly to the remnants of my strength, I staggered back to the cliff face.

Nine

As Dinan climbed, I squatted on the small ledge, my arm around Dagny. Her moans had grown fainter. Her eyes were half closed; beneath those drooping lids no pupils showed, only white arcs. The second rod I had taken from the cache lay across my lap, but I pressed my free hand against the still seeping wounds on my chest. The chill was bad. We should keep moving to stimulate circulation. But Dagny was a dead weight, and I was too weak. Also, I had killed two of the monsters, but that was not to say that more were not lurking among the ice pillars.

My thinking slowed, grew muddled. I was sleepy now—so sleepy. Yet some small spark within me sounded alarm. No sleep—that was the way to extinction. I fought to rouse, to listen. It seemed to me I could hear even from here the sound of the buried river.

River—water had to flow somewhere. Suppose we could trust to that stream for a road out? I knew of no major river in the lava lands. But that section of Beltane had never been fully explored. In latter days when men had been so few, and the majority of those engrossed in the labs, there had been little curiosity as to what lay outside the settlements. Only the Reserves of the animals had been patrolled to any extent. I believed that we had been the first to come this way since Butte Hold was closed.

So for all the evidence we had one way or another, the

river could be our way out. And if we discovered no other, it would have to be.

Dagny's weight against my good shoulder became heavier as time passed. I had forgotten to mark the hour when Dinan had left and had called from the crest that he was safely up and over. So looking at my watch told me nothing. The road back was straight—if he did not meet another blind prowler!

But he was a small boy, chilled, tired. I could not reckon his speed by the same effort I would put into that journey. I fumbled one-handedly with the ration bag and brought out a stick of Sustain. In the light I saw Dagny's face was smeared with traces of the same food. Dinan must have tried to feed her. But when I attempted the same thing, she allowed the nourishment to slip from her slack mouth, and I saw it was no use.

I sucked away. The stuff had a strong, unpleasant taste, but it had been meant to fortify a man through physical effort, and I forced myself to finish the bar. Still Dagny moaned. And time crawled with no real passing at all. A man could believe endless day-night drifted by.

The need for being alert was a constant spur. Finally, I learned to press tightly against the claw wounds. The pain from that touch broke through the haze in my mind. Yet as time went on and on and I heard nothing from above, though I warned myself that it was still far too soon for a rescue party to arrive, I lost heart. Would Dinan see that they would come with the right equipment? Why had I not made plain our needs before he left? I should have given him definite orders, outlining our needs. I could not trust to Dinan to know—

In that, though, I was wrong, for when they did come, I found that he had wrought better than I expected. They had the climbing ropes we had used to bring Lugard down the ledges. And Thad came down to adjust a sling about Dagny, climbing beside her inert body as those above drew her aloft.

When I tried to move, I found I was so stiff and giddy that I could not help myself much, so I had to huddle where I was until Thad made the return journey and slipped the same looping over me. That pressed against my wounds, and I cried out until, with pushing and tugging, we got the support lower.

What I could do to aid myself, I did, but that seemed little enough, and I progressed so slowly that I thought they must find me as much of a burden as Lugard had been. At last I was over the lip and lying face down, which was agony against the wounds until somehow I managed to roll over.

They had brought one of the large beamers with them, and the wash of light from that was all about me, harsh and blinding in my eyes. So I closed them while hands searched out my wounds, pulling from them the rags I had used to stop the bleeding. I felt coolness, a blessed soothing on those painful cuts, and knew that they used plasta-heal from an aid kit. The relief was so great that it left me weak and shaking, but I opened my eyes to look at Annet and Thad. A little beyond, Gytha sat on the floor, Dagny lying across her lap, while Pritha wiped that loose, drooling mouth and tried to dribble water between the uncontrolled lips.

"Can you walk?" Annet asked slowly, spacing her words as if she had need to reach the understanding of someone not quite of her world.

It was not a matter of what I could do, I thought, but rather what I must. To burden them with my weight even on a level surface was impossible. Time was of the essence for Dagny. And, since they had tended my wounds, a certain amount of strength flowed back into my misused body.

With Thad and Annet steadying me, I got to my feet, though that was difficult. Once up again I found I could walk, waveringly, but I was sure I could make it.

"Take her"—I nodded to Dagny—"on. She needs attention."

Annet gathered the little girl out of her sister's hold. That even her loving care could do anything for Dagny now I doubted, but she would have the best Annet could give her I knew. Perhaps that and time would heal—unless we might get top-world to the real attention she needed, again always supposing that the port and its people still existed. Would the enemy war against a child—a sick child?

I found Gytha by my side. As she had done once for Lugard,

she raised my good hand and put it on her shoulder, offering a support I did need. Of the rest of that journey I have only scanty memory until once more I awoke in the barracks.

This time the bunks around me were occupied with sleepers. Someone moaned, another muttered, both sounds born out of dreams. I felt cautiously across my body. My tunic was gone. My fingers slipped over the covering that healed and protected my wounds, and that light pressure raised no tingle of pain. We could thank such fortune as still smiled on us that medical supplies were at hand. I knew that under that coating I was well on the way to healthy scarring.

However, I was hungry, and that hunger moved me, so I crawled to hands and knees, eased up to my feet, and reached the mess section, leaving my blankets behind. There was a dusk here. The hut had been darkened for sleeping, but it was not the complete black of the caves. I could see the cook unit and the cans of ration and other supplies ranged on a shelf against the wall. I crossed to those.

Opening a ration tube bothered me. Though my wounds were better, I was still almost one-handed. So I twisted off the cap with my teeth and waited for the heat to be released in the contents. The stuff smelled so good that my mouth watered, and I did not wait for full heating but sucked it avidly.

"You—"

I turned at that exclamation and saw Annet in the doorway, a blanket draped around her shoulders. Her eyes looked puffy and her face haggard, and she was no longer a girl but a woman who had hard days and perhaps worse nights behind her.

"Dagny?"

She shook her head and came into the room, closing the door carefully behind her. Then, as one doing one thing but thinking about another, she swept one hand over a plate in the wall and the light became brighter.

"There's caff—on the unit," she said in a tired voice. "Press the button."

I put down the empty tube and did that, then picked up two mugs and set them on the table. She made no move to help me but sat down, putting both elbows on the table and resting her head on her hands.

"Perhaps—at the port—they can do something—" But she sounded very doubtful. "What about the passages, Vere?"

One-handed, I poured the caff into the mugs, surveyed her critically, and added to each two heaping spoonfuls of sweet cane crystals. And I stirred hers well before I put it down to deal with my own.

"Both stoppered. We haven't the equipment, or at least I haven't seen any yet, to open them."

She stared unseeingly before her, not noticing the mug or me. I felt a stir of concern. Her expression at that moment was far too near Dagny's withdrawal.

"I found something else, in the ice cave—"

"I know—the rod. Dinan showed it to us."

"It controls a force like a laser. Perhaps we can cut through. There is the river, also—"

"River," she repeated dully, and then with a spark of interest. "River?"

I sat down opposite her, grateful for having broken through her preoccupation. Between sips of caff, I told her of the fall of rock wall in the cave and the finding of the river.

"But with the rods you can burn a passage through one of the other tunnels," she observed, dropping her hand to the mug. "That's better than trying to follow a stream that leads you don't know where. And if you brought down the wall of the cave with that one, it ought to work in the passages as well."

I had to admit her logic was sound. Yet somehow my thoughts kept returning to that waterway, though I agreed to try the alien weapon or tool to burn our way out.

I did try, but to no purpose, for I discovered that, as with the laser we had found, it was a matter of power lack. I must have used all that remained in the ancient charge when I fought the monster in the ice cavern. When I tried it on the sealing of what seemed the better of the two blocked tunnels, it flared for several moments and then vanished. And all my working of its simple controls could not produce another spark, while the second one I had taken from the chest answered with only one quick burst. I made the trip back to the cache and brought out the other two, but neither responded in the least.

Whatever else was hidden behind that murky wall of ice was as well kept from us as if we had an ir-wall between. We could chip at the ice, and we tried. But the chill and the slowness of that labor showed us that was a task requiring more time than we had—for Dagny's sake.

With infinite care and effort, Annet managed to get enough food and water into the child to keep her alive. But beyond that she could do nothing. At last she agreed to try the river, since a return up the way we had come proved that at least one more cave-in had closed that path also.

By testing we discovered that the stream behind the wall was about waist deep, but the chill of the water, plus the fact it had a swift current, argued against wading. Under our beamers the liquid was so clear that you might step into it by mistake, thinking that some stone on its bottom was above the surface and not below it.

We drew on the supplies and set about constructing a raft that would ride high enough above the water to protect us and the packs we must take. In addition, we could make use of some pieces hacked free from the installations in the "missile" hut to serve as poles for guiding and for braking against too swift a forward sweep, while the climbing cords could provide anchors.

Of course there was always the dark chance that we might come to passages ahead completely water-filled. For that we had an answer in a roll of water-resistant plasta-cover, though whether it would make the raft and its passengers waterproof when carried under a surface, I could not be sure until we tried.

During our labors we lost all count of time. We ate, slept, and worked when we were hungry, tired, and refreshed. I forgot to check my watch, and the number of days we had been underground we could now only guess at. In fact, the very mention of that subject was apt to cause arguments, until, by Annet's suggestion, it was forbidden.

But at last we had the raft ready, which was as secure a

method of transportation as all suggestions could make it, and we loaded it with supplies we would need for the trails above, if we were ever fated to reach the surface of Beltane again.

I counted heads in the bunks on our last night in the base. One was missing. Once more I made that silent roll call, this time using my forefinger to number each.

Gytha! But where—?

I had my bedroll by the door, but I had visited Annet in her curtained cubby to see if she needed aught for Dagny. Her sister could have slipped out then. Where? Surely after the adventure of the twins she was not trying exploration on her own!

No calling yet. No need to rouse the camp until I did some searching on my own. I slipped out to look about. It took a moment for my eyes to adjust to the dark, and then I caught the faint glow of a belt torch as if radiating from some place among the rocks at the foot of the ledged cliff. With irritation at her recklessness, for we could never be sure, though we had found no more traces, that there were no more monsters in the caverns, I started after.

I planned to speak my mind sharply when I caught up with her, but as I saw where she stood, I paused. The shadows thrown by the debris were thick there until she went to work, for Gytha held in her hands one of the rods from the cache, its point to the cliff wall. From the point came a series of flashes, feeble indeed when compared to the blaze it had produced in my fight with the monster.

"Gytha!"

She turned her head, but she did not drop the rod. And there was a stubborn determination in her face, which at that moment clearly showed her kinship with Annet.

"You said these were no good for what you wanted," she returned defiantly, ready to justify her action. "But they'll work for this."

She was using the two rods, first one and then the other, to incise letters on the rock. Reading tapes have for so long been in use that manual writing had been almost forgotten. But on Beltane the lack of supplies had revived some of the ancient forms of record keeping, and Gytha had taken with enthusiasm to such learning.

"'Griss Lugard.'" She read what she had already set there. "'Friend'—It is true; he was our friend. He did the best for us that he knew. And I think he would like that said of him more than to list his rank or tell other things."

I took the rod from her, and why I did it, I cannot tell to this day, but below the rather shaky letters of her "Friend" I nursed every spark from that rod and the other to add five other letters.

Gytha read them one at a time as I set them into the rock.

"P—i—p—e—r—Piper. Oh, he would have liked that to linger in memory, too. It is just right, Vere! I couldn't go away and leave him without any marker at all!"

Romance learned from story tapes, some would have said. But I knew she was right, that this was what must be done. And I was glad she had thought of it. As a fitting finish I thrust both of the now exhausted rods into crevices of the pile so they stood upright, staffs without pennons, markers that perhaps no living creature would see again but that we would remember down the years.

As none had marked our going, so none witnessed our return. Nor did we mention it again, even to each other, but went directly to bed.

In the "morning," if morning it was above the layers of rock and soil between us and the open, we made a last check of our kits. We had drawn on the supplies Lugard and the earlier sojourners here had left. I now wore a Service tunic from which I had stripped rank badges that had no meaning. The one that fitted me best had carried a captain's shooting star, and I wondered who had left it here and what had happened to him on or between other worlds.

We made the descent into the ice cavern easily enough, having done with Dagny as we did earlier with Lugard, immobilized her in blankets and an outside wrapping of plasta that would protect her once we were afloat.

We had left the raft by the broken wall, and on it were already lashed the heavier of our packs. It cost effort to launch it and then hold it steady for embarkation. When I got aboard and loosed one of the hooked lines while Thad threw off the other, I had a moment of faint-heartedness and apprehension concerning the unknown that might lie ahead, wondering if we had chosen the best solution after all. Yet I also knew that we dared waste no more time if we would save Dagny.

Luckily, the current was not as swift as I thought, just strong enough to carry us along. One of the big beamers had been mounted on the prow (if a raft can be said to have a prow) so we would have a warning of dangers ahead. And Thad and I took the poles on either side to ward off any swing against the walls. The air remained cold, but as we were pulled away from the ice cave, it grew less frosty and finally became more like the temperature of the camp cave.

I turned to my watch again as a check upon our passage. We had left at twelve, but whether that marked midnight or noon I had no idea. By fifteen hours we were still in passage, and while once or twice the roof had closed over us so that we had to lie on the raft's surface, we had not had any real trouble.

We were ten hours on that voyage, and I had no way of figuring how far the waters took us. But suddenly Emrys cried out and pointed up, his hand outlined against the back rays of the beamer—

"A star!"

At the same moment the beamer showed us a bush that certainly could not have grown underground, though we still passed between rock walls. We were aware then of fresher air to fill our lungs, not conscious of the underground taint of what we had been breathing until it was gone. So we were out of the caves, but since it was night, we had no idea of where we were.

I crawled forward and loosed the beamer so that I could swing it a little from right to left. Bushes, but they were small and stunted-looking. Rocks, among them pieces of drift that argued that at times the river must run higher here than it did at present.

Then the canyon, or whatever it was in which we floated, widened out, and a long spit of sand ran out into the water.

The raft made one of its half turns, since Thad was alone at the pole, and grounded against that sand bar with a thump that rocked us all. I swept the beamer to pick up a sandy beach with tufts of coarse grass growing farther up. A good-enough refuge to hold us until daylight. I said as much, and the rest agreed.

We were stiff and cramped from the voyage. Thad and I fared the best because of our employment at the poles. We tumbled out onto the sand bar, and then all turned to drag our craft out of the pull of the current until we could be sure that it would not be tugged away, leaving us marooned.

So we made camp, and then I looked at the compass that had been among the supplies. The second map showed nothing of the river. That must have been hidden from the mapper. But according to the compass, we had come southwest—which meant we must be over the mountains, in the general direction of the large Reserves. This was all wilderness if I was right. But there were the Ranger stations, and if I could sight some known landmarks in the morning, I thought we might find one of those. Even to be out under the stars gave me such a feeling of relief that I suddenly had no doubts that all would go better from now on.

We ate and unrolled our beds. Fatigue settled down as might another blanket. I put Thad at one end of the camp, with his stunner to hand, while I took the other. I did not think that either of us was in shape to play sentry, but we must do the best we could.

Sound awoke me. A loud squawk was repeated. I opened my eyes to sunlight, blinked, and saw a bird walk into water and the river close over its head. A guskaw! We might have alarmed it by our presence here, but the fact that I saw it at all meant we were in the wilderness. I sat up to look around.

None of the other blanketed bundles stirred. It was quite early morning, the light grayish, and we were in a canyon. I looked back the way we had come and saw my landmark, one large enough indeed. Whitecone, a former volcano that now wore a perpetual tip of snow. So we had come over the mountains by underground ways.

With Whitecone in that direction, this must be the Redwater, though the clear stream lapping the sand only a couple of arms' lengths away had none of the characteristic crimson tinge it wore in the Reserve. I knew of no other body of water as large in this direction, and since my ambition had been to be a Ranger here, I had pored over aerial survey maps of this area.

If this was the Redwater, and I was sure it was, we need only continue our voyage and we would reach the bridge on the Reserve road. The Anlav headquarters was only a short distance north from the bridge. I gave a sigh of relief. It was good—almost as good as sighting the com tower of Kynvet.

I set about getting breakfast, using the portable cook unit. Warm food would mark our triumph over the dark and the caves. One by one the others roused, as eager to press on as I now was. There would be a flitter at the station. If we could not all crowd into that, why Annet could take Dagny and as many others as possible, and the rest of us could wait on a second trip. My plans spun ahead, and then I remembered. We might have come out of darkness into light, but what had been happening here? It could be that we were no safer really than we had been at the cave camp.

So I warned them that we must move warily still. I did not think they all agreed with me, however, and I made it plain by an order, though whether I could enforce that I did not know.

"We do not know what has happened. For our own safety we must be sure just who or what we face. There is a chance that any trouble at the port or the settlements would not have reached here. I hope we can get help at the Anlav head-quarters. There will be a com there, and with it we can learn more. But we must go carefully."

Some of them nodded. I had expected a protest from Annet, but that did not come. Then she gave the ghost of a smile and said, "Well enough. To that I agree. But the sooner we do find out, the better."

I had wondered at her change of position. Had she at last, to herself, admitted that Lugard had been telling the truth and that we returned to danger and not to aid and comfort? But I had no opportunity to ask her.

Once more we floated the raft and repacked it. But here the current was not enough, and Thad and I stood and poled until we grew too tired to push. Then Annet handed Dagny to Pritha, and she and Gytha took my place, Emrys and Sabian, Thad's. In spite of doing the best that we could, dark came and we still had not reached the bridge. The river, now running between banks of red soil, had taken on the color that made it a proper landmark.

Once more we camped, rose with the dawn, and bent to the poles. It was midmorning when the bridge came into sight. We forced the raft ashore, made a cache of most of its cargo, and took only trail supplies. Gytha, Annet, Dagny, Ifors, Dinan, and Pritha settled into hiding at the end of the bridge where there was a good cover of brush, and three of us went on, Sabian taking a sentry go at the other end of the span.

There were no marks of any recent traffic on the road. Ground cars were in general use here. Hoppers too often frightened the animals. And there had been a recent storm, which had left patches of red mud drying and cracking under the hot midday sun. No marks across that, save here and there a paw or hoof print where some creature had gone.

That unmarked road was disturbing, and I found myself drawing my stunner—the one that had been Annet's—looking from right to left and back again as if I feared sudden attack from the walls of brush.

Ten

"THIS IS THE LARGEST Reserve, isn't it?" Thad moved closer, his voice low, as if he shared my uneasiness and feared being overheard, while Emrys kept to the middle of the road a little behind.

"Yes. Anlav." I did not believe we need fear the animals. They kept mainly to the wildest parts of the Reserve, though I did not know about the mutants that had been housed here.

Anlav had once had top priority among the mutation labs. But that had been some years ago. The curtailing of such work had made them center on the nearer Pilav Reserve for a time.

We rounded a curve to see the Ranger station. Like all such posts, it had been deliberately fashioned to blend in with the natural scenery. Its walls did not run straight but were made of rough stone unsmoothed. The roof had sod and vines planted on it, growing as if their support were a natural hillock, and the vehicle park was concealed by a brush wall.

I cupped my hand trumpet-fashion about my lips and gave the recognition call. But though we eyed the patch of dark that must be the door with growing impatience, there was no response. Now there was nothing but to cross the open.

If the force field was up, we would know it soon enough. Warning the boys, I took the lead, my hand outstretched as a warn-off. Animals coming against that screen suffered, I

117

had been told, a mild shock. What effect it might have on a human I did not know.

But my hand met no barrier, and I came to the door, which stood a quarter open. The distrust of all about me grew with every step I took. Anlav was of such importance that the Ranger station should be manned at all times. What had happened here?

The door swung in at once under my touch. I crossed the threshold warily, coming into the main room. It followed the general pattern of such places, consisting of three rooms, the largest running the full length, a combination living-office space with a cook unit at the far end. To the back would lie the bunk room and, flanking it, a small lab and storage space.

I almost fell, for my eyes were bothered by the contrast between the light outside and this interior gloom. There was something on the floor to trip me. I switched on my belt torch and glanced down at a sheet of plasta, the kind generally used for storage protection. As I swept the light on around the room, I saw other signs of disorder. A chair had been pushed back so hurriedly that it had fallen on its back, the legs pointing at me like stunner barrels. There were dishes on the table with dried bits of food. And on the desk a com-ticker had gone on spewing forth report tape, which curled to the floor until the machine had finally run down.

The wall rack on which large-duty stunners usually rested was empty. There was a rustling as I approached the desk. A furred thing, moving too fast for me to get good sight of it, darted out from under that piece of furniture and scurried on through the door into the storeroom. The post had not only been left suddenly, but also some time ago.

I saw the control plate for the lights and passed my hand across it twice for the brightest beam.

Thad asked from the doorway, "No one here?"

I tried the bunk room. Small personal items were still on the hanging shelves there, and all four bunks were neatly made. Whatever had called the staff away, they had not packed. I made sure of this by trying the wall cupboards, peering at changes of uniform and underclothing.

The lab-storage was neat, but there were some signs of

rummaging at floor level—gnawed containers, rations spilled and half eaten out of them. I heard a warning snarl from behind one overturned box.

"They're gone," I answered Thad's question as I backed out of that room, not wanting to turn away from whatever might be hidden there. There are some small creatures that do not look menacing to the uninformed but are formidable if you underrate them.

There might be one possible answer. I crossed to the desk where the duty tape had twisted into coils on the floor. Though I could not judge the amount of use such a machine had in Anlav, I thought that more than one day, or perhaps two, had elasped while the machine ground out unread reports. And there was no way of telling how long it had been since it ran down entirely.

The loops of tape were in code, but it was a simple one, for condensation only. I read it without trouble—all routine dictation from Eye-Spies set up on feeding grounds and on game trails, reports of animal movements. There were two alarms about predators in grazing grounds, which would ordinarily have sent the Rangers on field duty out with a stunner.

"Com—" Thad pointed to the other installation.

One stride brought me to it. When I picked up the hand mike, I could hear the unmistakable thrum-thrum of an open connection. But there was no other sound carrying through. I levered the visa-plate, but that remained blank. The broadcast did not come through.

"Call in!" Thad was beside me.

"Not yet." I put the mike down and fingered the button that broke the relay. "Not until we know more of who may be there—"

For a moment it seemed he might question my decision, and then he nodded.

"Might be alerting those we wouldn't want to know—"

"Just so. Let's look for a flitter."

What we found in the vehicle park were a ground car and a hopper. The former had its engine box open, and tools lay

119

in disarray as if the one working on it had been hastily summoned elsewhere. Thad went to look at it.

"Putting in a new pick-up unit—just needs the tri-hookup, but it's based."

Emrys had gone to the hopper, climbed in, and was gunning for a take-off before I could stop him. But there was no purr of answer. Perhaps both vehicles had been abandoned because they were useless for those in a hurry.

"Get out!" I snapped at Emrys. "Remember what we agreed—go slow. We take a hopper, and we can be picked up on an income screen. If we use any transportation, it must be the ground car—that has a distort shield."

"And," I added as he came out, his look sullen rather than contrite, "if you need action, get back to the bridge and bring the others in. It's going to rain and soon."

The brightness of the morning was gone. Clouds rolled dark and heavy, and one could almost drink the gathering moisture from the air. As he went, I turned to Thad and the land car. He was right. About two-thirds of the work on it had been done. It needed only the final connections. And if that was the only repair needed, once we had completed that we would have a mode of transportation far better suited to our purpose now than any far-ranging hopper or flitter. Though it traveled only at ground level, it was equipped with screens that distorted the vision of those without so that it was, for all purposes, invisible. It could not travel fast, but it would be able to move without detection, though a radar could pick up some hint of it. Meant to get close to the animals on the open grazing ranges, it would be a type of transport unknown to the refugees, if they were now our enemies.

"Close it up now," I told Thad. "We can't do anything until the rain is over. Let's hurry the rest along."

We did not beat the rain, for we were all wet through when we at last dodged into the post. I laid Dagny down on one of the inner bunks, and Thad quickly switched on the heat-dry unit. When we closed the door to the storm, we were well sheltered, even better than at the cave base.

"What happened here?" Annet looked at the dishes, the

chair none of us had bothered to right, and the tangle of tape on the floor.

"The staff must have left in a hurry—I don't know how long ago. Meanwhile, let's make sure we have no uninvited guests." Stunner in hand, I went into the lab-storage. I warned the others to keep outside and turned my weapon from maximum to low, since what I hunted was small enough to take refuge behind a box only knee high.

I gave a swift cross spray of the deadening ray and then pulled crates and boxes around until I discovered my quarry, lying limp, its sharply pointed nose turned up as it slept, if not peacefully, well.

It was an inflax, always a camp.raider when it could get a chance, but not as harmless as it looked, for this was a male with the hollowed fangs for the irritating poison. I picked it up and laid it on a box top, while I searched for any other visitors. But this seemed to be alone. I carried it out and pointed to its armament in warning, then set it outside the door under an outcrop of the wall that would keep the worst of the storm from it. The outer air and the added whip of water would speedily awaken it.

Annet had found the com and changed the dial to the range of the port. I had just time to grab the mike from her hand.

"What do you—" she began fiercely.

"We agreed—no rash steps until we were sure!" I reminded her.

"We haven't time to poke and pry!" She tried to force the mike from me. "We have to get Dagny to the medico and as quickly as possible. If we call, they could send a flitter."

"First, try the incall." I thought that the fact I had not been able to pick up any broadcast might impress her. "Feeholme is the only settlement this side of the mountains. Try that!"

I gave the mike to her and clicked on the proper relays. If there was any broadcasting, we could pick up the chatter, even if our wave was not narrowed to either call or reception. Again we could hear the thrum of an open beam but no whisper along it. Once more I dialed for receive, taking a chance to do so much, my hand ready to break connection instantly were we to attract the sort of attention we did not want. But the sound of the system was all that came to us.

Annet stared at the mike in her hand and stooped to read the symbol above the switch I had activated.

"I don't understand. They should be on the air. At this hour there would not just be an open circuit and no broadcast."

"Unless there was no one there—"

She shook her head violently, not only in denial of my suggestion, I thought, but also against her own fears.

"But the com is *never* untended. Try the distress call—"

"No. Listen, Annet. If Lugard was right, we could trigger worse than what we have now. We agreed not to rush blindly. There is a ground car here. They were repairing it when they left, but I can finish off their job as soon as the weather clears a little. Ground cars may be slow, but they have protection which may be of benefit to us. I promise you, as soon as we can use it, we'll take off for Feeholme. And from there a lift over the mountains is nothing. But tell me, does this suggest to you that a normal state of affairs exists?" I indicated the room. "And when they left, they took all the armament this station had."

"All right. But as soon as we can—"

"We'll go," I promised her.

She moved away from the com and stooped to pick up the chair to set it straight again. Then she was at the cook unit, opening the supply cupboard above it, while I went to search the desk for any hint of what had happened here. There was nothing but routine record tapes. The tape from the floor, though I gave it more detailed study now, also held nothing but reports from the Reserve.

The force of the storm lessened by midafternoon. As soon as we could venture out, Thad and I were back at the ground car. He proved knowledgeable and was the kind of co-worker one could wish for. But since neither of us was trained as a tech, we were not as swift about it as we might have been. We had no more than made the last connection and slammed down the cover, than a second storm was upon us, driving us to shelter in the post.

That was a wild night. Perhaps our sojourn underground made it seem twice as bad as it might have otherwise. I had a sudden idea to fit another tape in the general report and click it on, centering its attention to details of what might be happening on the road between us and Feeholme.

It clicked away steadily, grinding out code for downed trees, overflow of some streams, animals fleeing before the lash of wind and rain. And as the worst of these possible delays were noted, I marked them in turn on a map from the desk so that we would have preparation for trouble the next day.

We started shortly after dawn. It was a wet world that faced us, but the violence of yesterday was passed. The ground car had been intended to carry equipment throughout the Reserve, and by stripping it of all but the seats, we had room for the whole party within it. I did not yet activate the distort, since I must save that for the approach to Feeholme.

The road was gullied and puddled, but the treads of the car were meant to take worse than that smoothly. We ground on at a steady pace. Twice we had to detour around fallen trees, and once there were a few anxious moments when we forded a stream and the storm-swollen waters lashed around the sturdy body of the vehicle as high as the seats within, sending a few trickles about the doors to wet our feet. But I went at a slant, more with the current than directly across, and the treads bit and pulled us up on comparatively dry land.

We caught sight of animals but always at a distance. At noon we pulled into the lee of a high rock spur that was capped with a pickup rod, one of the link of supervisory contacts across the Reserve. There was no sign anyone had been there, though one of the guidelines for the pickup had broken and whacked against the rod in the pull of the wind.

Annet, however, had no eyes for what was around us in the wilderness, for she had at last won a small response from Dagny, who asked for water. Not that she seemed aware of those around her, but as we ate, she sucked from an E-tube, and it was not necessary to squeeze it into her mouth and then try to get her to swallow.

I thought we might make it by dark and began to prepare Annet now for the further precautions I wanted to take when we reached there. When I spoke of halting the car, leaving them in it in distort while I scouted, she seemed amiable, but it was as if she humored me, not that she believed it necessary.

Feeholme I had seen only once, and then it had been an in-and-out visit, a point of departure and change from the flitter that had brought me with two other Ranger candidates from the port to the hopper that carried us into the Reserve. It was larger than Kynvet because it was the only settlement this side of the mountains. But it was no more than a village probably when compared to towns off-world. It was the headquarters for Rangers.

We crawled on, and I kept an anxious eye on the gauges. The worry over the reason for the half-repaired engine was always at the back of my mind. If transportation failed us here, it might be grave. But so far there were no signs of trouble.

Twilight came early as clouds were massing again, and I put on what speed I could to race another storm. We came to the foot of a rise, and there I turned off the road, creeping into a small copse of trees and through that to the ravine they guarded. There were rocks here to form a natural wall, and I backed the car against that. If the others kept inside, they would have the best protection I could find from any gale.

I did not take anything with me save the stunner, and it was my hope that somehow, somewhere, I would find a replacement for that, a weapon of greater power. I made Annet promise to keep the lights off while I was gone, while Thad took my seat at the controls with orders to switch on the distort as soon as I was out of range.

Then I moved up the rise. When I turned to look back, it was as if the car had vanished, and I knew a small lift of relief. They were safe as long as they stayed inside that.

There was no reason to return to the road. I cut across

country, where there was more cover. Below now I could see the dark blot of Feeholme, a very dark blot for not a single light showed, and that was an immediate warning of trouble.

The country around the settlement had been cleared of the thicker growth of trees and underbrush, leaving only enough to please the eye and give shade. Here the houses and the headquarters buildings were not set off by themselves but around an oval, the center point of which was a landing place for flitters and hoppers. I did not know the exact population, but I thought that those dark buildings should shelter at least two hundred. In addition to the Reserve headquarters, there was a shopping center, which had once sold off-world products but now served as an exchange for the output of various other labs and settlements—for there was a small trade in specialties from different sectors. Each of the settlements was practically self-sufficient, however—a reason for the dwindling interest in off-world trade, which had not, after the first ten years of pioneering, ever supplied more than luxuries and exotics.

I came now to cultivated fields, drawing back to leap the safe-current—until I saw there was no thin blue radiance stringing from post to post. A branch pushed forward to where that current should run did not shrivel. The protection for the crops, already near harvesting, had not been activated. I saw a small herd of verken taking advantage of that. Judging by the extent of trampled and eaten plants, I guessed that this had not been their first visit here.

They snorted, snuffled, and scattered at my coming, but they did not pursue their loping run far, facing about to see if I would give chase. When I did not, they shuffled back for such a feast as they had probably never known before.

Dark houses, inactive field protection—it added up in a way I did not like. Then I came upon a hopper, well off the road, its nose slammed into a wall until the front was crumpled. I flashed my torch into the cabin, then flicked it off and tried to erase from my mind what that instant of light had shown me. But having seen it, I came directly into the open. *That* would not have been there had there been anyone left in Feeholme to care.

So I tried the first house and again found—No, a single glance was enough to send me out faster than I had entered. But there was still the headquarters, and perhaps I could discover something there, if only a hint on a message tape. There were others who had died in the open. And there were scavengers from the Reserve come to feast. I avoided what I could. But I had to step over part of a skeleton to enter the building I sought. There I found men who must have died at their posts in the com room and elsewhere, but nowhere any sign of what had come so suddenly to end a settlement almost a hundred planet years old.

I made myself examine some of the dead. There were no wounds or laser burns. It would seem that these had simply fallen at their duties and died, perhaps in a matter of seconds.

Gas? But what of those in the open? Or had they been the stronger and managed to crawl as far before collapse came? I could not account for such wholesale slaughter by any weapon that I knew.

The off-worlders might have such. We had heard rumors of all types of things developed for the exploitation of enemy planets, things that would remove a population and leave their world empty. Had the refugees put into service such a one here—perhaps trying it out before they turned pirate as Lugard had foretold some of the remnants of the tattered fleets would do? But why such wanton slaughter?

I stood in the com room. The circuits were still open as they had been when a dead or dying hand slipped from the control board. I saw the steady light of clear channel on the board. Stepping closer, I read the symbol for Haychax over the mountains. But all that came through the amplifier was the same thrum-thrum we had picked up at the Ranger station.

At any rate, this town could give us no aid. And I was not about to lead our party into what lay here. But I did search for weapons. In the end, I found three more stunners and one long-shot laser meant for ground clearing, but that was too bulky to transport, and when I turned it on, the glow was so reduced that I knew it near extinction. The fact that in a settlement that supplied three Reserves these were all to be found in the way of arms was another disturbing point. It would seem there had been other searchers before me. When I came into the store place, I found evidence of that.

I faced wild confusion. Boxes and containers had been ripped open and much of their content wastefully spilled and trampled. The tracks in some of the wastage were signature enough to tell me that no Beltane settler had done this, for two or three boot prints were so clearly marked that there could be no mistaking—space boots. The looters must have been from the refugee camp. Had they also caused the death of the town? I went down on hands and knees and tested with fingertip the leakage of a broken canister and decided it had begun perhaps only a day earlier, while the town had met its fate long before that—perhaps even on the same day we had gone underground, or shortly thereafter.

Now I foraged in what was left, finding a drop bag meant to be parachuted to Rangers in the Reserve where there was no landing place. Into that I packed small cans and ration tubes. We had brought little enough out of the caves, and if we had to stay away from settlements, we would need all we could find.

It was too heavy to shoulder when I left, so I had to drag it after me, but it had been made for hard usage, and I did not worry. I had come out of another door into the landing place of the settlement. Here again was a scene of wanton destruction. I dared to use my torch, though only in quick flashes. What I saw were burned flitters, at least two of them. Half a dozen hoppers had been worked over with lasers until they were masses of half-melted metal. There was not one remaining unwrecked transport.

I had seen enough of Feeholme—the tomb that Feeholme had become. There were two other Ranger stations on this side of the mountains, but I doubted whether we could find help at either. And if we returned to Kynvet, it would only be by taking the car as far as we could run it, then hiking over the mountains on our feet. But perhaps there was no reason for such a return—

Dragging my pack of supplies, I went back across the fields. I was in the shadow of a copse of trees when I saw a spark in the sky. It was well away from Feeholme, but it was no star—rather the light of a flitter. Its course was erratic, moving up and down, side to side, as if whatever hand lay on the controls was either inexperienced or under some difficulty. I headed to where I had left the car, and I hoped that those I had left there would not strive to signal the pilot. What I had seen here made me more determined than ever that we must keep our guard.

Rain broke then, cold and heavy, and I found the bag a greater weight as I struggled up the rise. I could no longer see the light of the flitter. There was a roll of thunder and clashes of violet lightning, which made me flinch involuntarily and try to run.

Eleven

I LAY BELLY DOWN under the very dubious shelter of a bush my head pointing downslope toward the car I could not see as long as the distort shield was up. The rain water ran down my back, gathered in the hollow of my belt when I moved, and then, in sudden icy jerks, trickled down over hips and thighs. Though it was summer and the days were warm enough, this stormy night held the threat of coming autumn, and I wanted nothing so much as to be under cover. Yet the sign of that flitter had made me doubly cautious. Any signal I gave those waiting below might betray us.

Cupping my hands about my torch, I made a funnel so the ray I needed would be hidden to anything above, though no flyer with a grain of sense would keep a light-bodied flitter aloft amid such tossing winds.

Now I pressed the button on, off, on, off. As far as I could see they ought to be able to pick up those flashes easily. But when nothing moved below, uneasiness boiled in me, and I was ready to go charging down with a stunner. My ever-present fear was that they had attempted to signal the flitter with the car com, and if they had been successful, who knew now what we might have to face.

There was a flickering below, and then the dark bulk of the car came into view. No lights on in it—so my warnings had taken root to that extent! I got to my feet and went down, dragging my heavy bag.

"Vere?" Annet's voice in anxious inquiry.

"Yes!" I scrambled to the door. "Let me in—quick!"

I thrust myself in as I might have charged an enemy-occupied room. There were startled protests as I forced a place for my wet self.

"That flitter—you did not com it?" I leaned across Annet to thumb up the distort once again, only breathing easily when that defense was on.

"No," Thad answered. "You said—"

"Why shouldn't we?" Annet's demand overrode his answer. "He held the mike where I couldn't reach it, or I would have. Why—what has happened, Vere?"

I was so tired that I could no longer fence. After all, they were going to find out sooner or later, and they should have been bright enough to guess for themselves with all the clues we had had.

"I found a dead town," I replied flatly.

"You mean everyone gone?" She sounded more than startled—disbelieving. "But where did they go—to the port, over the mountains?"

"I said dead, not deserted. A town of the dead—"

I felt her stir beside me, as if she cringed away to the extent anyone could move on the overcrowded seat.

"But how—killed?"

"Those I—I looked at showed no signs of laser or blaster. They had apparently just dropped at their duty posts. But the town is dead. And its store has been looted at a later time. I brought two stunners—the rest of the weapons are gone."

"Then Lugard was right!" Thad cut in. "The refugees attacked—but why kill everyone?"

"No!" Annet was shivering. "No! It can't be true! Vere, we've got to get back to Kynvet. Take a flitter—there must be flitters at Feeholme."

"There were flitters. Someone systematically destroyed them. Lasers had been used on those—on hoppers, too. There is no workable transportation left."

"Then—then what are we going to do? Dagny—"

"We have this car, and I brought all the supplies I could

that were light and yet highly sustaining. Our best move now is to head back into the Reserve, cross the mountains—"

"That flitter—" Thad asked. "Do you suppose it was the looters?"

"It could be our people, hunting survivors," Annet said. "If it was and we didn't com them—" Her tone was accusing.

"Did you ever see a normal flitter following such a flight pattern?" Thad asked for me. "There was something wrong with the machine or the pilot. Do we go back the way we came, Vere?"

It was a temptation. There was the Ranger headquarters where we could find shelter, perhaps use it for a base while we scouted a possible route over the mountains again. However, it might well be that any structure would serve as a magnet for looters. There were maps in plenty; they could have found one in Feeholme that located every station in the Reserves.

"I think not. We strike due southeast from here, into the hill country. There is a reception point for mutants at Gur Horn. We can head for that—perhaps pick up more supplies there."

We would go nowhere this night, however, uncomfortable as it would be; rather we would try to shelter and rest in the car. I was in no mind to switch on driving lights, which would be beacons in the dark. Rough cross-country travel was impossible, and to seek the roads was to ask for discovery. I thought Annet would raise opposition to this decision, but she did not. Instead, she set about reorganizing our seating so as to give maximum comfort in our minimum of space. Some of the food was shared out.

We slept, I think out of sheer fatigue. Twice I was awakened by cries from the sleeping children and knew that they dreamed. But I did not, and for that I was thankful. Annet was quick to soothe and comfort. The last time, when Pritha whimpered herself half awake, Annet reached out her hand as if seeking support, and I grasped it. There was no other sound from Pritha, but Annet turned her face nearer mine and whispered, "Vere, *can* we get over the mountains?"

"If we take one step at a time, we can. This is summer; the Reserve pass will be open. If we use that, we shall come out not too far from Butte Hold." Then I hesitated, remembering those visitors Lugard had faced down with a far more formidable weapon than any we possessed. If a hint of treasure had drawn them to the Butte, they might be there now, hunting for Lugard's rumored find.

"Vere—" Her whisper was now such a thin thread of sound I could hardly hear it. "There was something—"

"What?" I prompted when she did not continue.

"You know, at Yetholme, they did controlled experiments for the forces." I could hear her swallow as if the words were being forced out of her.

"That was years back, and didn't they close down entirely?"

"Everyone said so. Dr. Corfu—you know what he did."

"Took a double cold-sleep pill and never came out of it."

"He—he wouldn't go ahead with their last experiment, and they pressured him terribly. I heard Mother—she had seen the initial steps. They were working on a mutated virus. Vere, it would kill off intelligent beings—it affected the brain—but it left a world intact, to be taken over later by jump troops. It had no affect on animals unless they were specially sensitized to it. Vere, what if—?"

Again I remembered one of Lugard's warnings. There might be secrets here which would-be raiders would welcome as part of their armament for future attacks. A virus with such properties, seeded in secret across an unsuspecting city, even a continent, or a world, a period of waiting—then easy picking for the seeders. But a virus—my hand caught at the latch of the car door—if such a thing had been loosed in Feeholme, then I could now be a carrier, already a dead man myself! Perhaps it was too late for all of us. I had spent the night here, in close quarters, breathed the same air, touched them. They could all be dead because of me!

Those in the town had died so quickly and at their posts that my guess had been some type of gas loosed off to blanket the settlement. Would a plague have worked in that manner?

"I might have—"

"No. You said they had been dead for some time." Her whisper was ragged.

"Yes."

"What they worked on at Yetholme was a forty-eight-hour strike. Then the virus died, unless someone came too soon. And there were immune shots. If we could find records, we would know. But you can't take this car up to the pass, can you?"

"No. But we shall use it as far as we can. Gur Horn first. If I remember rightly, there was never more than a small staff there. It was a mutant introduction point, and all they did was watch over the high types. They may have been summoned just as the other Rangers were. We can get more supplies there, shelter. It is the highest of the permanent Reserve bases."

"What mutants were there?"

"I don't know. The time we visited Anlav, we didn't go there. They simply informed us as to what it was when we sighted it from the flitter."

"Would the staff have transportation?"

"A hopper maybe, a ground car certainly. They had to be ready to transport injured animals for treatment. There was always the danger of a mutant being attacked by a control. And in order to study them properly, they couldn't keep them penned or caged."

A hopper, yes, we might just find a hopper there. And that would lighten our mountain journey by about half. I found myself impatient to set out for Gur Horn.

The storm blew itself out by dawn. And as soon as we had light enough to see before us, I put the car on steady power, though that was drained by the energy to keep up the distort, which was never intended to run steadily. These cars were meant for very rough usage, but I had no idea how long or how far their unit charges would take them. We might be put afoot before we reached our goal, though I tried to make the best time possible.

Luckily, the southeastern way took us mainly across open country. It was rolling, though, with an up-and-down hillock route, which, before noon, forced us twice to pause when Pritha and Ifors became ill from the motion. Dagny lay inert, wedged in with blanket rolls. She ate and drank, but she lay with her eyes closed, and Annet could not tell whether she slept or was in a stupor.

We nooned beside a small stream, eating E-rations rather than trying to heat any food. The sun was hot outside the car, and it bore down on one's head and burned any exposed portion of skin. We did not tarry long, and I filled all our canteens before we pulled out. I had no notion of water supply in the hills to which we were pointed.

Those grew higher about us, and I had to find a twisting path among them instead of taking an upgrade and downgrade route as I had before. It seemed I was right about the lack of water, for the terrain grew more and more desert. Storm waters had torn through gullies, leaving drift behind, and our progress grew slower and slower. Then we hit upon a cleared trail that could only be that to Gur Horn, and recklessly I turned into it, determined we must make speed.

Distances as seen from the air and the ground vary a great deal. When we had flown this route on the instruction trip, it had seemed that the mutant station was a very short space removed from Ranger headquarters and that both were about within shouting distance of Feeholme. Now I wondered if I had mistaken the way and missed Gur Horn, to travel lost into the hills.

We moved down an alley between high-growing spiggan bushes. Since it was fruiting time for those, the branches were so loaded with their purple burden that they bent far groundward, and our road was crowded. Insects, from small ones to those large Zand moths that I could not cover with my hand, wore their brilliant wings outspread as they clung to the overripe and rotting berries already fallen in a mucky carpet across ground and road. There were birds in plenty, and here and there small animals that had glutted themselves into a drunken stupor and lay, some on their backs, their limp paws pointed skyward as they slept off their indulgence. I knew it was good we drove enclosed, for the odor of the too ripe fruit was nothing anyone would want to smell twice.

We were away from the far end of this feasting place when I stopped, for the creature standing in the middle of the way facing us had not fed here, and its stance now could only be explained by the fact that it not only saw us (though how could that be with the distort on?) but also that it wanted to halt us purposefully.

"An ystroben!" Gritha leaned forward until her head was level with my shoulder. "Vere, it's an ystroben!"

134

At first sight I would have agreed with her. It had the thick red fur, the rounded head, the fan-shaped, fur-edged ears, the rounded muzzle, the black paws, and the stub tail. Yet there were differences, and the longer one stared at the animal, the more apparent those differences became. In the first place, the head—it had a higher and wider dome of skull. Also, it was larger than any ystroben I had ever seen. And it was far from timid. Also—it saw us!

"Vere, it wants us to do something—see!"

Had I not watched what happened, I would not have believed, for the beast arose from its plump haunches, came a little farther toward us, and deliberately raised a forepaw to beckon. There was no mistaking that gesture—it *had* beckoned.

"A mutant!"

"It wants us to do something," Gytha repeated, emphasizing that with a firm grip on my shoulder.

"But"—Annet's hand went out to touch the lever among the controls—"the distort is on. How can it see us?"

"If it is a mutant," Gytha retorted, "it can do all sorts of things. Vere, we must see what it wants."

But I had no mind to play games with animals. And mutants could be untrustworthy. Who knows what could be roaming about now, freed from some lab control by the failure of a dead man's hand to touch the right buttons?

I activated one of the safety devices of the car. And, while we felt nothing at all, the things feeding on the berries seemed to go mad. Those that flew and could still depend upon their wings and their equilibration arose in the air, some so sharply that they collided. And the four-footed ones still conscious rolled on the ground or ran as fast as their legs could carry them, scattering from the vicinity of the car as if that had exploded.

The ystroben shuddered and strove to stay where it was, making a visibly great effort to do so. Then, its mouth opened in what must have been a shriek, though whether of rage or pain we could not hear within our soundproof cocoon. And it fell to its four feet, to weave drunkenly off the center, staggering into the wall of bushes.

"What did you do?" Thad asked.

"Sonics—used to ward off animal attack."

Gytha's hand on my shoulder became a fist, which she brought down with bruising impact on my flesh.

"You didn't have to do that!" she cried. "It wasn't going to hurt us. It wanted us to do something—"

I closed my ears to her protest and stepped up the speed of the car, wanting to be out of the overpopulated bush as quickly as we could. We came into an open space where there was more luxuriant growth than we had seen for hours. The reason for that was plain, for a fountain played on a level space, and from it flowed a stream, to reach a little hollow, puddle into a pond, and again seek a way on a pebbled bed until it was swallowed up by reeds and water-loving vegetation.

Beyond the fountain was another of the artfully constructed houses blended with care into the landscape. Behind that soared the unusual formation of rock that gave it its name—Gur Horn, for that towering spear of stone was indeed shaped to the fashion of a gur horn, even having the spiraled markings one sees on the adult male of the species.

We had come so suddenly into the open that I had no time for any hide and scout precautions I wanted to take. But there was no sign of life, and the parking space to the side of the house housed not even a ground car.

I pushed off the distort, and instantly the world was alive with the noise it had cloaked. Noise it was—a mournful lowering, a moaning, and now and then a scream or rumble or growl, all of which seemed to come from the house.

"What—?" Annet had her stunner ready.

I had been about to open the door; now I hesitated. The amount of that sound and its plaint suggested trouble, bad trouble. Yet I could see nothing moving.

"Vere, the ystroben—" Gytha demanded my attention, pulling at the arm she had bruised minutes earlier. I turned my head in the direction she pointed. The animal that had tried to withstand the sonic, or its close twin, staggered out of the berry-walled lane. Its eyes were half closed; it shook its head from side to side as if it had been deafened. But doggedly it kept on its feet and passed us, heading for the house. Now it was uttering sounds, too, a kind of rumbling, and the other cries began to subside.

"Vere, look! It's asking you again!"

It had reached the level of the fountain and was standing there, its flanks heaving, its mouth hanging a little open as if the effort that had brought it so far was exhausting. Now it did indeed balance its weight on three paws, raise the fourth, a fore one, to make a clumsy beckoning gesture.

There was no denying its urgency. And somehow I could not. But as I slid through the door with stunner in hand, I gave orders sharply.

"No one follow. Close this after me, and wait for an all-clear sign. If I don't show again promptly, take off—"

I did not give them time to protest but slammed the door and started warily toward the fountain. The ystroben, seeing that I was on my way, seemed satisfied. It turned and made, not for the house which I first thought its goal, but to the right. And I hurried after it.

There I found the beginning of tragedy. There must have been a shipment of mutants from some lab just before whatever devastated our world struck. They had been housed in pen cages for eventual release into the Reserve and then, apparently, forgotten. No food, no water, and there were some pitiful bodies on the ground that testified that, for some, release would now come too late. The ystroben hunkered down, its nose against the wire of an end cage. And there within was another of its species, lying on its side. It tried to raise its head at the coming of its comrade and failed.

One look told me there was no danger here for us but much to be done. I hailed those in the car, and soon we were all busy opening cages, carrying food from the containers in view, which must have been an added torment to the animals, and water in pails from the fountain.

Some of those already lying prostrate were still alive, and we worked over them. Those first to recover went down the hill into the wilds of the Reserve. For the others we left cage doors wedged open and plenty of food and water, to let them recover at their own rate of speed. Five were dead.

The house was deserted, with the same signs of haste the Ranger headquarters had shown. To have gone with caged animals on the premises was so foreign to all training that I knew

137

the need must have been great. Had some message gathered in all the outlying personnel to Feeholme where they could be conveniently disposed of? That was the only explanation I could see as logical.

But this was not a house claimed by the dead, so we settled into it thankfully, though it had been intended only for a staff or two, and we found it crowded. What pleased me most was the discovery of a recharging unit on the wall abutting the parking space. We could spend a day, or a part of a day here, making sure that the power in the car was fully restored. I hoped we could continue to drive well into the heights.

"Vere"—Gytha came up as I was studying the charge dials and trying to remember the necessary steps for a full hookup—"these animals, they're all mutants, aren't they?"

"I think so."

"How smart are they?"

I shrugged. Without lab reports how could anyone estimate? The ystroben had certainly displayed intelligence in its struggle to win our aid for the caged ones. We had all heard tales, of course, of the beast teams—mixed collections of animals working with and under the direction of a trained human leader. There had been some exciting stories of those out of the war. Survey and exploration were using, or had used, animal aides on newly discovered planets, the men depending on the keener senses of the animals. But not all mutants were successful telepaths, which was necessary in both beast team and survey work.

There had been twenty beasts in those cages, of fifteen different species, some of which were totally new to me. Five were dead—among them two of the unknowns. They would all be loose here now, but the tests they had been sent here to make would never be set up. I wished them well but thought they were no longer our problem.

"I don't know—maybe no one did," I said in answer to Gytha's question. "They could have been sent here for just that reason—to discover what they could do," I told her as I began uncoiling the hookup wires.

"Were—are any of them dangerous?"

"No. They should all be conditioned. They will protect themselves, but they should not be aggressive. The normal wild ones, though, are not adjusted to man. There are some parts of the Reserves you never visit without distorts and sonics."

"That wart-horn—"

For a moment I did not know what she was talking about, it was so long past.

"What wart-horn?"

"The one we saw on the Butte com. Vere, was that a mutant?"

"Couldn't have been. There was no work done with native animals that I ever heard of."

"But there could have been and not reported?"

"Anything is possible—"

She was nodding vigorously. "You know, after the commandant left, when everyone said they were through working on war projects, a lot of the labs never reported to Center any more."

That was right. But why did the wart-horn bother her now I asked.

"I don't know. But Pritha keeps mentioning it. She said it was watching us, that it didn't like us—"

"Even if that were so, which I don't believe," I replied, "that thing was over the mountains to the north and a long way from any place where there is any settlement now. It could be no danger to us."

"But, Vere, if everybody—" She hesitated and then went on. "If everybody except us is dead, then the mutants—they could be people, or like people in time, couldn't they?"

It was possible, but it was not a thought to dwell on.

"We cannot be sure all are dead," I told her firmly. "Tomorrow we shall do some scouting. As soon as we can map out the best trail up and over, we'll take it. You'll be back home before you know it."

"I don't want to be, Vere. Not if Kynvet is like Feeholme."

"Winter is coming; we must get home before the passes close," I continued as if I did not hear her, for I did not know any answer to an observation that matched my own feelings. It would be better to shelter at the Butte, or in a Reserve cabin, rather than return to a dead Kynvet. I knew that I could not take the children into a place of ghosts and expect them to stay. Not all parents had been so remote with their offspring as the Ahrens, and those who had had a closer family relationship must not be allowed to see what had happened if the fate of Feeholme had also been visited on Kynvet.

"Vere, look up there—" She caught my hand and brought me half around to face the Gur Horn.

It had been put to good use by the Rangers, for the spur had been turned into a lookout to give a wide view of the surrounding country. Thad had climbed there at my suggestion not long before, and now he was waving vigorously, pointing north. I signaled to him to come down, hurrying to the foot of the climb pole to meet him.

"A flitter, crashed over on the hill due north—" He gasped. "And it's afire!"

The one that had passed over us the night before? Crashed and afire—there would be little hope for her crew.

"Sabian, the aid kit." Annet had come up behind us. "Thad, can we reach it by car?"

He shook his head doubtfully. "I don't know; it's pretty steep. But you might climb up—"

"Where do you think you're going?" I demanded.

"To the people on board!" She looked at me as if I had grown wart-horns. "They are probably badly injured. We had better hurry."

And I could see that at that moment there was no argument I could raise that might move her.

Twelve

"THAD, YOU STAY—take guard duty here." There was no detaching Annet from what she believed was a duty, but we could not just go off without some order.

I almost expected him to protest, but there was no longer any trace of sullenness in him when I gave orders, as there had been in the days before we entered the caves. He nodded, and I handed over one of the extra stunners.

"Stay under cover. You know what to do." I paid him the compliment of not amplifying and again he nodded.

Annet and I only. She had shouldered the aid kit and was already striding off in the direction Thad had indicated. I had to hurry to catch up. But we needed no real guide. In the twilight the fire was a beacon no one could miss.

She set a punishing pace over rough ground, and I did not try to deter her. She slowed of her own accord quickly enough and stood panting on a rise before she could take breath to go on. I pulled up beside her. The scene of the wreck was plain. The flitter had met a cliff head on, and the blazing tangle was a crumpled wad at its foot, as if caught in some giant fist and squeezed into a lump.

"There are no survivors of that," I told her.

Her deep breaths were close to sobs. I pressed the point. "Go back—"

"And you?" She did not look at me; her eyes were still on

141

the wreck as if something in her did not allow her to look away.

"I'll look—" But privately I thought a journey to that pile of mangled metal was useless.

"All—all right—"

Annet was shaken as I had not seen her since the cave passage when she had come upon the fall-in and realized we were sealed from the surface. Beltane life had been so unmarked by violence and tragedy that we had not faced death often. She had seen Lugard die, but she had not seen Feeholme, and no amount of description from me could make that real to her. This carried the impact of a blow.

I watched her turn back. She did not once look at me; rather her head was bent as if she focused her eyes only on the ground under her feet. I again centered my attention on the wreck.

It had fallen in one of the barren places, and for that I was glad, since the fire could not start any grass blaze. Of course the storms of the past two days had thoroughly soaked the vegetation, but there was always a chance that a smoldering could start up again, given wind to fan it. And of all the dangers to be feared on a Reserve, fire was the worst.

There was probably no reason for me to go closer. I could not approach the wreck to identify it and whatever—whoever—had been in it. But there was always the slim chance I could pick up a hint of what had happened to Beltane, so I went.

I was right. The heat reflected from the rocks kept me well away from the general proximity of the burning machine. But as I tried to trace the lines of the flyer, I was suddenly sure this was not a ship from any settlement. Even crumpled and broken as it was, it had an unfamiliar look.

Then I found on the ground, thrown well away from the crash as if the cabin had burst wide open and scattered cargo, a blaster. It was regulation Service issue, though meeting with a rock had split it past repair. I had not seen one of those on Beltane since the forces had left. I did not try to touch it. Annet's virus story was too much in my mind. If the flitter—or whatever it was—had been piloted by men dead or dying (which could account for its erratic flight), then contagion might still lurk in their possessions.

But the victims I had found in Feeholme had been settlers. Had the plague spread to the refugees? Had they been too greedy, raided some settlement before the "safe" period? A man could guess and guess and piece together a logical surmise, but that did not necessarily mean his guesses were correct.

So I did not touch the blaster and stepped carefully over and around other bits and pieces of debris. There was enough remaining to make me sure my conjecture concerning this ship had been correct—that it was not a regulation flitter and its origin was off-world.

The fire was dying down, having consumed most of what fed it. There was no reason for me to linger.

When I returned to the station, I discovered that Annet and Thad had moved our belongings in. Dagny lay in one of the bunks, and the girls' bedrolls were in that room, while Emrys and Sabian had spread ours in the main portion. Annet had the cook unit on and was heating food, which smelled so good that I could believe it would draw us as Lugard's pipe had done.

"Anything?" Thad asked as I entered. I noted with approval that he had stationed himself by one of the window slits from which he could see the approach to the cabin and that he had one stunner in hand and the extra one lying beside him. With the cabin backed against the wide base of the Gur Horn, we had only that front sweep to defend.

"No. Except I don't think it was a flitter. Perhaps a ship's scout flyer. But there's not enough left to make sure. And— we stay away from there."

Annet caught my eye. "Yes," she agreed quickly, "yes!"

We ate, and I set up a program of watches. Annet was to be immune from that duty since Dagny was her special charge. But Gytha, Thad, Emrys, Sabian, and I would split the time. What I expected might come on us out of the night, I could not have said, but it seemed wise to make sure we could not be surprised.

I took a torch and made the rounds of the mutant pens.

Already the majority of the creatures had gone. The ystroben that had hailed us was inside the cage beside its fellow. It was pushing food to the weak one's mouth, while that one ate feebly, seemingly yet unable to get to its feet.

Seeing an empty water pail, I brought more, set it close to the enfeebled animal, and cupped my hands full of the liquid for its lapping. Its companion moved aside with not so much as a warning growl. The other drank and drank again, but the fourth time I offered water, it turned its head to one side and nosed at the feed with more vigor than it had shown before.

It was a female, and I thought it was in cub. The other must be its mate. I did not know much of ystrobens. They were off-world imports and quite rare. That they had been only so recently brought to the Reserve made me wonder if they had not been part of some long-time experiment just concluded. And if they had been lab-housed, perhaps during the whole of their lifetimes, how would they manage turned loose to forage in the wild with no Rangers for their protection? They were omnivorous, of course. No animal was ever sent to the mutant stations for release unless its feeding habits had been adapted to the range. But—However, I could not worry about these unhappy wayfarers now.

I brought still more food and water. The male followed me to where the containers of food were piled. He stood on his hind feet and pawed at the top of one as yet unopened, looking at me meanwhile with some of the same entreaty he had exhibited in the berry-walled lane. I used a rip bar on the top of that box and stood back to see what he would do.

He bent his head to give a long sniff, but he took nothing—rather went to four feet again and padded back to his mate, apparently satisfied that the food was there if they needed it.

I spent a little time in looking over the remaining animals, hoping they would leave soon on their own, for I did not believe that we ourselves should linger too long here. Again I was tempted to make this our headquarters, though it was less roomy and not as good a base as the Ranger headquarters.

I had no idea how long it might take us to get over the mountains, and sometimes storms hit the heights in late summer to close the pass. If the Butte was unoccupied, it was a far better camp for us than anything this side of the range.

I had selected the last watch of all, so I took to my bedroll as soon as I returned to the cabin, knowing that Thad would wake me when the time came. Again I slept heavily, the exertions of the past few days acting, once I had relaxed, as a drug, but I roused quickly enough in the dark when Thad shook my shoulder.

"Nothing—" His lips near my ear carried a thread of whisper. "Some of the mutants came back for food, but nothing near the door."

"Well enough." I took up the duties. So much time at one of the slit windows, cross over, and an equal time at the other. But there was nothing to see under the light of the full green moon, one of Beltane's natural wonders.

I had left the car hooked up for recharge, and that would run without tending until it reached repletion. How much longer we could use that transportation was the question. Though Annet assured me she saw an improvement in Dagny's condition, it came very slowly indeed, and I thought she would have to be carried once we left the car, which meant we must also limit the supplies we could pack. E-rations were best, designed to supply bulk of energy with minimum of substance, but at the same time we needed water and clothing for the cold of the heights—for even in summer snow powdered the pass at times. We could strip down what we carried now, but there were things we dared not leave behind. I listed those in my mind as I kept watch.

Against the wall at the far end of the room was the com that had linked this station with Feeholme. We had tried the night before with faint hope, quickly extinguished. I had decided to set the com in the car on the widest band, though that would necessitate some extra wiring in the morning. Suddenly, it was needful to hear a voice, any voice, even if it were that of a potential enemy, to let us know that we were not alone on Beltane.

What if we were? One must be prepared for the worst.

Then there was the port SOS, which could be set on automatic to continue to beam a distress signal into space. Any ship passing within range of that must answer, unless it was a warn-off signaling some contagious plague. In that case, the answering ship must relay that call to the nearest Patrol center.

Patrol center? For centuries of planet time the Patrol had policed the star lanes and such planets where trouble had broken out endangering life. But if Lugard's dismal prognosis was right, did the Patrol still exist hereabouts? Or had the remnants of it been pulled back, closer to the wealthy inner planets where civilization might continue to exist for a while?

I had heard dire stories of worlds where law and order vanished overnight, sometimes as the result of natural disasters, sometimes because of war or plague. The settlers of Beltane had used the war-ravaged ones as horrible examples for their pacific arguments. What if we faced both here, or rather their aftermath—war and plague? And if there came no answer from space?

Technology had begun to fail already. It would regress faster under the circumstances. Thad and I knew enough of mechanics to keep a hopper, a ground car, or even a flitter working. But once there were no more spare parts, nor charges, nor—There were draft animals at some of the settlements, kept for experimental study. There were plantations of food under cultivation by robos. And how long would those continue to carry out their implanted orders to sow, reap, store? I had a sudden vision of a plantation where the robos kept on, laying up foods for men who never came— until the storage bins burst with rot, never halting until their inner workings wore out.

Ten of us and a whole world—but that could *not* be! Somewhere there were—there must be—others! And in me the need to find them grew stronger until my impatience was such I longed to wake the company, to set out at once on the search.

I throttled down that impatience, and when morning came and the rest were astir, I made preparations with all the care I could summon. We sorted supplies, those from the ground

146

car, those I had brought from Feeholme, and those we had found here, setting aside those easiest to transport but high in energy. Our old trail kits, which had come all the way from the Butte, were turned out. All that was not absolutely necessary in them was thrown out, and they were repacked with what we must use once we left the car.

A hunt through the tapes and records of the station uncovered another map giving the western face of the mountains and the approach to the pass. There was a marked trail that might serve the car.

Once our kits were stowed, we turned to the packing of the storage space in the car, putting in all the food and water we could. We then went over our clothes, substituting parts of the uniforms in the cabin for those garments too worn or torn. Annet, Pritha, and Gytha worked with seam-seal to fit them better to the smaller members of the group. Such preparations took us all day.

In midafternoon Ifors reported that the two ystrobens had at last left the cage and were going downstream. At his summons we gathered at the door to watch them go. The male padded ahead, very plainly on watch, his mate moving unsteadily with frequent halts, during which her head hung low and her breathing was labored.

Gytha waved, though neither turned to look at us as they left. It was as if all their energy and determination was centered now on the need for getting into the bush. "I hope they can find a nice den," she said.

"Vere"—Pritha looked up at me—"there will be a lot of mutant animals left loose now, won't there?"

"I suppose so. But most of them are already free on the Reserves. Remember, the Committee suggested that some months ago. It was too hard to get special lab foods for some of them since the off-world ships haven't come."

"But will there be others left in cages with no food, no water?"

"I don't think so. There was only one big mutant lab left— at Kibthrow. These came from there. I see the markings on the food boxes. They were probably getting rid of them all."

"Kibthrow," she repeated, as if that made an impression. "That's over the mountains, north of the port, isn't it?"

"Yes."

"Then, Vere, when we get over the mountains, could—could someone go there—just to be sure?"

"Yes, I promise you we shall!" I did not mean that lightly. I might not have been ready to yield to the entreaties of the ystroben in the lane, but what I had found here made me sure that wherever we went in search of survivors from now on, we would also make sure that no animal had been left to die because a man did not release it.

"In the morning." Annet smoothed the last jacket they had cut down and fastened together with seam-seal for the small frame of Dinan Norkot.

"Yes," I agreed to her unasked question. In the morning we would be on our way.

Though we had seen nothing during the day to suggest that we might be in any danger, we kept guard for the second night. It was clear, and the moonlight very bright. The last of the living mutants had left the pens. But I spread all that was left of their food along the side of the brook so that, if they returned, it would keep them away from the house. Not that any of them had shown any interest in us once their wants were satisfied and they were free to go—It was almost as if we had a distort about us.

I wondered, as I took my sentry turn, about what Gytha had said. Suppose with mankind on Beltane reduced to a handful (I refused yet to believe there could be only *us*), what then would happen to the mutants? Some of the experimenters had made high claims for the intelligence of those they had bred and trained. The continent was wide and mostly wilderness, and those that might withdraw beyond the nebulous boundaries could continue hidden for a long time. Could another intelligent race ("men" as we must judge alien men) arise here, unknowing its original seed? But that was supposing we would vanish—

We had our last meal in the camp and packed into the car. For the first time Dagny appeared awake and really aware of her surroundings. She sat in the curve of Annet's arm, pressed tightly against her, looking about as if she saw the land and us, though she said very little. Annet confided that she was sure coming from the caves and the fact that we had had no more alarms, but traveled through a peaceful countryside, had wrought some healing. We warned the others against mentioning in Dagny's hearing anything of the past or what might face us. If her still cloudy mind accepted that we were on a camping trip such as we had taken before, then all the better.

Our path led by the cliff face where the flyer had come to grief, but I made as wide a detour around that as I could. There was still a small sullen plume of smoke ascending from the wreckage, but the frame was so tangled and melted that I could not identify it.

We came upon a wash leading up into the mountain country, and according to the map this was the best way, as long as no more storms could push a flood upon us. The flotsam from the last was still caught among the rocks to serve as a reminder that this desert did not always lack water.

On we crunched and crawled, our pace such that a man walking briskly could have left us behind. I kept off the distort since we moved mainly in the shadow of rising canyon walls and there were few beasts that came here that were formidable enough to fear.

Midmorning we came upon a galophi—rounding a curve to front it. As a specimen of its species, it was a fine example, one of the few creatures native to Beltane to attain any noticeable size. Its back scales were coarse and thick, as wide and long as fingers, and each edge where it fitted over another displayed fringe that resembled bristly fur but was really a fleshy growth. The same made a frill about its throat and a kind of mane stretching from between its large faceted eyes back to become a spine ridge ending only at tail tip. The front paws were clawed and the back feet wide and flat for swift travel over sandy soil. When really disturbed, it would inflate its mane and ridge hair into a spiney bush, flick out its forked tongue, and run two-legged.

This one was not about to run, and I knew why a second or two after our surprise meeting. It was of the dull green

149

shade of a female that had recently laid the yearly clutch of eggs. Somewhere in the rocks around us must be the nest site, and we were facing now a truly formidable opponent, some six feet long and able, if it were really provoked, to tear open the ground car.

I brought my fist down on the sonic as the galophi reared, not to turn tail but to charge us, and saw its tongue slap back and forth as if a laser beam had touched it. A galophi hears through that appendage, having no ears as we rate them, and that eerie blast must be torment for it.

It writhed and twisted and finally lost its balance altogether, falling behind the rocks from which it had been about to leap. I gave the car extra energy as we grated by.

Emrys, wedged in at the rear, gave us a report. "There's its head! It's still waving its tongue around, but it isn't following, Vere. No, now it's lying down with its back to a crevice."

"Nest," I replied briefly. I silenced the sonic. We were far enough away so I did not think the galophi would follow. Instinct would keep it close to that nest until the young hatched, and it could not be drawn from that vicinity. But the episode had been a warning not to accept the country at its bland face value but to be better prepared.

"Dagny!' I glanced at her. Would such a happening throw her back into that twilight state where she had lain so long?

Annet shook her head at me in both warning and reassurance. Dagny leaned against her, and her eyes were closed. "Sleeping."

We scouted our noon stop well before we left the car to eat. Though the sun was high, it was cool here. We had come well up into the heights, and by studying the map, I thought that we would have to leave the car not too far ahead. So I suggested that when we reached that point, we should spend the night in its shelter, even if some hours of daylight remained, beginning our foot travel with the new day.

At last we ground to a halt on a ledge. To reach it, I had taken some risk in forcing the car. When I got out, I worked with the boys to wedge rocks under the wheel treads for safety. It was chill here, though the sun was still up. I sealed my outer tunic and said I would scout the trail for at least an hour but that we would camp here for the night.

The going was rough, but it had been marked by blaster cuttings and some smoothing over bad stretches. So I was on course, and the pass lay beyond. If we started at dawn in the morning and climbed well, we should be through that gap and part down the other side before dark. And on the down side was, or had been, a trail shelter.

I found an outcrop and perched on it, lying full length to use the distance lenses back over the country through which we had come. There was no sign of movement there, save for a lazy winged flying thing or two. Indications were that the weather was in our favor.

Annet sheltered a portable cook unit behind some stones, and when I returned, she had a steaming mug of caff for me. That was one of the small comforts we would have to leave behind, and I applauded her wisdom in giving us a heated meal and drink. We would be having nothing more save E-rations until we reached the Butte. I hoped we could make that in two days, though thought of the lava country worried me.

We stood sentry again this night, Annet taking a turn, so we cut each period shorter. However, the sleeping quarters in the car were so poor, I think only the smallest rested easily enough to sleep well. I know my long legs were cramped, and I had an aching back when I crawled out to face the dawn.

Once more Annet heated caff and rations before we stored the unit and the rest of the extras back in the car. Then all of us, save Dagny, shouldered packs and took up two canteens apiece. I was pleased to see Dagny was on her feet, seeming even nearer to her old self than she had been the day before. She was to march with Annet, Pritha immediately behind them to lend a hand if needed.

I took the van, then Gytha, Emrys, Sabian, Annet and the two girls and Dinan, Ifors and Thad bringing up the rear. We would trade positions, except the lead would remain mine. Thad and I both carried the hooked metal ropes, which had

151

served us so well and which might be needed as life lines aloft.

Thus, just as the first rays of the sun appeared, we set off on the pass trail. And I do not think any of us looked back.

Thirteen

WE TOOK THE CLIMB at a slower pace than I would have journeyed had I been alone, but this was a case of conserving strength. The longer Dagny could walk, the better it was for the rest of us. It was cold, as cold as it had been—almost—in the ice cave. And there were winds to search out the thin parts in one's clothing.

No more trees, only patches of grass here and there, and scrubby wind-trimmed bush were to be seen. A pacca sat on a rock unafraid, watching our passing with round eyes, the wind ruffling its long blue fur, though it kept its tail tight folded about its toes. Its cheeks were puffed far out from early morning gleaning, which it was taking back to a burrow, for this was its harvest period when it laid up food for winter.

From every level place where we paused for a breather, I turned to sweep the lenses over our back trail. I did not really know what I expected to see. Surely no one had survived the wreck. Yet there was always the possibility of a bailout before the final moment of crash.

Now and then I would pick up a dot that must be one of the larger animals from the Reserve, but nothing on the path we had taken, nothing near the car we had left with its wheels braced by stones.

Though no rain fell, the sky was overcast, and that was enough hint of bad weather to keep us going. So far Dagny was doing better than I had hoped, keeping pace with Annet and Pritha. She even noticed the pacca and commented on it, which was heartening.

We came to where nothing save lichens grew. There were pockets of snow in the shadows of some rocks, hollows as deep as cups into which the sun must seldom penetrate. The wind made us tuck our chins into tunic collars and pull tighter the hoods that usually flapped as small capes on our shoulders. It was here that Dagny faltered, but we could go no slower— we must get through the pass and down as soon as possible.

There was a crevice between two pinnacles of rock, and we huddled in that shelter, bringing out E-rations. I looked at the map from the mutant station. There was no fear of losing the road; the marks left by those who pioneered it were easy to see. I tried to measure the distance to the cabin on the other side of the pass.

"How far?" Annet asked. Dagny was on her lap, the child's head resting against the older girl's shoulder, her eyes closed. I thought she breathed overfast, though all of us did in the rarefied air of these heights.

"Through the pass, then perhaps a little more than the distance from where we left the car on this side." I gave her the truth. This was no time to coat it with hoping.

"She cannot do it, not walking." Annet was definite, and I knew it was a fact.

I unbuckled my pack and squirmed out into the open to unwrap it. We had pared and pared its contents. But we had also foreseen that we might have to pare again because of just such an emergency.

I began to divide up what we could not do without. The extra charges for the stunners I stowed away in the front of my overtunic. E-rations could be shared—most might be eaten soon anyway—while the blankets—

Thad laid hand on one. "I'll take this. You'll need the other to put around her. And this"—he selected the largest of the remaining necessary items, one of the beamers—"I can strap to my belt."

So when we set out again, I carried Dagny in a webbing of ropes on my back. She had not roused but rested with her head against my shoulder, once more in a condition approaching coma.

Luckily, the rocky path was not one to require exertion, and I blessed over and over again the Security men who had cut this road. It was not as smooth as a plains trail but better than I had dared hope for.

The pass was a deep notch between two peaks, each almost as spectacular as the Gur Horn. It was twilight dark in that cut, and the wind thrust through it with full blast force, so that we hugged one wall or the other, keeping hand holds, going one wary step at a time. Dagny's weight was greater than the pack, so I had to be doubly careful I did not overbalance under the push of that blast.

Beyond, the way sloped down. We would come out at a lower level than we had entered. That I welcomed. We could no longer talk—it would require a shout to better the moan of the wind—but communicated by sign when there was need. Once a tongue of snow licked out from a crevice, and we crunched through it. But at the end of that cut, we ran into real trouble.

Still in the lead, I came to a crosswise break in the rock that slashed the trail as neatly as if some giant hunting knife had been used to bisect the puny efforts of my species to make a road. Whether it had originally baffled the surveyors of the pass, I did not know. At least it was not marked on the map. But it was too wide to leap, and I did not see how we could bridge it.

We drew back into what small shelter we could find in that place, huddling together. There were the ropes with hooks. Employing those, it might be possible to lower ourselves into the crevice and use that for a road, hoping that either of its ends would give access to the surface on the other side.

I left Dagny with Annet, ordering the others to gather the blankets around them for warmth. Thad made fast the ropes and oversaw my descent into the cut. There was unsteady footing at its bottom, for rubble had long rolled into it. The right-hand way was of no use, for it soon narrowed into too slim a slit.

The left was more promising. I picked my way along and finally found a wall that could be climbed with the aid of the ropes. It took us much effort and time to cross, and the last haul up the other side was exhausting. Thad went ahead a little, to return with a slightly encouraging report that he had found again trail markings, plus the fact he had been able to sight what he believed to be the roof of the shelter. But that still lay a goodly distance ahead.

Night was coming. We ate and conferred. Annet was opposed to spending the night in the open. She was worried not only for Dagny but also for the rest of us in these heights, and I was inclined to agree with her. We had our torches, though to use them could draw the kind of attention we were better without.

"That is only a possible danger," Annet pointed out when I voiced that as a warning. "A night here is a more probable one. One light carefully used—"

"Shielded," I mused, "bent only on the trail. To travel so will be slow—"

"But better than staying here."

"Thad," I said, "you take scout." Carrying Dagny, I could not be properly alert and unencumbered. "Emrys will serve at the rear."

I was putting a burden on the younger boy that I had not yet done. But he had marched well, and he was level-headed. Annet could drop behind near him. We must, however, keep close together and not string out in a place where a misstep in the dark could mean trouble.

Through those hours of deepening dusk, I did not consult my watch, so I have no idea how long that down-mountain crawl lasted, for crawl it was. What might have seemed not too difficult a trail for the rested and unburdened was harsh going for those carrying packs and already weary. We had Thad's torch, and he used it well, shining it back to guide us all when he struck a particularly bad section.

The night was cloudy, but I thanked Providence, whenever I had time to think of more than just my footing, not stormy. Then I noticed we were in scrubby brush and that the wind no longer tore so relentlessly at us. Once more there

156

was the suggestion of a cleared trail. But this had been much overgrown, and I saw the rise and fall of Thad's arm and realized he had out his long-bladed hunting knife and was cutting free our path.

Some time, what seemed a *long* time later, we came out into a clearing where tough mountain grass grew tall enough to wreath around our boots, and Thad's light illuminated the front of the shelter.

It was not as substantial or as well constructed a building as the Reserve cabins had been. Its door hung on one hinge, while drifts of leaves and earth had blown over the threshold. In a way, I welcomed those signs of long abandonment, for they meant safety to us in the here and now.

We stumbled in and collapsed almost as one on the gritty leaf-strewn floor. Thad swung the light from side to side to show us the poverty of our refuge. There were bunk frames along one wall, mere empty shelves. But there was nothing else to show occupancy—no other furniture, no cook unit, nothing at all. A tangle of dried grass and leaves in one corner and in it the gray-white of small, well-gnawed bones said that, after man had left, it had offered a lair to some animal. But the bones were old and the bedding of last season, or perhaps the season before that, so even that use was no longer made of this place.

Annet unhooked her pack, got our blankets, and spread them hastily on one of the bunks, taking Dagny from me to rest there. I wanted nothing more than a hot drink, which there was no chance of my having. Those who had no bunk room rolled up on the floor. I leaned against the door frame, my stunner unholstered. Tired as we all were, there was still a need for a sentry, perhaps more so this side of the mountains.

The wind that had been with us in the pass and on the mountainside died away. As I sat there, I was so tired of body that it was a great effort to move, but I was not sleepy. It was as if I had passed some point where sleep normally waited. I could hear the heavy breathing of the rest. There were no moans, no signs of nightmare tonight, only the deep rest of exhaustion.

Once there was a rustling, and my hand was ready on stunner grip, though my reactions were woefully, almost frighteningly, slow. But that sound had come from without, and whatever made it did not seek to enter.

How far we might now be from Butte Hold I did not know. Perhaps the map could have told me, but I could not consult it tonight. And whether we would have to cross, on foot, the devilish waste of the lava country was another point on which I had no briefing. If that were so, it might be well not to try to return to the Butte—in spite of the fact that we had left a hopper there and that we would have a wealth of supplies.

I was too tired to think clearly, yet thoughts marched, counter-marched, milled about in my overactive brain. In so much was I ready to follow what Annet had urged from the first, a scouting expedition into the settlement lands. Going on foot would make that a longer and slower journey, one the whole party could not take. Therefore, we must find a base from which to operate. And such a safe base I could not see, save the Butte.

"Vere—"

I turned my head away from the door to the dark shadow that crept across the floor as I recognized Thad's whisper of my name.

"I'll take guard—"

I wanted nothing more than to relinquish even this small portion of my responsibility, but I knew sleep was beyond me.

"I can't sleep," I told him as he crept closer until his shoulder nudged mine. "I'll stay on—"

"Vere"—he did not accept my unspoken suggestion to return to his blankets—"where do we go now?"

"Butte Hold, if we can."

"You mean, we may not get over the lava fields?" He must have already considered that himself.

"That—and the fact it may be occupied." In a few quick whispers I told for the first time of that meeting between Lugard and the refugees.

"So you think they may hunt the treasure, that stuff we saw in the ice cave?"

"It would draw them, yes."

"Then what do we do?"

"The best we can. In the morning we'll look over the maps, see if there is a back way to the Butte, one that will give us any advantage of approach. If there is and the Butte is clear, we move in. It has defenses."

"But Lugard knew them; we don't."

"Then we'll have to learn, by trial and error if need be," I retorted. The exchange with Thad was, oddly enough, quieting my nerves, as if I needed only this stating of near and far objectives to drain the tension. All at once sleep assaulted me so I could not keep my eyes open.

"Take over, Thad," I found the energy to say. I remember faintly starting to crawl to the pile of blankets he had just left, and then nothing.

I awoke with the sun hot across my face. It was a good heat, one my body welcomed. I heard stirring sounds, whispered talk. When I sat up, rubbing my hands across my eyes, I saw that some pretense of order had come into the shelter.

The leaves, the mess of the old lair, much of the drifted grit and sand, had been swept away. Blankets were neatly piled on the bunk, save for where I now lay. Annet sat in my old place by the door. A stunner was near to hand, but she was occupied with hulling berries, which she dropped onto a wide leaf. Pritha was similarly busy, and Dagny sat between them, now and then reaching out to take a berry and eat it. Of the rest there was no sign. Pritha glanced up, saw me watching, and smiled.

"Vere's awake, Annet."

"It's about time! You can sleep sounder than anyone I ever knew!" Her words might have been an accusation in another tone, but she was smiling. Now she got to her feet. "Go wash up. There's a spring out there. Then get some breakfast— you'll need that as much as you needed sleep."

"Now that you mention it, yes." I was aware of a vast empty space somewhere in my middle, but I still blinked. There was a different atmosphere. Annet almost might be on one of our old camping trips, certain that we would return to the home we had always known. Was it because we were now back on the fringe of familiar territory? Did she think we would find all the same when (or if) we returned to Kynvet? At any rate, I was not going to break the spell; I was too grateful for the easing of the tension that had ridden us all since the closing of the caves.

A small spring had been channeled into a basin of rock, and I made good use of it. To be able to wash added to my feelings of well-being. The clearing was largely overgrown, and the berry bushes where Annet had done her harvesting were a major part of that encroachment.

I was still on my knees by the water as Thad pushed through. Seeing me, he headed quickly in my direction to report abruptly.

"I looked at the map this morning. We have lava land between us and the Butte. But"—he was frowning—"I went up to the highest point for a look-see. There's something—I didn't tell the rest, not yet. I wanted you to know first."

"All right." I wiped my hands on a tuft of long grass. "Where?"

"Vere, are you ready? Breakfast—" Annet called.

Thad's frown grew.

"Something which"—I nodded to where the girls waited— "is better not spoken of yet?"

He nodded. "Gytha saw it, but she'll keep quiet. It—it won't go away. You might as well eat, or they'll wonder."

"Vere"—Gytha came through the bushes in turn—"there's a—"

Thad made an emphatic gesture, and for a second she looked mutinously indignant; then comprehension dawned.

So I did not enjoy my breakfast as much as I might have done, but I swallowed E-ration, which no longer tasted like a guesting banquet, and praised the berry pickers for their addition. I could guess that both Thad and Gytha were curbing their impatience better than I would have believed they could. At last I was able to give the excuse of inspecting the lookout and leave. For the first time Annet did not ask when we were moving on, and I was eager to get away before she did, as I had no answer for her.

Thad led the way to an improvised ladder leaned against a wind-twisted borgar tree. The ladder was a fensal topped in some storm and thrown until its branches had become entwined with the borgar. Its weathered red trunk, now missing most of the aromatic bark, was sharp in color against the borgar, which had lost its early season leaves to produce the pale blue flowers of the second stage.

With Thad perched on a neighboring limb of the borgar to direct me, I used my lenses. What came into clear view as I adjusted the distances was a hopper. As far as I could see, it was in no state of disrepair. Clearly, it had been landed on a strip of level, unwooded land, not smashed in a crash.

"Take us to the Butte without trouble," Thad commented.

Which was perfectly true, but the mere fact it was sitting there within perhaps an hour or two hours downhill walking did not mean it was usable.

And I think Thad also had doubts, for he added, "Don't know what's inside. But we've watched it, Gytha and I, turnabout, for most of the morning. No sight of anyone around. Could be bait in a trap—"

Good thinking, but he might be going too far with it.

"If it is bait, not for us," I said. "We could hardly have been tracked here without our knowing it. There's only been that one flyer, and that cracked up. On the other hand—"

Gytha hung halfway up the fensal. "You think there's someone dead in there, just as they were at Feeholme—"

There was no reason to deny the shrewdness of her guess. "It's very possible."

"But if they died of the virus, it won't hurt us now, will it? And we do need the hopper—"

"What do you know about the virus?" But I might have guessed. We had been in close quarters in the ground car, Annet and I, when she had told me of her fears.

"We heard. Thad and I know, and Emrys and Sabian. But we didn't tell the others. Pritha believes her mother's waiting for her. And Ifors, he talks all the time about his father. They mustn't know until they have to. But, Vere"—she returned to her main question—"couldn't we use the hopper if we didn't have to worry about getting sick?"

"I suppose so. Only we can't be sure that what has struck or did strike at Feeholme was that virus."

"You aren't sick, Vere, and you went in there. You brought back food. We ate it, and none of us are sick—except Dagny—and that isn't from any virus." Gytha hammered home her logic point by point.

"True enough. All right. You stay here. Thad, I turn command over to you. I'll go down and scout. If it can be used I'll lift it up here." I snapped the compass from my belt and took a bearing, then marked what guiding landmarks I could. "If I start right now, I might be able to return before dark. Tell the others I am scouting a trail down."

"Will do." Thad waited for me to leave before he swung down after. Gytha was already on the ground to face me.

"I want to go too, Vere."

"No."

"But, Vere, suppose it is a trap. I'm good with a stunner, and I won't go up to the machine. I can cover you while you look at it."

"No." Then I lightened that with an argument that I hoped would satisfy her. "It is because you *are* good with a stunner, Gytha, that I want you here. One person alone can slip around and get away. And believe me I shall take every precaution. But if a trap *was* set for us, if we *have* been trailed in some way, then they may be up here. I want everyone in the shelter, ready with lookouts—understand?"

The threat was remote, but it was there; in that much I did not stretch the truth any. She still had a mutinous expression about her mouth, but she turned toward the clearing with no more protest.

"If I'm not back by dark," I told Thad, "take cover. I still think the Butte is the best place to go—if it is empty. But—"

I was at a loss. How could I foresee all that might happen to me, to them? And why burden them with suggestions that might not be right if I did not return and the situation altered?

"Use your best judgment." That seemed a weak ending but the only one I could give.

"Yes. And Vere—"

I glanced around, for I was already two strides on my way.

"See you take care," he said almost angrily. "We can't afford to lose you."

So far had we come from the feeling I had had—was it only days earlier?—that Thad was waiting to challenge my authority. It struck me that, as I had looked to Lugard at the beginning of this fated venture, so now Thad was looking to me. And that I did not like, for it pushed me into a role I shrank from. I raised my hand for an answer and pushed into the brush.

Thus far we had not planned much into the future. I had speculated, as must all of the older members of the group, that something very wrong had happened. But to look beyond tomorrow had not been done.

What if the worst had happened and we were the only humans? Go to the port; set the distress beam. But there was no promise that that would be answered for years—or ever. Then what? I shied from such forecasting. It was safer all around for me, perhaps all of us, if we looked no farther than the duty immediately to hand. And mine was now to investigate the hopper.

If it had been abandoned or if it housed only the dead, then it was a gift from fortune. We need not fear the trek through the lava lands. Having seen that country, I shrank from attempting such a journey on foot, with limited supplies, no guide, no detailed map.

In order to follow my present compass bearings, I had to leave the old trail and strike off to the left. This was a forested country, though the trees at the timberline were not the giants one might discover farther down. I took frequent bearings, intent on not getting lost. The knowledge that had made me a Ranger cadet was all I had now to depend upon.

The trees grew taller, the ways under them more shadowed. I paused now and then to listen. But never did I hear more than the usual woodland sounds. Then there arose a screen of brush, and beyond it was the clear space in which stood the hopper.

I kept to cover, working my way along to where some of

the bushes thrust forward. The door of the vehicle, which could now see, hung open a little.

And when I saw what held that door open, I got to my feet in spite of the churning of my stomach, and walked out to face what I would rather have shrunk from.

Fourteen

THERE HAD BEEN four passengers and one of those unwilling. He was in the pilot's seat and wore the coveralls of a settler, while the one behind him had the semi-uniform of the refugees with a laser close to hand. It was easy to deduce that he had been holding that on the pilot when the end came. The other two were also in uniform.

I do not want to recall the next hour. I had nothing with me for digging. The best I could do was heap loose earth over them. In the end, that was done, and I had a hopper that was in running order.

Where they had been bound I could only speculate. Perhaps over the mountains, perhaps even to Butte Hold, for there was no other camp or settlement in this direction. But they had all been dead for some time.

At last I was able to lift back to the shelter on the mountainside. This machine had been well kept, even better, I thought, as I relaxed at its quick response to controls, than those at Kynvet. Since it had been left on manual and not a journey tape, I could not tell from whence it had come any more than its destination.

It was twilight when I set down in the small clearing. And I was glad to see that none of the children was in evidence as I climbed out of the cabin.

"Home!" Annet ran her hand almost caressingly along the side of the hopper. "Now we can go home!"

"Not yet."

"What do you mean?" she demanded fiercely. "We have to get back to Kynvet, learn what has happened."

"I know what happened, a little of it," I told her and all of them, for the sooner they knew the need for caution, the better. "There was a prisoner and guards in here. And the prisoner was a settlement man, the guards from the refugees."

"Who—?" Annet asked.

I shook my head. "I don't know."

To my relief she let that subject drop, but instead asked, "Where, if not home?"

"To Butte Hold. Remember the com room?" That was all the bait I had to offer to win her compliance. Would she argue in exchange that the coms elsewhere had done us no good? And if she insisted upon going to Kynvet, would my authority be strong enough to deny her? We had never reached a point of absolute contradiction, and it was the last thing that must happen now.

"The Butte," she repeated, and was silent as if thinking it over.

"It is the strongest refuge I know of. And we don't know all its resources. Lugard said it had defenses nothing on this world could crack."

"Defenses against what?" she asked bitterly. "So far we have found no menace to us—here. And we must know—"

"Yes—"

She must have caught my thought and the significance of the swift glance at those about us, for she looked startled for an instant, and then, perhaps because she felt guilty, she surrendered.

"The Butte then. Do we go tonight?"

"In the early morning." I had no mind to land in a nest of Zarvna vipers. And if the Butte was occupied by treasure seekers, it could prove just that for us.

So we spent a second night in the bare shelter. But we were this much favored by fortune—we had transportation and need not face a perilous trek across the lava country.

I tried the com of the hopper. It was open and working,

166

answering with the thrum of a waiting channel. But I did not try to send, only pick up any hint there was still life in the valley. Nothing came.

In the morning, at dawn, we loaded into the cabin. As with the ground car, it proved a tight fit, but we were happy. To have again the familiar about us was heartening—to a point. I set us a course I thought would be a direct line to the Butte.

As we passed over the lava lands, I was thankful we were not making that journey on foot. The desolation of which we had had a taste on our way to the cave entrance had been modified by the fact we used a road Lugard had already pioneered. Looking at this tortured, twisted land, I could see we might have been lost forever in its hold.

We raised the Butte before noon. Annet, seated beside me, had manned the snooper scope. The skies were clear of any flyers; not the faintest beep gave warning. And now, as she turned it groundward, she reported the landing space also clear.

That surprised me. "The hopper we took in—" When? How many days ago? I could not have numbered them due to our sojourn underground.

"Yes!" That struck her, too. "Where is that?"

Picked up by prowlers who came after us? And Lugard had locked the big door when we had gone. If he had left all guards up, we were now deprived of what I wanted most for us, a secure base. I thought of my folly in not making sure, back in the cave, that I had the metal plate that unlocked all for Lugard.

Then Annet reported the main door open, so one small barrier did not exist. However, I did not land the hopper here, but rather maneuvered with all the skill I had to set down on the roof. If there was some trap within that door, we might so escape it.

As soon as I had magna-locked the wheels on that surface, I dropped out, stunner ready. There was the faint wailing of the wind among the queerly sculptured rocks, the heat of the sun pouring full force on my head and shoulders, making me instantly aware that the clothing meant for the mountain was not for the lava lands—nothing else.

I made for the door of the watchtower. Annet took my place at the controls, and I had her promise to lift should there be any trouble, whether I could make it back or not.

It was an eerie business, this step-by-step descent into the deadly quiet of the Butte, for it was thus that the silence impressed me—with a perilous promise, as if each forward press of an unwary foot could plunge one into disaster.

I stopped frequently to listen, but there was nothing to hear. Inside these walls even the sound of the wind was lost. Down and down I went until at last I was in the main hall from which opened the com room, the grav lift, and the mess hall where we had eaten so long ago. I had met no challenge save that raised by my own unease.

In the mess hall I found that first proof that the Butte had been visited. As in the raided storehouse of Feeholme, there were signs of hasty pillaging, though there was not the wanton breakage I had seen. Whatever they had taken still did not greatly deplete the supplies.

The com room was my next objective. There was no disorder here, so I could not tell whether or not it had been in use. I did not try to activate its installations. I ran to the open door and saw that it had been forced by laser, so that that could not be closed again. That was something of a blow to my hopes for defense, but we could see to that later.

However, the place was now clean. At my signal the rest disembarked, and we moved into the Butte.

For two days we worked to make it the fortress I believed we might need. I expected Annet to object to this as a waste of time. But to my surprise she did not, though she spent time in the com room. I did not doubt that she tried to pick up some broadcast to reassure her.

The grav lift still worked, though I did not trust it too far, but we discovered a second opening into the underground depot. I hunted for this since I knew the machines Lugard had used had not been brought up via the lift. This opened directly into one of the narrow lava ridges.

We experimented with the machines until we found one

like that which must have been used to seal off the cave camp. It mounted a laser and could be pulled, by a great deal of effort, around to the front of the Butte.

Into the burned-out door space we then packed material as tightly as we could and melted it all into a solid stopper with the laser until where there had once been an opening was now a lump as unbreakable as the walls it joined. We now had no ground entrance—only that via the roof and the one in the lava cut. I thought it would take a massive attack to break in.

There were piles of supplies in the depot, and we need not want for sustenance for a long time. On the night of our third day within those walls, I lay on my bedroll, tired to the point of exhaustion, but with a feeling of real security such as I had not known since this whole adventure had begun, but I was not left to enjoy that long, for Annet came to stand over me.

"Kynvet." She said only that one word but with such determination that it was both promise and threat. Then she added, "I can pick up nothing—we must know."

She was right of course. Only something in me, now that we were so close to the final revelation, wanted to delay it.

Then, perhaps seeing that reluctance mirrored in my face, she said, "If you do not go, I do—even if alone."

And that, too, was a promise I knew she was determined to keep.

"I'll go." My sense of security fled. It had been such a short time of well-being. It was as if I stooped to pick up again a shoulder-bruising burden I had only set aside.

"If—if the worst has happened," she continued (now she did not look at me, but rather beyond as if she did not want me to see what lay in her eyes), "there is the port and the signal."

"You know, Annet, that the signal—"

"May go unanswered for years, yes!" She caught me up with some of her old fierceness. "But that is a chance we shall have to take. Kynvet and—and then, if necessary, the port. But, Vere, not this time alone."

"Not you," I countered.

"Not me," she agreed at once to my relief. "Only we must be sure, of Kynvet, of the port signal. Two are better than one. Thad—"

"But—"

"Oh, I know. You look upon him as the eldest in line, the one to step into your shoes. Certainly he is not Vere Collis, just as you are not Griss Lugard. But you must take him for the very reasons you wish to leave him here. He is the next to you, the best we have."

Thinking it over, I could see she was right, though I did not want to admit it. Thad did have the qualities that would enable him to carry on the needed tasks if anything happened to me. And the very fact that Annet foresaw such a possibility suggested that she no longer cherished the hopes that had made her so stubbornly set on coming over the mountains. But I did not question her, for that all was better unsaid now.

I took one more day, though I knew Annet begrudged it to me, to make sure I would leave the Butte in the best possible shape to withstand trouble. Then we left on foot, for that was one thing in which I did not yield to Annet. The hopper must remain as a final possible means of escape for those in the Butte.

It was also my argument that we could move better under cover, even if it took us longer. And the ability to keep out of sight might be our best protection.

The trail out from the Butte was largely overgrown. For ten years it had been left to nature, and all recent traffic had been by hopper or flitter. But enough traces remained to guide us. We took only very light packs and stunners with extra charges. I had searched and researched the supplies for a more formidable weapon. But, as in the cave base, they must all have been taken when the forces left. My final act at the Butte had been to dismount the laser we had used to seal the door, get it by painful effort to the roof, and there afix it as a defense. I did not think that Annet looked upon it with any favor, though, and I was not sure she would use it, even in extremity—though no one knows what he will do facing death.

We might have been moving through wilderness as little

tamed as that of the Reserves, but at noon we came upon the first of the far farms. There we found another kind of tragedy. As at the mutant station, animals had been penned here, and they had, for the most part, died in captivity. We freed two of the burden beasts still alive—they had eaten to stubble the grass of their paddocks—and fed and watered them, turning them loose to go as they willed, though I had the thought that if we could find them upon our return, it might be well to lead them back with us. But for the smaller creatures—the gleex with their fleece for garments, the obor birds, and two pidocks—there was nothing to be done.

The house was empty, and we found no sign of what had become of the owner and his family. No raiders had been here, but it was a dark beginning to what, I am sure, had no light ending, nor could have.

We pushed on, keeping to the road as a guide where we could. I think we needed that road for our spirits, as it was a link not only with what civilization Beltane had possessed, but also with the secure past. But we did not talk much until Thad suddenly burst out, "You think everything—everybody's gone, don't you, Vere?"

"That is a possibility."

"The refugees, too?"

"Those in the hopper were dead. They may have loosed something they did not know how to control."

Thad stopped and looked at me directly. "Is it better—really—to know?"

"We have to."

Thad's position at Kynvet was not far different from mine, or had been. His parents died as a result of a lab experiment gone wrong, and he had been taken in by the Drax family, who were relatives of his father. So he had no close kin to miss. Yet it did not follow that he could be as detached as I had always felt. After all, he was not of a Service family and so not set apart from the rest of the community.

"I suppose so," he said reluctantly. "And what do we do Vere, if it is true—that we're now alone here? Oh, I know we set the port call. But who knows if that will ever be picked up."

171

"Boat law," I said briefly.

"Boat law?" he repeated. Then understanding came. "Oh, you mean the space regulations. We start a colony because we are marooned. Only we aren't survivors of a shipwreck.'

"Near enough to follow the law. And we shall be starting with more than many such survivors ever had. We have all that is left here. Always supposing that it *is* ours now without dispute."

"The machines won't run forever. A lot of them need more servicing now than we can give. And when everything stops running—"

"Yes, we'll be on our own. We'll have to do all we can to establish ourselves before all the machines stop."

But that meant planning for years ahead, and I still shrank from that—until I had to. I think that perhaps Thad liked such thoughts no better because he was quiet. What we said for the remainder of the day was limited to matters of our traveling.

We made a cold camp that night in a small copse beside a stream. We shared watches through the dark hours, ate E-rations in the morning, and went on.

It was past midday when we came into familiar fields. Animals had been loosed here and wandered aimlessly. Some trailed us, making plaintive sounds as if they wanted our company, but we eluded them when we could, not wanting to call attention to our passing.

So we came to Kynvet, or where Kynvet had been. We had seen tapes of wartime destruction on other worlds, but I did not believe they meant much more to us than those of fiction or history tapes, displaying events far out of our range of direct feeling. And the force of this was now like a blow in the face.

There was churned earth of sickly yellow, bits of material that might once have marked homes and labs we had known all our lives. But not one landmark remained to say that once a settlement had been here. It was as if a giant fist had crushed and blotted out all men had done.

"No—" Thad's denial was half moan. He did not move out

172

into the area of disaster in any search for what had once been, but he looked to me, his face stricken.

"What—"

"This is what we must have heard in the caves."

"Why?"

"We may never know."

"I'll—I'll—" He swung up his stunner as if it were a blaster and he had the perpetrators of this within its sights.

"Hold your fire—until it is needed."

That got through to him, that promise of retribution.

"Where do we go now?"

"The port." But I had little hope we would find better there.

We had meant to camp at Kynvet, but we did not want to stay anywhere near. Instead, we pushed on at a swifter pace than we had followed all day, striving to put between us and that scar as much space as possible. And it was well into dark before we halted—for we felt as those fleeing a disaster—in a shed meant to store harvest on the edge of another line of fields. Between Kynvet and the port the land was largely under tillage.

Those crops were very near harvest. In fact, it must have begun because we had passed some fields with only stubble left, though there had been no bagged grain, no reaping robos in sight. It might well be that once we were—sure—we should see to that harvesting. Though the yield would be far more than would be needed for our small band, yet letting it rot in the fields sat ill with me. We had been so trained to thrift and economy since the wartime breakdown of interworld commerce.

The next morning we crossed the edge of Yetholme land. Perhaps the settlement had not been treated as Kynvet, but in the caves we had felt the shock of more than one bombing. At any rate, on the way back we could detour to pass both Yetholme and Haychax, but now the port mattered most. I had the idea that if any life remained, it would center about there anyway.

We covered ground at the steady trot, rest, trot that was a part of Ranger training and that they had, in turn, learned from the Security men. It was as speedy as any foot travel, and across fields one could keep it steadily. But we were still outside the port when we saw those two tall pillars of metal, sky pointed.

"Ships!" Thad cried aloud.

"Easy!" I caught his arm and pulled him back with me into a screen of brush that had been set out to fence field from field. With those in sight, we must use all the caution and cunning we had.

They were certainly not government ships, nor did they have the round-bellied, cargo-carrying look of Free Traders—though such might have planeted only to be captured.

"Patrol?" That was no identification but a question from Thad.

We crept now, flitting from one piece of cover to the next. Perhaps we were wrong; the settlers might have set an off-world call, and these come in answer. If so, we were safe. But I accepted nothing untested.

There were signs of disorder and fighting among the buildings around the port gate. Seared marks and melted patches told of laser beaming. We passed broken hoppers and a flitter crashed into the roof of a house, its wreckage still hanging there. But there was no sound, no sign anyone had been there for days.

At last we reached the gates and crouched behind an upended and partly lasered hopper. I got out my lenses, determined to make sure before we advanced.

The ships had been a long time in space—that was certain from the scouring of their sides. The nearer would not rise again. Its tubes were badly eroded. I wondered at the skill of the pilot who had brought her in, three points down, on those. Perhaps he himself had been left speechless at such fortune.

There was insignia on both, half effaced. It was of some old force, I was sure. The refugee ship had not landed here—but maybe these were the two who had followed her and demanded similar privileges.

Their hatches were open, the landing ramps out, but about

them nothing stirred. I focused on the ramp of the far one, looked for a long moment, then got to my feet.

"What is it, Vere?"

"There's a dead man on the ramp. I don't think we need fear the ships. Let's go to headquarters."

We did not approach the ships but were emboldened enough to walk across the open end of the field to the headquarters. Our soft-soled woods boots made no sound in the halls where the magnetic plates of space boots had once sounded a welcome clatter. The signs of neglect had been here even before the disaster—doors long closed, sections of hall and concourses where nothing waited to be shipped, no off-world passengers gathered, nor had they for long years. It was like a monument—not to a dead hero, but to a dead way of life. And I found, in spite of the stuffy warmth, I was shivering.

The com room was our first objective, and it was in wild confusion. There had been a fight here. Rays had seared and wrecked installations, and there were splotches of dried blood on the floor. Also there had been some attempt at repairs. Tools lay about one board, which had been loosened and laid back to display fused wiring. It was, I believed, that meant to signal ships in orbit.

But the repairs had hardly been begun, and what remained was beyond my knowledge to continue if I had wished. However, what we sought was still farther in the small room opening off this. Avoiding bits of wreckage, we crossed to that.

The door resisted our pushing until we both put our shoulders to it with all our strength. Then it grated harshly as it moved. Within, on a central base, was the beacon—or had been the beacon! What stood there now was a melted mass of metal with no possible use for us or anyone on Beltane.

"No beacon," Thad said after a long moment. "They were fighting here, too."

"Someone may have tried to set it and was caught—"

Though I had never really believed in any help from space, yet now I felt a sense of loss, of closing in, as if the room about us grew darker even as we looked at the failure of the last link with the world of the past. I turned away, and when Thad did not at once follow me, for he was still staring at that melted lump, I put my hand on his shoulder.

"Come on. It's past use now."

There was one other place in this building that I must visit. Not that I could get any aid, except an answer, perhaps, to a question, but answers I wanted.

The headquarters must—should—hold some clue as to what had happened. Report tapes from all the sectors came in here daily, were sorted and stored by the memory banks of the computer. If that unit had not also been destroyed, we could find the final reports and glean from them information. I said as much to Thad and we left the wreckage of the com center, padding down the hall in search of the memory banks of Beltane.

Fifteen

I FULLY expected to find that the computer banks had also been damaged or destroyed, but that was not so. Either the fight had never reached this point, or no one had been interested in the records. I went to the control seat in the center of the room and studied the buttons on its board. The wall ahead was a vast visa-screen, meant to give visual as well as audible answers to questions. And built into the walls were the relays to carry not only the full history of the colony since First Ship landing, but also all data from the research labs. Most of that was classified, though, to be released only in codes I did not know.

Now I hesitated, not knowing just what combination would give us an account of what had happened in the last days. And for want of a better key word I decided upon "refugee," for it would seem this had all been triggered by the arrival of the first ship. Therefore, I set up that simple pattern.

"On the fourth day, sixth month, year 105 PL—"

The voice of the recording rang startlingly loud through the chamber, and I hastened to cut the volume. The bare facts continued—that the refugee ship had asked for landing, had been granted such to the north, and had planeted there. Then were added some facts concerning the new settlement.

From this the recording went on to the coming of the next ships, the appeal for the second landing, a meeting between representatives from the ships and the Committee—plus the voting of the settlements. That brought us to the end of what we already knew. I leaned forward eagerly to hear what would follow.

"On Twelfth Day, seventh month, year 105 PL, it was decided in open meeting to ratify a second treaty, admitting the second ships, on the understanding there would be no more. This was voted in general meeting 1,200 to 600—"

The voice was silent. It would seem that was the end of the refugee problem as far as the memory banks were concerned. There was one other place we could perhaps find out more—Once more I punched a code and waited.

What came in answer was code, a series of numbers and allusions intelligible only to those who set it up. So it ran on and on, and I wondered what good those reports on experiments and sector progress would ever be now. Then—

"Sector 4-5. Refugee party came early this morning. Wanted medical aid—took Dr. Rehmers by force. Left men on guard behind—killed Lofyens and Mattox—looted the Rytox lab. Have most of our personnel now under guard. Warning: they took the old records—" Once more the voice fell from that stark report into code. But I marked the numbers in my mind, signaling to Thad. He nodded, and I saw his lips move, so I knew he was also striving to memorize. The voice ended abruptly, and we heard the snick, snick of unfinished tape.

"6-c-r-t-tex-ruh-903." I repeated from memory.

"Yes," Thad agreed.

Now it remained to be seen—or heard—whether the information answering to that was also in code beyond our translating. I set up the call numbers and activated the banks.

"Classified, classified—" chanted the voice. And on the board a red light flashed. I knew an alarm had gone to the quarters once occupied by the commandant. But there was no one to alert now, nor would any guard come pounding down the hall to investigate.

Having given its warning, though, the machine was ready to oblige with the rest filed under that heading. Most of it

178

was formula that meant nothing to us, but finally it shifted into understandable speech.

"Highly volatile and unstabilized, not to be recommended. Results as follows. Plague possibilities: will kill within forty-eight hours. No symptoms except slight headache. Produces cerebral hemorrhage. Contagious as long as subject is living, but cannot be communicated except from living to living. Will destroy only intelligent life to the—" Another rush of code, then: "Classified, fifth level, double code. We shall destroy all but master formula, which shall be coded in lock-files—"

Again an end. Thad moved forward to stare down at the keys that had brought us that report.

"They must have found that formula. But why—?"

"Lugard had fears of this." I told him what the veteran said concerning a pirate fleet using biological weapons known to researchers here. It seemed, though, that this weapon had gotten out of hand.

"Then they used it, and everyone just—died—" Even though he had seen the port and Kynvet, I do not think that before this moment Thad had really believed in the end of Beltane.

"We'll probably never know exactly what happened," I said. I was setting the code again for daily reports. There were two more, one from Haychax, the second from Kynvet, and that was broken off in mid-word, though neither had held any hint of danger.

"That's that." Perhaps sometime we could return here, experiment to break codes, or find a way to open fully the secrets of the memory banks. But we had no time for that now. I rose slowly from my seat, glancing from one wall to the other. There was a wealth of knowledge locked in here, but it was largely too specialized, with little to help us now. But there was something—I had been here several times on errands, and I knew what I wanted and where it was stored.

I crossed the room to the far wall and punched a request pattern. There was a clicking of relays, and two rolls of Zexro tape fell into the open trough below. I picked them up and was about to leave when there came another and louder click.

179

"Sign, please. All requisitions for tape must be signed for."

I heard a choking sound from Thad, half laughter, half something else, which warned of his state of mind. But I turned and set my thumb into the sign block, repeating my name and the fact I was from Kynvet on official business.

"Stop it!" I caught the boy's shoulder and gave him a hard shake.

"Sign—" he repeated. "Sign—as if nothing's happened and you just came in for supplies!"

"Yes." It had struck me, too, that indifference to all but a patterned programming. A world might be dead or dying, but the machine demanded a signature to release two rolls of tape. To us, it brought home with a rush all the wastage and horror about us.

We turned and ran, out of that room of unfinished, or perhaps now, finished history, down the corridors beyond, out of that building, and into the field where the silent, dead ships stood pointing to the stars from which we were now perhaps forever exiled.

But once out in the open, some of the feeling that had set us fleeing the headquarters vanished. Under the unchanging sun, with fresh wind about us, we could be sure we were alive. Though our principal reason for coming to the port was a failure and hope of rescue was gone, there were other things here that could be of service to us. I decided to do some exploring for what we could eventually transport to Butte.

Also, if we could find a flitter in working order, we would be even more fortunate. It would have been easier to split up and do our searching alone with an appointed meeting place, but neither of us wanted that. To roam a town of the dead alone was at that moment beyond our courage.

However, what we needed could be only in a few places—the park where all the in-use vehicles could be, the warehouse for off-world shipping (though that must be near empty), the machine shop where repairs were made on transports and machines still running, and the supply depot. I listed them, and Thad agreed. We needed more than what remained of this one day to search, and we decided to risk

180

a stay in town overnight, camping out in the warehouse. Neither of us cared to enter a dwelling.

The vehicle park was a disappointment. Like that of Feeholme, the majority of the flitters and hoppers had been systematically destroyed. The one or two that had escaped were near the repair center and needed work. Given time and a chance with the instruction tapes, though, I thought we might put at least one into service again.

What bothered us most was the silence. Oh, the wind blew, and we heard the calls of birds (too many birds for a place where men lived), and now and then the sound of some four-footed scavenger. But this place made one look uneasily over one's shoulder and glance about sharply now and then. There was an odd feeling that someone had just left each room we entered or that someone had vanished around a corner only a second or so before we came into view. And that tension grew until Thad put it into words.

"They *are* here!" He made it a statement rather than a question.

"No—at least we have seen nothing." But my feeling of being watched made me so modify that negative. Was it because we knew this was a place of the dead that we were so haunted by what we could not see?

After the park we searched the warehouse. I could dimly remember coming here with my father when I was small. Then it had been a busy place. Why, there had been four or five ships out on the pad at once, discharging cargo, taking on the exotic side results of lab experiments, while this building had been crammed with cargo.

Now it was largely empty. There were a few bales at the far end, and we walked toward those. It was dim in here. The lights must have shifted to "low" long ago. And even the soft pad-pad of our boots sounded too loud.

"Looters—" Thad said abruptly.

He was right. The remnants of those off-world supplies had been looted. We saw broken boxes, torn bales, and again wanton destruction of what the raiders had not wanted. A careful search might reveal something worth carrying away, but since we had no transport save our legs, we were not going to add to our packs any except very exceptional finds.

"Supply depot—" I took the next on my list.

"It'll just be another write-off," Thad replied. "Food is what we'll need most—"

He was right. When I thought of it, breakfast was a long while back. We went into the office where the customs and the cargo masters had once dealt together and looked about. The room had two doors, one giving on the vast emptiness of the warehouse, the other on the outer street. I opened that to look out—into silence. When I closed it again, I set the thumb lock. Why, I could not have told, save that with the door locked against the silence and the coming dark, I felt safer.

There was a small heating unit in the cupboard, probably intended for the brewing of caff. And a moment later Thad, peering into a drawer, found half a jar of that and an array of mugs. They must have been for official visitors, for on each was the insignia of one of the settlements.

I noted that when he picked out two, he did not take those with names on them we knew well, but rather set out a pair marked for over the mountains. I measured caff into the brewmaster and set it on the unit. Small tasks to keep the hands busy were good. When we sat down to wait the heating on either side of the desk, which served us for a table, we tried not to look at each other.

"What do we do now?" Thad broke the silence first.

"Go back to the Butte."

"You think that we—we are alone here?"

"There may be someone left in the north, but I doubt it. They would have come into the port, too."

"And the refugees?"

"Would also be here—with those ships—if they still lived."

"I suppose so." He glanced over his shoulder to the door into the warehouse, which we had left a little ajar. "I can't help feeling that there *must* be someone, some place. And"—his voice became more rapid—"I don't want to meet—whoever it is!" He picked up the mug of caff, sipping, but as if he still listened. And I knew what he meant.

We put our blankets on the floor—hard beds, but they suited us that night, for in this office there was no hint of ghosts." There might have been far softer rests in the port, but this night they were not for us.

Though we had seen nothing to make us think a guard was needed, we agreed to share sentry goes. Thad took the first, and I rolled into my blankets. We had turned off the light in the office, preferring the dark with the subdued light from the warehouse. I thought I would not sleep, but I did—until I awoke to Thad's shaking. His other hand was over my mouth, impressing me with the need for silence.

As my sleep-dimmed wits cleared, I heard it. There was the rap of footsteps on the warehouse floor, and only one kind of boot made such clatter—a spacer's. One man—no, I thought I could make out the sound of at least two.

Thad's mouth was close to my ear. I felt his breath on my cheek as he whispered, "They came in from the field. I heard a flitter set down there."

Together we crept to the door and peered into the warehouse. There was the glow of a beamer at the far end where the looted cargo was. And we could see two figures moving around there. So we were not alone—

Once more Thad whispered, "Do you think they were watching us? That they know we are here?"

"No—or they would have attacked," I answered. "They have the superior weapons; no need to worry about jumping us."

From what we could see, they were searching through the already tumbled containers, a kind of haste in their movements that suggested they were pressed for time or were frightened men.

If the virus was already seeded in them, then they were walking dead and must know it, having witnessed the fate of other victims. Also, they were more menace to us just living than if they hunted us with laser beams crackling through the air.

"Pack and out," I murmured to Thad. "Leave nothing to let them know we have been here."

We moved cautiously, assembling our packs. Thad col-

lected the mugs and restored them to the drawer, while
snapped shut the door of the cupboard with the heating unit
We dared not turn on the light to check, but I thought tha
should anyone glance in, it would appear untouched. The
I loosed the lock on the outer door, and we slipped into the
street.

It was just when I was sure we had made it safely that we
heard a shout behind. We were a block away from the ware
house, needing to skirt the landing field to reach the ope
beyond the town.

"Lasers!" I warned Thad, and we jumped to cover in a dee
doorway. The door gave inward, and we half fell into a hal
I had the door slammed again in an instant. They could bur
in easily, but even the small portion of time needed for tha
would give us a fraction of head start.

Thad stumbled over something in the dark and nearl
went down. He uttered a wild, gasping cry and shrank fron
what had tripped him, breaking past me down the hall.
dared flash on my belt torch for an instant, saw—and fol
lowed him as precipitously.

The hall ended in a grav shaft, but I took the first roon
to my left, pulling Thad with me. I was rewarded for m
choice by a large window. This was open to the night, an
it took us only a second to drop through, landing in a garden
almost in a garden pond.

The space was walled with a lattice vine, so thickly en
twined that nothing short of a laser beam could cut throug
it. But the strength of our fear and revulsion was such that
in spite of the cuts the thorns made, we went over it, hardl
aware that we climbed until we dropped on the far side, onc
more in a street.

We still heard a distant shouting, sounding at interval
as if the shouters were not giving an alarm but calling ques
tioningly. Did the hunters believe we were of their own band
And if so, why would we run—unless all men had becom
very wary of each other since the plague hit.

For some moments I was confused as to which way w
should head. To get away from the port and into the ope

184

country would, I was sure, give us the advantage. And I said as much to Thad.

"Where then—back to the Butte?"

"No. We dare not let them trail us." Though we had tried to make the defenses as strong as possible there, I had seen too much here at the port to believe we could hold out if they brought their strongest weapons against us.

We ran down the street, using every pool of shadow to cover us. There was a flash of beamer, centering on Thad for an instant, before he threw himself flat and rolled.

"Hellloooo—"

Not the searing rays we had expected, but rather a call. Were we wrong after all and those who chased us were not the enemy but our own people? But I was too certain of the click of space boots in the warehouse.

"Wait—!" Again a hail instead of fire.

But wait we did not. I hauled Thad to his feet with a quick jerk, and we slipped between two buildings, striving to put the rows of structures between us and pursuit.

"Flitter—" Thad gasped.

There was no mistaking the beating sound of a low-flying flitter. We ducked instinctively, hoping to melt so well into the shadows around us that we did not register for the pilot. It skimmed the roof near us and went down in the street we had just quitted, perhaps to pick up those on foot there or to join them.

"Come on!"

We used every trick we could think of, and enough of them worked to take us out of the port. A backward glance was startling. Lights had flashed on there. It was such a blaze as I could remember from my childhood—a reckless burning of lately hoarded energy. They must believe us holed up somewhere in there.

"They didn't fire," Thad observed. "Why?"

"They could have enough of killing," I said bleakly. "Or else we were out of their reach before they discovered we were not their own kind."

"Could they have been ours?"

185

"Not wearing space boots—and I heard space boots in the warehouse."

"What do we do now?"

"Circle north. If they try to trail us—"

"How can they? If they are off-worlders, they have no tracking experience."

"They don't need any. All they need is an infra-scope. And those are to hand. That's why we stay as far from the Butte as possible as long as we know they are after us—or even casting about in search."

Infra-scope—another thing meant for a good purpose, which could now be used to put an end to us, unless we could get out of range. There were plenty of those at the port. The Rangers used them regularly for tracking animals. And they could easily be adjusted to human warmth broadcast—since they had also located men lost in the Reserves.

So we headed north, in direct opposition to the path that had brought us to the port. I tried to think of some way we could baffle the scopes. Underground—yes. We must keep away from the lava country, lest a pickup from the Butte betray what we wanted most to guard. But there were other caves in the hill country. Our supplies were low, and I had had no chance to replenish them from storage.

By dawn we were well out in the wild, but a flitter could run us down with ease. We needed rest, so we chose a thick copse and settled down. Thad slept first while I mounted guard.

It was cool under the low-hanging branches of the trees. I was sure that even hovering overhead a flitter could not sight us. But they would not need to actually see us. If the scope told them where we were, they need only train a laser in our general direction, and that was that.

I heard a flitter coming from the south. The woods were thick here, and if we separated for a short space, that might give them two targets, spoiling their aim. I shook Thad into wakefulness.

"What—?"

"Move!" I shoved him a little to the right. "We go north—but not quite together."

186

"Yes." He shouldered his pack, and we veered from one another. The flitter sounded as if it hovered just over us. I waited tensely for a burning lash to strike about me. Instead, I heard the booming voice of a throw-com, hollow and ghostly in the night.

"We know you are there. Come out! You have nothing to fear—" The speech was in Basic, the off-world trade vernacular.

"Come out! We mean you no harm!" It blared away.

Did they think us so stupid? Why stop to talk? It was plain they had not wasted talk on the settlements.

Yet they did not fire, though by the sound the flitter still hung there. I could hear Thad moving through the brush, keeping pace with me but some distance away. Had our split-up, which seemed such a desperately futile precaution, really baffled our trackers? Or was there some reason why they were reluctant to loose death now?

We had seen their dead as well as ours. Could it be that they were reduced to as small a company as we were and that they now thought that those who had worked in the labs here might have some counter to the plague? My imagination supplied such an answer. I would probably never know whether or not it was the truth.

"We could cook you," the broadcast shrilled, "you know that, beam you right where you stand. But we haven't. Come out. We're all the same now—we die, you die. Only you'll die the quicker unless you come out!"

Pleading and then threats, but manifest reluctance to carry those out. They wanted us in their hands, not dead, which meant they had a pressing use for us.

In the end, the land saved us by a route we could not have foreseen. This section must have been one of those once included in a small Reserve for study purposes. We came to where the tops of the trees met to veil a narrow ditch, a hidden observation walk.

I found it by tumbling in and seconds later heard Thad crash after me. That it was artificial was proven by its pavement. When I stood, the edges just topped my head. I whistled the call of a tree lizard and was answered by Thad who moved to join me.

We felt our way in the dark, buffeted and torn by briers, tough roots, all the impediments protruding from the sides of the cut, unable to use our torches. To my surprise I heard the flitter swing away, no longer hanging directly overhead and I wondered why, unable to believe that its crew had simply given up the chase.

If they did not want us dead, they must be baffled as long as we stayed in thick cover. It might mean they were now seeking a place to set down from which they could move in on foot. If so, the advantage would be ours.

"I think they are setting down," Thad said.

If they were considering a landing, they had chosen wrongly for their purposes, for the sound moved far from us. We continued through the cut, which must end somewhere ahead.

Sixteen

THE CUT GREW shallower, though the thickness of the brush about it did not thin. Twice we came to spaces that must have been intended for observation posts, with seats before shelves on which snoopers or scopes could once have been bolted, but from the growth and uncleared condition of the runway, I thought it had been a long time since these had been used for such a purpose.

What lay to the north of the port was unfamiliar to me. This had always been the less populous section of the continent, with only a fringe of settled land, backed against wilderness, where only a few Security posts had been garrisoned by rotation. The projects once set up here had been the first abandoned.

Somewhere ahead were the hills that eventually joined the mountains across which we had come. I thought if we could reach that stretch of country, we would have a curtain from the flitter, for the infra-scope was notably erratic in broken country.

We came to the end of the slit when I struck my shin painfully against an obstruction. With searching hands I discovered a set of steps, so narrow as to hold but one foot at a time. There had been no sound of the flitter for some time. If they had come to earth, we now had the advantage, since we were trained to this, and they must be surer in space than planetside. Now was the time to put as much distance between us as possible. I said so.

"Can we get back—to the Butte, I mean—if we go north all the way?" Thad asked.

"Not soon. We shall have to circle west."

"There are no trails there."

"No. If we get far enough out, there are the Security posts."

Those posts, they must all be in ruins now. I remembered the one we had picked up by chance on the com. The warthorn, sitting in the chair as one with a right, staring back at us. Somehow that memory now sent a small shiver coursing down my back.

We issued from the slit into what had clearly once been a road.

"Where are we?" Thad moved closer. "We—we are in woods, aren't we?"

His uncertainty was well founded. Visibility was almost nil. I explored gingerly, and my hands encountered a springy wall of brush. By following that up as high as I could reach I discovered they bent, or had been trained, inward, to meet in a thick mat overhead. I recognized this as one of the blind ways used in a mutant Reserve for the coming and going of observers.

But a mutant Reserve to the north? All I had ever heard of were over the mountains. However, general knowledge on Beltane was limited. There had been so many Security projects begun in the early years—and many of them abandoned later—that a hundred such could have had being in remote portions of the continent, unknown to settlers not directly concerned.

Now I dared to use my torch, knowing of old how well constructed and secret such ways were. We looked both ways down a tunnel formed from growing brush. This had been trained over a mesh of ro-steel, which resisted all assaults of weathering for years, and its matting made as thick a wall as one of the settlement structures. We had a choice, right or left, and the compass said left. No flitter could spot us from overhead. If this followed a pattern set on other Reserves, a number of low grade distort patterns had been installed in

190

hat mesh that would interfere with an infra-scope. Luck had brought us into a safe way—for as long as it lasted.

It continued to puzzle me that so elaborate an observation installation had been so near to the port and yet unknown, for while I had not explored possible informative tapes with the same fervor Gytha applied to such research, I had prided myself on knowing as much as the next about the Reserves.

"What—where is this?" Thad drew closer. Though we went single file here, he was near to treading on my heels.

"A mutant observation run, as far as I can tell. As to where—no Reserve listed now. Ah—" We had come to what was apparently a dead end of brush, but this I knew how to deal with. I had Thad hold the torch while I hunted among tendrils of vine and twig ends for the release that must be here. Only, after I had found it, I had a struggle to force it open, proving that this way had not been used for a term of years. Branches parted and vines tore as we united our strength to break through.

Before us was what I wanted least to see, open ground— and not only open ground, but also boggy territory. Clumps of vas reeds were almost as tall as the trees we had left. They still wore their wide summer crowns as fans to catch even the smallest breath of wind, so they were always in motion, striking one against its neighbor with click-clicks of stiff fronds, dislodging with every blow some of the fruit developed at the end of those fronds.

In addition to the vas reeds, there were grotesque humps of hortal, a fungi growing in weird lumps, to die quickly, riddled by flying things and animals for homes. They were unsafe to touch simply because they were so occupied that one never knew what kind of stinging or biting inhabitant might be decanted in a fury.

Straight into the bog led a pathway of rocks, now overgrown and discolored by algae and mosses, while above the muck, the slime-ringed pools, and all the other traps for the unwary danced or stood, like evil greenish candles, the swamp fires. This was as foreign to the Beltane I had always known as if, in coming through the tunnel, we had crossed space to another world.

191

"Do we go through there?" Thad wanted to know.

Someone once had and often enough to need the road bu I had little inclination to follow. We could retrace our step and explore the other end of the covered way, though it rai directly opposite from where we wanted to go.

The effluvia of the swamp reached our noses as the va reeds rattled loudly under a rising wind. This way was risky even by day I decided. I was about to turn back when I hear a shout from the trail we had followed. It must be that ou hunters had fallen into the slit and so were still on our track If we retreated, we would come face to face with them.

I studied that broken stone road with closer attention tha I had earlier given it. As far as I could see, it must follov some ridge of high land. None of it disappeared in a scumme pool, nor was it matted by reeds. Then, startled, I realize that in spite of the dark of the night, I was able to see thos stones, that they appeared to be coated with some phospho rescence, which made them clear to sight. Thus, this patl must have been meant to be traced in darkness. Were wha the observers wished to spy on nocturnal?

"We'll have to go this way," I decided. And I took the firs step.

I believed that those who followed after, wearing metalli plated boots, might have trouble, for the stones seemed coate with some slippery substance, but our soft-soled forest gea planted us firmly as long as we did not hurry. For a time w went straight out into the bog, the odors of its foulness risin, about us. The vas reeds now grew thicker, and when the roa curved to the left, they curtained off the back trail.

Since our eyes were well adjusted to the dark, the glov of the stones was enough to lead us on. I did not try to us a torch. We were well into that dismal land when we cam to an island rising so much higher above the general leve of the bog that five of the stones had been set in the slope c the hillock to make a stair to its surface.

The top of the hill-island had been smoothed, thoug bushes and matted grass proclaimed that it had gone unvis ited for years. In its center were a series of pens resemblin those we had seen at the mutant station—a place wher mutants had been kept before release into an environment attractive to them?

This could also be the dead end of the road, and I began to think my choice had been stupid. I wasted no time in crossing to the other side of the hill. Here again steps, but these only brought us down to what had manifestly been a landing place for flitter or hopper.

That was walled in with the glowing stones, others of which had been set around as markers to be seen from the air. Why had it been necessary to deliver cargoes here by night? All this suggested nothing else.

We paced along the wall of the space on three sides. There was no break in it anywhere to say that the road led on, but finally I dared to use belt torch, beaming beyond the wall, hunting some possible foothold on through the swamp.

What it brought into view was a ridge of higher ground, much the same as the one that had supported our road in, save there was no pavement of stones on this. If it were a continuation of the road, then it could support us, but to use it was a gamble.

We climbed back to the place of cages. For the first time I saw a small structure, no larger than the cages but with walls of mesh covered, as had been the tunnel, with living growth.

Its door was open, but the vines of the wall had laced across that, barring entrance until we cut our way. This had been, I thought, as I flashed the torch cautiously about, fashioned for the same blending-with-the-landscape concealment as the stations on the Reserves. And it was never meant for more than a temporary shelter.

Like the mountain lodge, it was bare of any furnishing, save for two bunks built into the walls, now covered with a layer of evil-appearing fungi. It smelt vilely of damp.

Thad gave a quick exclamation, and I saw the flicker of stunner beam shoot to my right. Then his torch caught and held a thing that lay kicking very slowly until the full effect of the ray took and it was still, its belly upturned, its tearing claw starkly revealed.

A koth crab—nasty enough when it leaped before one

could bring it down. And behind it a web of its fashioning with some swirling movements in it—

"Out!" I backed, Thad with me. Not just one crab, but a nest of them!

What other unpleasant dwellers this hillock might have I did not know, but I had no desire to discover. We would have to turn back now—only when we reached the end of the hill, we heard that sound, saw the wedge of a beamer aimed from above—the flitter had trailed us!

I grabbed the torch from the fore of my belt and thrust it back into the hut, having set it to give the appearance of someone inside.

"Come on!"

We hurried to the lower landing space, over its wall, to that ridge of hard ground that might or might not run to the other side of the bog. If they were hunting by sight now and not by scope—but we dared not hope for such a favor from fortune. At least, seeing the light, they might delay by the hillock.

Now we had to move by the feel of the ground under us, and that was a treacherous guide. After we had gone a short way, though, the surface under my boots felt as solid as the stone had been. I slashed with my woods knife and cut off a length of vas reed. With this in hand, I tapped the way ahead, testing for any change in the surface or for a turn we could not see, though the eerie marsh lights played here and there, giving a faint light.

The unmistakable sound of a flitter settling came from behind, and for that I gave a sigh of relief. They had caught a glimpse of the landing stage and set down there, perhaps beaconed in by the torch left in the hut, which meant they no longer hunted by scope—or they would have known that for a decoy.

Suddenly, under my rod there was no surface. In panic I quested to right and left, hoping that loss meant a change in direction and not an end to our narrow margin of safety. It did, for slightly to the left once more there was firm meeting of reed and ground.

From then on it was a matter of nerves. We fought tension,

for the path no longer ran straight but wavered right and left, then right again. Each time it changed made us fear we had reached its end.

I began to think that this ridge was not natural but had been thrown up for some purpose, though it was not paved. It wove back and forth too much to be normal high ground. Now the marsh lights were fewer and behind us. We still moved through the stink of stagnant pools, and things slid, slipped, and splashed away from our coming. We expected at any moment that which might not flee but stand to dispute our passage.

At last the ridge skirted the edge of a small lake. I heard Thad gasp and might have echoed his exclamation of astonishment.

What we saw were lights—not the marsh fires, nor any torches such as those the flitter might have used, but pale living bars of a chill glimmer that had much in common with the earlier road stones.

Of the stones! It did come from stones! They had been set in rough pillars, not in any regular pattern, but here and there. Between those pillars, which rose out of the surface of the dark water, were rough mounds plastered together above the surface with mud and reeds in rude masses.

"Wart-horns!" Thad cried in a half whisper.

Wart-horns, yes. But never had I seen a whole village of them so gathered. Wart-horns were generally solitary creatures, a small family perhaps in a single pond. Yet here I counted some twenty of the mud and reed mounds with the pillars between them.

Nothing troubled the water's surface, and as I saw from one of the nearer mounds (there was a hole in it a little above the water level), they might be abandoned. Yet it was something so far out of the normal for that species that it was worrying, and one learned early on Beltane that it was best never to let the extraordinary pass without note.

We edged along the narrow path and so passed very close to one of the pillars. I saw that it was indeed a makeshift erection, the stone having been plastered together with the same mud and reed mixture as formed the sides of the domes.

Wart-horn doing? But why? Wart-horns were not intelligent enough to work out such a system of lighting.

The stones were uniform, exactly like the blocks that had formed the roadway to the island. I suddenly went down on one knee and ran my hand over the ground. So doing, one could feel indentations, though they were seasons old and much worn away. The pillars had been built of road stones!

Watching those domes warily, we felt our way along. There was this to hearten us. While the wart-horns liked water to base their dwellings, they did not live entirely within the swamps, for they needed certain foods that grew on higher land, so they must here be near the edge of the bog.

With the graying of the dawn sky, we were again on solid land, the swamp well behind us, and we had not heard the flitter again. The road that had guided us through the morass ended abruptly at a second park for transportation. I searched the ground ahead for some sign of a cave or like shelter. We were lagging, and we could go little farther without rest.

"Vere!"

I turned my head. Thad was pointing eagerly at the cliff wall a little ahead.

"Eeopoe, Vere!"

I saw it, too, the turn of broad-billed head, the flash of brilliant orange and white. It soared high and then shot down and seemed to disappear directly into the rock of the cliff. We started for that point. The eeopoe is a cave dweller, liking to set its nest, a plaster of feathers and moss and a secretion of fluids from its mouth, directly on the side of some opening. It nests in the dark but comes forth to hunt insects. Thus, our fortune had held that we saw it at all.

Had it not been for the bird, we would never have found the cave, for there was a towering rock to mask the entrance. One had to squeeze through a narrow slit between that and the parent cliff in order to enter at all. We found ourselves in a twilight, sandy-floored space.

This was not lava formation, and I had no intention of going too far in—just enough to deaden any scope the hunters

196

might have on us. But we were free now to light the remaining torch.

The narrow inlet was like the neck of a bottle and, through that, was a strange place indeed. Though our travels through the lava caves had been good practice in underground oddities, the light showed us something new.

From the cave floor sprang a dense growth of pure white vegetation about knee high. It had rooted from seeds dropped by the eeopoes, whose murmuring calls sounded in strange, echoing moans over our heads. Some of the sprouts had already withered and died; others still fought for a doomed life. Thad lifted the rays from that ghostly growth, and it shown in the eyes of the birds on the nests until they stirred restlessly.

There was another sound at floor level, a scurrying. Thad flashed his light downward to catch a furry rump and puff tail—a weaver-brod. That tail whisked out of sight into a huge topple of nest, made partly of withered fronds from the ghost garden, partly of debris brought from without. The whole mass was almost waist high where it was packed against the far wall and must have been gathered by more than one generation of brods. The characteristic weaving of grass lengths was broken and crumbling in places, but it was clear the nest was still very much inhabited.

We avoided the ghost garden and the brod nest, also those portions under the eeopoe nests where there were showers of an unpleasant nature marked on the walls and fouling the ground sand. That left us a narrow strip on which to hunker down, the torch burning to the continual worriment of the birds, while we ate sparingly of our supplies. Then I brought out the map to try to plan ahead.

Sentry watch we took by turns. Twice more we ate. The eeopoes became accustomed to our company when we turned off the torch and would make their swift flights out and back. Timing by my watch told us we spent a day and a half in that hiding. This would, I hoped, baffle our pursuers into giving up. Yet I could not risk staying too long for fear they might cast southward and pick up the Butte.

The folly of our com calls was now apparent. Should Annet

try again during our absence, she might beam in their destruction. The last hours spent in the cave were hard; we wanted so much to be on the move.

At last we followed the eeopoes out at dusk. There was no sign we had been trailed this far. Now we had to aim directly by compass, south and west once more. This was not easy country in which to follow any straight bearing, for it was rough, foothill land.

We skirted the swamp for the first night's journey. But we had the moon, sometimes entirely too much of it. There was no need to feel out every step, and we moved at a faster pace. I kept watching for a wart-horn trail. Such a group of them as suggested by the village in the lake would certainly leave a very noticeable regular swamp exit.

When we finally came upon that "road," I was startled, in spite of my anticipation, by the width and depth of the paw-pounded expanse. It was wide enough to accommodate a ground car, and it was worn below the surface of the surrounding soil as if it had been a main thoroughfare for generations of the creatures.

I had certainly no curiosity as to where it led. Having seen traces it was still in use, I wanted only to leave it behind. Wart-horns were not formidable creatures alone, but a pack (unknown heretofore) might be prudently avoided.

We hurried on until the swamp veered to the south, and we took a path more to the west. Meanwhile, we listened for the flitter, but when we were able to make such good time without hearing or seeing anything that suggested we were still the object of a search, we relaxed somewhat, but not enough to walk into the trap they had set.

I had no scope, but I did have something that anyone with even limited Ranger training developed speedily or else was no aid to such service at all—a sixth sense of warning. I stopped short as we came to where we must round an abutting pillar of rock, throwing out my arm as a barrier to halt Thad also.

Instead of advancing, I inched back, pushing Thad. I listened, tried to sniff any alien odor (though scent is the least

f all warning for my species). There was no sign of danger
head—except that I *knew* something waited for us there.

With a last rush I threw myself back into a pocket behind
he rock, carrying Thad, half under me, to the ground. We
ay there for a long moment, listening.

I do not know how they knew their trap had failed. Perhaps
hey had the scope at their service to tell them we were near.
'hey were hard driven, so hard driven that they tried now
penly what they had failed to accomplish with their ambush.

"We know you are there."

The voice boomed among the rocks as it had in the air
ear the port. "We mean you no harm. We need your help—
ruce oath."

Truce oath? Yes, once there had been such promises, and
nen had kept them. But for what had happened here on
3eltane—after what we had seen—there was no trust in the
honor" of those we faced.

"You need us, we need you—" the voice continued, and
here was a note of desperation in it.

"Look, we'll disarm. See—"

Out into the moonlight beyond the rock spun weapons,
our of them. They clanged down on the stone and gravel and
ay with the light shimmering on them: a blaster, two lasers,
nd another piece I could not identify but had no doubts was
ast as deadly as the other two—perhaps more so.

"We're coming out now—empty hands—truce oath—"

I could see their shadows moving before I saw them. I
eadied my stunner and saw Thad do likewise.

There were three of them, and we did not see their faces
lain, for they had their backs to the light. They moved
lowly, as if each step was an effort. Though they held their
ands high, palms out, I saw one come to a halt and touch
is forehead with his right hand. I remembered the disease
ymptoms, and I froze in fear.

"Now," I whispered to Thad, "give them full beam!"

Seventeen

THEY WENT DOWN, crumpling to earth as if they were indeed made of clay that dissolved under a stream of well-directed water. They were not dead, but we had no fears of them for a time.

"Thad, stay away!" I ordered sharply, for he was moving toward the flaccid bodies. I did not know how to look for signs of the plague, or even if it had visible signs, but that these men had so pressed after us was a warning. I believed I could guess only one reason for that—they knew us to be of Beltane and thought we might have an answer to the demon that had been released.

"Contagion from the living," I reminded Thad when he looked at me. "Take their weapons, get away before they come to—"

He nodded and scooped up the nearest laser and blaster, while I gathered up the other two arms. We made a careful detour to avoid the men themselves.

"The flitter—" Thad said.

"Yes."

If we could find their transport and make it ours, we would not only leave them afoot and unable to trail us south, but we could hurry our own return to the Butte. We had not heard the flitter in passage, but that did not mean that they were not grounded somewhere nearby, so we began to search for it.

I had no idea how long the stunner would render them unconscious. That varied with individuals. But with all the weapons now in our hands, we were in control of the situation. They had only one arm, though that was a formidable one if they realized it—they need only pass the infection to us and we would be dead men, though we still walked, talked, seemed alive.

Together we scrambled to the top of the cliff along which we had been traveling. From that height I made a careful survey of the surrounding territory, to spot what we sought in a small meadow strip around the point of the cliff.

I focused on the flitter with the lenses. The door of the cabin was open—and, in the trampled grass there, a man lay prone. He might have fallen from the cabin or collapsed while he stood sentry duty by the doorway. But he lay very still, and not from any stunner. I was sure of my foreboding—the party carried the plague with them. But the flitter—dared we take it? It would mean so much to have such a means of transportation to hand. And to leave it where any of the enemy continuing to live would have it at their service—A questing flight south could bring them to the Butte. It only remained whether the machine was infected.

"He's dead, isn't he?" Thad sighted on the flitter. "Plague?"

"I'd say so. If we dare take the flitter—"

We had no idea of the size of the hunting party. There might be others, dead or dying, inside.

Thad, watching the flitter, tensed so visibly that I was aware of his surprise.

"What is it?"

"Look at the tail—beside that stand of red grass."

The growth he named was vivid, its blood-scarlet stems and narrow blades doubly visible because it was flanked with drab zik leaves. For a long second or two I made out nothing, so well did the lurker blend into the background with the natural camouflage of its species. Then it moved, and I was instantly able to trace the ugly, horn-snouted head lifted to peer at the motionless body.

"Wart-horn?" I wondered, for its present actions were those of no wart-horn I had ever heard of.

Normally wart-horns were not dangerous, though their ugliness was apt to repulse. They were amphibian, a well-grown specimen standing some ten hands high at its humped shoulders. Their wide faces with gaping slits of mouth and the three warty growths, one mid-section where a human would have a nose, the other two above pop eyes, were exceedingly ugly by our standards. They also had the faculty of being able to alter their skin shading to blend with their surroundings. Mainly, they were timid creatures, preferring their mud sinks, fleeing when disturbed, though the males had fangs, which at certain times of the year exuded poison. Their method of fighting was to leap from behind on their prey, grasping tightly with sucker-padded paws, tearing for the throat with their fangs.

This one was larger than any I had seen recorded. Its head, held at a strained angle above those hunched shoulders as it struggled to see better, was out of shape, having a wider and higher expanse.

It moved now with one of its characteristic hops, a tremendous effort that brought it from the tail of the flitter to thud to earth beside the body. Then it bent forward, its face very low above the man, head swinging from side to side, either inspecting or sniffing.

Apparently satisfied, it suddenly reached out with its front paws, planting one on either side of the door, drawing up in a very awkward and visible effort, to put its head inside. Again it remained so, its warted back presented to my lenses, as if it were carefully surveying the interior of the cabin.

Dropping back to the ground, it turned its attention once more to the man, putting out a forepaw to fumble over the body.

"Vere! Look what it's doing!"

I had seen that, too. The creature from the boglands now had in its paw a long bush knife. Light flickered along the metal blade. It was holding up that find, studying it with bulbous eyes. Everything in its movements suggested this was no longer an animal but a thing with intelligence who had found something it could put to future use.

"Vere, why—?"

"Mutant." I gave the only possible explanation. What I had just seen, coupled with the village in the pond, meant—So there had been mutant experiments with the native animals as well as with imported ones! But for what purpose?

Once more the wart-horn bent to survey or sniff the man it had despoiled. Then it turned again to the flitter and made a futile effort to climb into the cabin—so extraordinary a departure from the norm as to keep me breathlessly waiting. But the squat body prevented that feat, though it strove with determination and effort. At last it left in two great bounds that carried in it the direction of the swamp. The knife had gone with it, carried in its slit mouth.

It had done one thing for us. Its actions at the flitter had made plain that there were no passengers in the cabin who need trouble us. And we needed that machine.

Shouldering our small packs, we climbed down from the crag. We did not hurry. And we scouted the strip of meadow before we moved into the open in a quick zigzag run.

We avoided the body as we had the stunned men, though I noted in passing he wore what had once been a space uniform. What alliance he had once owed, we would never know.

While Thad stood on guard, I followed the wart-horn's lead and looked inside. It was a six seater, one of the large ones from the port. Behind the passenger section was a muddle of boxes, as if those who had brought it here had been looting. I swung up and in and went to the pilot's seat. As I thought, the controls were not set on a journey tape but on manual.

"All right." I summoned Thad.

He obeyed with no waste motions, slammed the cabin door behind him, and settled in the co-pilot's place. I triggered the controls, hoping it would fly. The charge dial wavered near low. Since I had no time to waste going for a recharge at the port, I could only hope it would get us as far as the Butte.

I had never pretended to be expert with a flitter, and I had not had much practice with such a machine. Hoppers were left to the less expert at this period on Beltane. However, I got us airborne with only a jerk or two. Then I sent it south and west at the best speed I could reach, which was better than a hopper's best. I picked a course not too near the port, having no wish to alert any remainders of the enemy force that could possibly be there.

"Vere"—Thad broke the silence—"those wart-horn mutants—"

"Yes?"

"There was never a public report of an experiment such as that."

"No." And how many other such secrets were now to come to light? Perhaps experiments had gone on that had never been reported at all—even in code to the memory banks.

"What if there are other things, Vere?"

"I think we can almost count on some more surprises."

"But we can't get any help from off-world now. And—"

"And we may have to share Beltane with mutants, unchecked?" I finished. "Just so—something to consider."

"The Butte, it's out in the wastelands, far from any Reserve. Vere, do you suppose we could open up the caves again. The base would make a safe place—"

"Always supposing some of the wild life wasn't indigenous there. Remember the ice caves?" I reminded him. He was right in that, though. Lugard and those before him had thought to make it a final refuge.

"Vere, look—over there!" It was Thad who spotted the movement, for I had been concentrating on the controls.

What he had sighted might, under other circumstances, have been a very common occurrence at this time of year. There were harvest robos at work in a field below, gleaning, threshing, spitting out at the end of every three rows a bag of grain. But who had programmed them? There were two more fields beyond, now only stubble. So they had been busy at least a day, maybe two.

The refugees? Had they any survivors who had had the foresight to set the robos going to save the crops, even as I had speculated on doing earlier? Robos had to be programmed carefully, since our fields of food stuffs were not too large, and a robo was apt to go on working through fences, even into heavy brush, unless it was supervised. These could not have been running long, and the fields had been correctly harvested. Yet no one with control in hand was in sight. Nor was there any near farmhouse. And—

"Gusset oats!" My identification of the crop brought my hand to the controls in an almost involuntary gesture and sent the flitter off course to circle the field. That was no food for human beings! This coarse grain the robos now bagged normally went to the Reserves, where it was kept to supply some of the wild life in a bad winter season. Why would anyone activate robos to harvest gusset oats now?

The robo working below us came to the end of the field. I fully expected to see it crash on, into the fence. There was always the chance that some half-delirious dying man had activated the machine without knowing just what he was doing.

But it came to a dead stop inside the boundary. I made another circuit of the fields, noted the row of bags waiting to be carted away, the now quiet robo. The fields had certainly been recently cut, not more than a day or so earlier. But the bags that should have represented the harvest were not all there. Only three beside one fence remained. The rest were gone.

"Someone's alive!" Thad cried. "Let's look for him. Vere, we must!"

There was a lane leading from the field. But a spurt along over that did not bring us to a farm or to any small settlement, only to a warehouse meant for storage. And no one moved there.

In spite of the pressing need to return to the Butte, I could not pass up the chance that some settler might be alive, so I set down in the open where cargo carriers had parked.

The doors of the warehouse were wide open. And inside, nothing—no bags. We called, and when I saw a com mike on the wall, I tried to raise an answer from it. But there was not even the thrum of an open line.

It was when we returned to the flitter that I saw the marks in the dust. They had not been left by a hopper or a ground car, nor were they the tracks of forest boots or space footgear.

Hoofprints, and ones I knew. Very recently, since the last vehicle or men had troubled this dust, more than one Sirian centaur had stamped this way. Gusset oats and centaurs made a neat pattern. But the robo harvester—who—or what—had guided that? Suddenly, I thought I did not want to know, I wanted to be back at the Butte, among my own kind and a wasteland where the unbelievable might not have been set free to roam.

"Vere, look—these dragging marks—" Thad pointed to lines. Manifestly, something of some weight had been dragged. Feed bags or—? I wanted no more of a place that now seemed alien. It was as if we had lingered too long where we were not wanted. Not that I had any feeling that we were being watched, or that any scouts of a nonhuman kind lay hidden out there, their attention on us. It was rather as if we had returned to a deserted house where no one of our race would live again.

Telling myself to curb an imagination that was only too ready to visacast pictures one should see only with the aid of one of the more fantastical amusement tapes, I settled in the flitter. As we lifted with all the speed I could safely muster, I determined not to be pulled off course again.

We did swoop over other fields awaiting harvest. What grew down there was for the filling of human stomachs. Nowhere were robos busy. Another month, even three weeks or so, might be too late to save these crops. The feeling grew in me that this was something we of the Butte must seriously consider. We should keep the supplies for emergencies and live off the land where we could. A margin for safety must be maintained.

It was necessary to detour around the port, and thus we crossed two small settlements—Riveholme and Peakchax. Neither had been bombed, but they were clearly tombs for their inhabitants.

By twilight we headed into the wastelands that cradled the Butte. On a chance that Annet might still be manning the com as she had continued to do from time to time, I channeled the instrument on the flitter to the port call, which, I thought, would not give away our true destination, and rapped out in our own code: "Vere here, Vere here—come in, Griss—" Trusting she would catch my meaning, though I did not really expect any answer, I set the broadcast on repeat and allowed those clicks to continue until they were drowned out by a strident series of louder clicks.

I read them aloud as I translated: "Condition red, condition red."

I flipped my own button and tapped out a demand: "What happens?"

"Mutant force, mutant force. Under siege by mutant force—stay off!"

She must believe us still afoot and vulnerable. But a *mutant* force—what could that mean? The wart-horn that searched a dead man for a knife, those centaur tracks and robo harvesters that might have served no human master— what had been loosed on Beltane now?

In the past I had not discounted the rumors of unusual experimentation with mutants. The beast teams sent offworld during the war were matters of certified record. But always those and the survey teams had been animals of intelligence linked with man, a human commander of a scaled, furred, or winged force, amenable to human control and discipline.

What if there had been rogues among such adaptations— or what might be considered rogues by the lab people, mutes unwilling to acknowledge human rule? The safe answer would have been to destroy such mutineers, make sure the strain was not used in breeding. Only, with all curbs on experiments removed in the past few years, there were scientists so immersed in their own work they could have deliberately chosen to raise intelligence and pay no attention to any aberration that accompanied it, as long as the specimens were safely housed and so, they would believe, not dangerous.

"Mutants," I rapped out. "What kind?"

"More than one—cannot tell. Stay off—" came her answer. And it was Annet who replied, for I recognized her touch in the tapping, there being as much individuality in such as in a man's thumb seal.

"We have a flitter." Since it was not a refugee force that

207

threatened, I dared be plain. "Is there room for a roof landing?"

"No! They have ungers with them—"

Thad gave a low whistle, which I could well have echoed. Among the things native to Beltane were these giant hunting birds of the open plains. An unger was large enough, and brainless enough, to not only attack a flitter, but also to damage it. An attack by more than one at a time could knock us out of the sky. But to try to land and reach the Butte on foot, through a force of mixed mutants, especially with the ground level sealed against us, I could see no sense to that.

I glanced at the weapons we had taken from the refugees. Two lasers—

"I'm going to set on steady flight," I told Thad. "You take that window, I this. Use the lasers—if you have to. We'll cut our way through."

He pulled the nearest laser across his knees and inspected the firing mechanism as I did the other. It was simple enough, no more complex than the stunners we were accustomed to. There were sights and a butt button. One aimed and then fired by pressing that.

"We have weapons," I told Annet. "We are coming in."

Go in we did, even as the dusk closed about us. I saw a beamer ray pointing up into the sky as a beacon. Back and forth through that column of light flapped ungers, seeming to patrol the air above the Butte. There was no sight of our people on the roof, but the hopper we had left there was now drawn well to one side. The beamer had been broken from its stand and battered, but its light did not fail.

"Going in!" I warned Thad. The sound of our motor must have alerted the flying guard. One wheeled and came straight for us. I waited until I was sure it was well within range and used the laser. The flame caught the unger in mid-body, and it was over in an instant, the charred carcass falling heavily.

I saw the tracer of another ray catch the wing of a second unger and shear that off and knew Thad was alert. We took out six before they left us alone, beating up into the streaked sky from which the sun had gone but not all color faded. I left Thad to the defense and loosed us from the set course. Now came the tricky part, to set the flitter down on the roof. I was not sure I had skill enough, but that was our only possible landing place.

Three times I made a circle in, all but the final swoop. And on the fourth, sure that I would never have a better approach and that I must do it this time or utterly lose my nerve, I buttoned for a landing.

I was not sure we had made it safely until I sat a whole moment in the now stationary flitter and knew that we were down. I cut the motor and unlatched the cabin door, slipping out, laser ready to repell another attack from overhead.

There was a barrier at the door at the foot of the tower. I slammed at it impatiently with the butt of the laser, then swung around as I heard a whistling cry from the sky. Thad ran across the roof, turned halfway, went to one knee, and fired. I saw the dark mass of the unger glide on and knew he had missed, but a second later I did not.

Then came a pattering sound, and something struck the roof, first not far from the flitter, then closer to a point between Thad and me. He stumbled on, to where I was by the blocked door. Once beside me, he switched on his belt torch, and I saw what caused the pattering—darts of some silvery material, with an ominous stain about their points. They came from below, beyond the walls of the Butte. They continued to fall, moving ever closer to where we stood. We could not return to the flitter save through that rain, and I had a strong suspicion they were even more dangerous than they looked.

"Lasers—" I said to Thad. "Burn me a path. Aim into the air and get them as they fall!"

He did that, leaving me scant space to dart under his beam, the hot breath of it scorching. I laid hands on a smoking carcass of unger and dragged it back to shelter us. Now, if those below were only alert enough to loosen what they had built up to secure the roof, we had a chance, always providing they did know we were here and worked fast to tear down the barricade.

The darts continued to fall. Thad wanted to burn them,

but I thought caution was indicated. We might need all the charges the lasers carried before we were through. We could only wait and hope.

"What kind of mutants—" Thad said. "Wart-horns? Centaurs?"

"They could be anything. There were lots of imports." Yes, my mind added, plenty of imports and no one among us now with the knowledge of just what part of the memory banks to explore to learn the nature of this unexpected enemy.

We heard a sound from behind the tower door.

"Vere?"

"Here!" I shouted.

It seemed a long, long time up there on the roof until they pulled aside enough of their barrier to let us in, only to have Emrys, Gytha, Sabian, and Annet, with hardly a glance at us, return to its rebuilding. Annet looked at me over her shoulder as she rammed a box back into a cranny.

"They made an assault on the roof not three hours ago. We were about to seal it forever."

"Good you did not." I helped her at the building. "Who— or what?"

"We don't know, Vere, we don't know! They came so suddenly. Some we recognize, some we don't. Animals that aren't animals. Vere, has the world gone mad?"

"No more so than the men responsible," I told her. "We stand alone now."

She caught my meaning, and her face aged as I watched.

"All dead—"

"Or dying." I thought of the refugees.

"And how do we—we make peace with those?" She flung out one hand at the wall of the Butte and what lay beyond.

How indeed? I had no answer for her, nor had anyone in that hour.

Eighteen

THE MUTANT BAND had arrived out of nowhere as far as they could tell us. Of their number, or even of all the species that comprised that company, we gained but little idea during the siege—for siege it was, to hold us within the walls. Finally, I took the flitter aloft again, in desperation flying low over the ground where they lay in hiding, while Thad and Emrys sprayed from the cabin windows with stun beams. After that one fight with the ungers, we did not use lasers again.

For a long day after that stunning, we saw no movement among brush and rocks. On the second dawn, being on look-out in the tower, I witnessed the withdrawal of that strange force, fading back and away toward the mountains. For three more days we dared not believe they were really gone, or at least had not left a holding force behind.

The reason for their attack we did not know, unless, having at last been freed from human control, they were not minded to come under it again. How they had known we were in the Butte was a mystery. Gytha suggested that one of those we had loosed at the station in the Reserve had followed us through the pass. Only that spoke of some organization already existing among them. To weld such diversified specimens into an army was so complex an action that I found it difficult to believe the mutants could rise to it.

For some time we speculated as to whether they could have been under some human commander—if some survivor

211

of a Ranger patrol, perhaps crazed by what had happened, had sent them against us thinking we were the enemy. But Annet said that until the arrival of the ungers, they had all repeatedly shown themselves on the roof of the Butte, so that any human watcher would have recognized another human.

At any rate, that attack and its conclusion was to remain unsolved—just as we shall never know exactly what happened to set off the attack on Kynvet and the loosing of the plague.

We knew that with the withdrawal of the mutant force, we were in perhaps the strongest position we could now find on Beltane for the preservation of our kind. Perhaps the fact that we had to face such harsh reality was the saving of us, for there was so much to be done that we labored from dawn to dusk, and exhaustion gave us dreamless sleep.

The flitter was our salvation. We dared not try to get through the country at ground level. Although we did not see any mutants, nor were we again attacked by any, yet we could never be sure that they were not lurking to pick off any straggler.

Thad and I never took the same trip out, lest a pilot be lost. He became as competent as I had ever been, then better than I at the flying and maintenance of our precious machine. We went out alternately on scouting trips, though never again did we see any traces of refugees or of any survivors of our own people. The machine shop at the port was Thad's principal point for visiting, and he took Emrys with him as a guard while he loaded with tools and supplies, transporting back to the Butte enough of both, he assured me, to keep the flitter and hopper running for years, barring accident.

Gytha, Sabian, and I made two visits to farms and activated the robo harvesters, leaving them to work during the night, for night or day meant nothing to those, returning at dawn to ferry back as much of the harvest as we could carry during the days, loading warily under guard every time we touched down at the edge of the fields.

We saw other robos in action and were sure the mutant had put them to such tasks. But these were busied by da and the harvest collected at night. So the mutants had reversed that order, probably because some were nocturnal.

Then came signs that their organization, if there had been one in truth, was coming apart in a bloody fashion. We went into an orchard of hyborian apples to discover we were not the first there. The ground was cut by the sharp hoofs of centaurs, and there were, in addition, paw marks of a type I had not seen before except in the dust around the Butte. There were also patches of blood still congealing, though no bodies.

My small hopes for us arose after seeing that. If our enemies of the four-footed kind now broke the truce kept among themselves, we were in less danger. They would be more occupied with their own quarrels than with us.

Three times I returned to the port and tried to make some sense of the records. I could pick out bits and pieces, but only scraps. Gytha, whom I took because of her long acquaintance with tapes, did little better. But we did dismantle a small reader, which ran on neutro power. This with all the tapes Gytha chose in searches of the central library files, we brought back to the Butte and installed with a hookup to the large com screen. What knowledge was within our grasp (too much of it was highly specialized and so of little use) we tried to gather.

It was at that time I began this record of the immediate past so that it could be added to Beltane history. Yet I feared there were so many gaps that we were losing or overlooking information we would need sorely in days to come.

We could bring medical supplies to the Butte and the information tapes from the medical library. But none of us had training to use the complex diagnostic or surgical techniques, so we lost much of the health protection known for centuries.

The lower rooms of the Butte became crammed with a vast miscellany of material from the port and from some of the settlements where, emboldened by no more attacks, we sought for what we could find. As yet we did not try to sort it all, merely brought whatever seemed worth carrying and was small enough to pack into the flitter.

The fall rains began, pouring their floods even across the

waste of the lava country that was usually desert. Their fury was such that we staked down flitter and hopper and covered them with sheets of plasta, which had protected the machines in the underground depot. Then we turned to picking over what we had brought, sorting out items of immediate use and putting aside others to be stored.

There were some brisk exchanges of high words when classifications did not agree and tempers wore thin. But with so much that was interesting and needful to be seen and handled—for our foraging teams had made widely varying choices—we soon forgot disputes.

At last, since our badly organized sorting had led to greater confusion than ever, we held a council, and it was determined to draw up a list and reduce our rummaging to plan. Thereafter, though we worked as hard, we did so to more purpose.

I had wanted to try to reenter Lugard's caves. Not only were the supplies in the base cave there, but we would also have a refuge if need arose. In addition, there was the cache of ancient things in the ice cave, which might hold even greater wonders than the rod that had accounted for the monster. But to work out in the wastes to open the caves, even under guard, was folly.

Along with our search lists, we also drew up study programs, putting on each one the need to learn all he could of some specialty, as well as such general information as was needed for survival.

It was then that we became strongly aware (when I say "we," I mean Annet and I) that these were the children of people who had for generations been specialists and workers by mind more than body. The first settlers of Beltane had been picked for their knowledge, and while these descendants of theirs lacked the advanced schooling their parents had known off-world, they had inherited the inquiring turn of mind that sent them seeking information.

Thad chose technical learning and pursued it doggedly, with Emrys trailing him as lieutenant. They would descend to the depot beneath the Butte and take out manual repair tapes for the machines there, disembowel the motor section of such as we thought we would not use and reassemble them to the best of their ability. I thought that there could be no more useful training for us now.

Annet's bent was biology. She gathered and read all the tapes I thought might explain the mutants, and was buried in them whenever she had a spare moment, while Gytha, always more interested in general rather than specific information, became our librarian and record keeper.

To my surprise, Pritha took up medicine, coming into that field through an interest in healing herbs, which she had always had. Sabian had been fascinated by the robos and their field work during our quick harvest season. Now he wanted all we could feed him on agriculture.

Ifors showed no special bent, but I found him often with the reader. The tapes he had chosen covered so wide a range of general material that I thought he was following Gytha's path. Dinan, too, made no choice as yet but studied stolidly whatever we put before him.

I have made no late mention of Dagny, for that was our first sorrow and a lingering one. During the fall the improvement that had come by slow steps after we left the caves continued. Pritha and Annet spent hours with her, but there were so many regressions, less patient tutors might have given up in despair.

Gytha played simple story tapes over and over, and we were all joyful when she responded to such tales. But it was as if some important function in her mind worked now by erratic jumps. We would be encouraged over what seemed a significant gain, dashed when she slipped back into her old withdrawal.

I do not think she was ever completely aware of what had happened, nor why life was now lived behind the thick walls of the Butte and not at her home. She showed no curiosity—which seemed to Annet the most ominous of symptoms.

As the rainy fall progressed, she took cold often and spent much time in bed, coughing, falling into sleep. Her appetite was poor. There were times when she must be fed spoonful spoonful and then would turn her head stubbornly away

215

before Annet or Pritha had gotten more than half a cup of soup down her.

Though there was a heating unit in every room of the Butte and Thad and I worked on the relays, using every manual we could find to aid us, we could not keep the hold warm on the days when our autumn rains turned to sleet and then to snow. Dagny spent all her time in bed now, and I noticed that those periods when she sat up with pillows behind her grew shorter and fewer each day.

What tore at us most was the fact that had we had the knowledge, we might have saved her—or at least knowing what the medics had done in the past, we believed that. As it was, all we could give her was comfort and loving care until the end.

That came before Midwinter Day. She roused one morning much her old self. Dinan spent a long time with her but finally came to Annet much disturbed and demanded to know what he should tell Dagny, for she wanted to go home and kept asking where their parents were. With wisdom beyond his years, her twin had said they were visiting another settlement on lab business, and Dagny had been satisfied for a time. But now she was very restless and wanted to go to them.

Dinan, remembering how she had taken him into the ice cave during a similar search, was frightened by her insistence. Annet found her sitting on the edge of her bunk, pulling a blanket around her shoulders, ready to set out. Annet's coming calmed her, and she consented to rest in bed, sharing a special ration treat with Dinan.

From that overexertion she slipped into a deep sleep, from which she did not wake. We laid her to rest as we had Lugard, since the ground was ice-bound. This time I used a laser beam and cut the name and dates, though we had lost track of time and moved now by seasons and not set days, for we were never sure how long we had been in the caves.

Thus, we lost the second of our company. And so small a band were we that, though Dagny had not really been one of us for months, there was now a gap we could not fill. Annet, Thad, Gytha, and I worked hard to keep the young ones busy.

We had a celebration on Midwinter Day, checking the date as best we could. We hoped that the children would not contrast it with the feasts of a year ago. Annet made us a fine dinner, using off-world supplies, which she now hoarded jealously. When we had done, Gytha rose in her seat and came to me, her hands holding a slender package.

What she had was a pipe—not such a one as Lugard had carried, certainly lacking the magic that had clung to his. But she put it eagerly into my grasp, and I saw them all look to me expectantly.

So I, who had once made small music on hollow reeds during our carefree days but had never done so since I had heard Lugard, raised it to my lips, doubtfully at first, because the making of music had long been lost to me. But then I recalled note by note one of the trail songs.

It came jerkily and then with greater ease. Straightway, Annet began to sing, the others following her, until their lusty voices drowned out my piping—which was perhaps all for the best.

When the song was finished, Gytha said, "No song now, please, Vere—just music."

That put me on my mettle, so I dared try one of those rippling series of notes such as I had once made at campfires when we had been the Rovers and not survivors in a dead world. I played it through to the end, noting they listened with an intensity, as if the music I drew from that rod was a key to better days.

After Midwinter Day the cold increased. We shivered and tinkered with the heating units, not often stirring out of the Butte, though there were days of bright sun on the dazzling banks of snow.

Though the Butte meant safety, yet I was troubled now and then by the thought that another season should mean a move for us. I had not too much liking to return to any settlement. Memories clung there. But a settlement of our own nearer the port might be prudent to consider. I had no hope of repairing the off-world signal. On the other hand, if the chaos following the war was not so great or lasting as

Lugard had foreseen and someone seeking contact with Beltane did come, it was at the port such a ship would planet.

If they found that in ruins and searched some of the nearer settlements without result, they would probably not penetrate this far into the wastes hunting survivors.

Finally, I mentioned this at one of our weekly councils. None of the port buildings could, without labor we could not undertake, be made as secure as the Butte. If we tried, it would entail more than one season's work. Also we must plant, Sabian insisted with more force than I had ever heard him use before. Though we could not put under cultivation, even by robo help, all the fields that had been utilized before, we must do our best to keep in growth the most essential food stuffs.

Those fields lay nearer to the port than to the Butte. Once the robos had been programmed, they could take over the bulk of the field labor. We had not forgotten the mutants. While the only evidence we had of their continued interest in us were tracks in the snow encircling the Butte (and we could not even be sure those were made by mutants and not wandering animals), we did not want to be cut off from our fortress in need.

Thus, it was decided that I was to fly into the port and make a general survey of the prospects for adapting one of the smaller buildings to our need. Emrys would go with me to keep the flitter aloft while I scouted, so there would be no danger of losing our most precious possession.

We set out in the very early morning of a day that promised to be clear. For the past two days there had been warmer winds. The snow in drifts around the lava ridges was beginning to melt. I wondered if I would ever be able to return to the caves—perhaps not for years to come.

The quickest route to the port took us cross-country, where the snow could not disguise the arable fields. We winged over the site of Kynvet, now all hidden from view.

At the port, one of the refugee ships still stood pointing to the stars, but the one with the eroded tubes had crashed, its nose having beaten a hole in the wall of the warehouse.

There were no tracks marring the white surface of the field or the silent streets.

We circled once, and I decided on a small house to the far side of the field, where the commandant of the port had lived in the good days. It had been built when the port was laid out, solidly constructed of poured plus-stone, almost as durable as the Butte.

I swung out of the cabin, and Emrys immediately took the litter up to cruise the surrounding area while I searched the dwelling.

It might do, I decided. Luckily, it had been unoccupied since the leaving of the last commandant, so death had not been here. We could do as we had at the Butte, block up the lower doors and windows and then we could rig a movable outside stair to an upper room. It would be difficult work, and perhaps we would take all year for it.

Emrys winged back at the appointed time, and he was highly excited.

"To the north, Vere—a town!"

A town! The refugees? Or settlers who had fled earlier homes?

"Show me!" I demanded. Obediently, he pressed the course button.

A town it was, if a collection of straggling huts could be given that title, though on Beltane now, I supposed, it could. The town had inhabitants we could see pouring out of those makeshift shelters as we winged down for a better look, Emrys switching on to hover.

"Up and out!"

His answer to my order was, luckily, instantaneous. I had seen enough to know that we might have done as ill as the man who plants a stick in a hor-wasp hole and turns it to incite the dwellers therein.

"Those—those were mutants!" Emrys said a little dazedly as the flitter leaped up and away. "But they had houses!"

What *had* gone on in those experimental labs? I had, even in those few moments when we had hovered over the untidy mixture of huts, counted at least three species—all of herbivorous types to be sure—but *three* living together appar-

219

ently on good terms. If this could be true of the herbivorous, what of the carnivorous or the omnivorous species? How many such haphazardly organized "villages" were there scattered around?

At least, though I was sure the centaurs had put the robos to work last summer, they were still not able to use, perhaps because of their body structure, mechanical transportation and so could not follow us.

But to discover such a settlement close to the port negated our plans for moving there. We could only leave some message that would make sure we would not be overlooked if a relief expedition ever came. And this I determined to do— not because I had any even faint hopes of such an arrival, but because it would satisfy our need to believe in life beyond Beltane, life of our own kind.

So now we live in a fortress, and we go armed when we venture forth. We preserve what small remnants of human civilization we can by treasuring our knowledge and striving to enlarge our learning. We tend machines with care, knowing only too well that they will not last even our lifetimes. We realize that those of our small colony coming after us will slip farther and farther down the ladder of civilization, perhaps, in time, to meet those others climbing up.

It is now three years since we followed that Dark Piper, Griss Lugard, into the safety of his caves. Two years ago Annet and I stood up before our small company and took the vows of life companionship. This spring, while the snows still lay, our son Griss was born, the first of a generation who shall never know the stars, unless some miracle occurs.

We have lost no more of our company, though at last harvest Sabian and Emrys held off an attack of mutants—this time an all-one-species pack of carnivorae remotely of canine breed.

Gytha has hopes that someday we may be able to deal with at least a few of the species on a more tolerant level. She cites our freeing of those left to die in the station pen as a beginning and has wanted to return over the mountain to try to contact the ystrobens. But we dare not do this—we are too few. One more member lost might endanger the whole colony.

The mutant settlement near the port has been a success. They ran the robos in several fields for two harvests; then these broke down. At Annet's and Gytha's urging, as a gesture of friendliness toward those most likely to accept us, Thad and I flew in by night and repaired the machines, setting those going at dawn. But though we left also some food as a gesture of peace, notably blocks of salt, they have made no return.

They still spy on us, and we only go out in pairs, though we do not kill, using stunners only.

Thad and I spent long days at the port, hooking up alarms and tapes. We hope our makeshift installations will work if any ship comes. The ship that fell is rusting, and that left standing is now canted to one side. Had we been trained, we might have taken off in that—but where?

It would seem that Lugard's prophecy of the end of a star-wide civilization is coming true. No one has visited Beltane since the refugee ships. I do not believe anyone will soon, maybe not until the beginning of another era, when somewhere, on another planet, a race will crawl once more out of barbarism, relearn old arts, and take to space.

If such rediscover Beltane, we hope they will find this record and the others we shall continue to tape as long as we have Zexro reels, for as we finish each tape, we set it with the permanent records at the port. Thus, they will learn how one world ended for us and another began.

This is the end of my part of the story. It is agreed that Gytha will carry on the recording. Tomorrow I shall lift to the port and place this one in the custody of the memory banks.

It is harvest time again. We shall watch the fields of the mutants, give them what assistance we can, always hoping that someday there will be a breakthrough and our species will face one another in friendship. If it is otherwise, our future is as dark as the caves we traveled through. Then we found again the open world and light. Now we ask each day that that may prove again.

ABOUT THE AUTHOR

Andre Norton, born Alice Mary Norton, has long been regarded as one of the best writers of science fiction and fantasy. She was born in Cleveland, Ohio, and began her literary career as an editor of her high school paper. Before the age of twenty-one she had published her first book.

After attending Case Western Reserve University, she became a member of the staff of the Cleveland Public Library in the Children's Department. Failing health caused her resignation and she then became a full-time writer.

In 1979 she was awarded the BALROG for professional writers in the fantasy field. She has also been awarded the Phoenix, the Invisible Little Man award, and a plaque from the Netherlands government for her past work.

THRILLS * CHILLS * MYSTERY
from FAWCETT BOOKS

This offer expires 1 May 81   8400